MAKE RUSSIA GREAT AGAIN

A NOVEL

CHRISTOPHER BUCKLEY

SIMON & SCHUSTER

NEW YORK LONDON TORONTO SYDNEY NEW DELHI

Simon & Schuster
1230 Avenue of the Americas
New York, NY 10020

Copyright © 2020 by Christopher Taylor Buckley

All rights reserved, including the right to reproduce this book or
portions thereof in any form whatsoever. For information, address
Simon & Schuster Subsidiary Rights Department,
1230 Avenue of the Americas, New York, NY 10020.

First Simon & Schuster hardcover edition July 2020

SIMON & SCHUSTER and colophon are
registered trademarks of Simon & Schuster, Inc.

For information about special discounts for bulk purchases,
please contact Simon & Schuster Special Sales at 1-866-506-1949
or business@simonandschuster.com.

The Simon & Schuster Speakers Bureau can bring authors
to your live event. For more information or to book an event,
contact the Simon & Schuster Speakers Bureau at 1-866-248-3049
or visit our website at www.simonspeakers.com.

Interior design by Kyle Kabel

Manufactured in the United States of America

1   3   5   7   9   10   8   6   4   2

Library of Congress Cataloging-in-Publication Data has been applied for.

ISBN 978-1-9821-5746-3
ISBN 978-1-9821-5748-7 (ebook)

For Kathy and Pat, with best love

And to the Deep State: thank you for your service

Author's Note

This is a work of satirical fiction.

Names, characters, places, and events are either the product of the author's imagination or used in a fictitious manner.

Any person finding any resemblance between themselves and persons depicted herein should probably be ashamed.

1

"**H**ow could you work for a man like that?"
   "What were you thinking?"
"What possessed you?"

All the time I get this, even in here, which frankly strikes me as a bit rich. Who knew inmates at federal correctional institutions had such keenly developed senses of moral superiority?

Let me say, at the outset I had no illusions when I agreed to serve as Donald Trump's White House chief of staff. I did not seek the job, nor did I imagine, even for a moment, that it would be a "picnic," a "walk in the park," or some other metaphor for "wonderful, life-enhancing experience." I certainly didn't imagine that it would culminate in having a mailing address consisting of an acronym and numbers recognizable only to the US Postal Service.

Call me old-fashioned. My view is that when your president calls, you pick up the phone. My wife, Hetta, urged me—literally—not to pick up the phone when she saw "POTUS" on the caller ID.

1

"Hetta," I said, "I can't not take a call from the president of the United States."

"Yes you *can!*" she hissed, sounding like an inverted Obama slogan. She remonstrated, as only Hetta can. But I picked up. Let history record that when the president called, Herbert K. Nutterman took the call.

The operator put me through to the Oval Office. I heard the familiar voice: "How's my favorite Jew?"

Hetta was now shaking her head, making violent "No!" and "Hang up!" gestures. It's distracting to have your wife do this when you are talking to the most powerful man on earth.

Mr. Trump often called me "My favorite Jew." (When he was pleased with me, that is.) Sometimes just "My Jew." I didn't especially enjoy it, but I emphasize it was not anti-Semitism. Mr. Trump is many things, but anti-Semitic is not one of them. It's just his way. Many people who grow up in Queens, a borough of New York City, talk this way. Mr. Trump called one of the White House butlers of color "My favorite African American." There was a navy steward in the White House Mess he always greeted with, "How's my favorite Mexican today?"*

I told Mr. Trump that his favorite Jew was fine, thank you. I quickly added—for Hetta's sake—"I'm finding retirement very pleasant, sir. Very pleasant."

Hetta shook her head as if to say, "Oy!" (a Yiddish expression generally meaning "My husband is an idiot"). She stomped off to the kitchen. Soon there came a cacophony of Calphalon pots. Hetta copes with stress by cooking. From one especially resonant *thunk*, I guessed that she had dropped the large soup pot. Perhaps on purpose. A great maker of soup is my Hetta. I hoped it was borscht, as I was very partial to Hetta's borscht.

---

* The steward was actually Filipino, but he never corrected the president. To be honest, I don't think Mr. Trump had any "favorite" Mexicans.

We Semites of Jewish persuasion turn to soup in times of trial; and indeed, in times of nontrial. I don't know if this is also true of the Arab-variety Semites, but it's certainly true of us Jewish-variety Semites. We're very big on soup. It's comforting. Considering historically what we as a people have been through, it's no surprise we seek comfort where we can find it.

"What was I *thinking*?" the president said.

I had no idea to what he was referring. His abrupt decision to abandon the Kurds, America's staunch allies? His "bromance" with Kim Jong-un? The trade war with China? Calling former vice president Biden a "douchebag"? Calling Angela Merkel, the German chancellor, "an old hag"? Why address this rhetorical question to myself?

"Why did I ever let you go?" he said. "You were the best manager I ever had. I'm not saying I'm not a genius. I am. But that was nuts of me. Must have been temporary insanity."

I won't pretend I wasn't flattered. But I had an uneasy feeling about where this might be headed. To the clatter of Calphalon was now added Hetta's sobs. She tried to hold them in, but they came out. Hetta's sobs sound like a large bird—an emu, say—choking.

Careful, Herb, I told myself.

"Thank you, sir," I said. I felt I should say something recip-rocally flattering, but now Hetta had appeared in the doorway, holding her favorite paring knife. I didn't want her to think that I was encouraging Mr. Trump. I said, "My years working for you were a major part of my life, sir." That seemed neutral enough.

"You're way too young to be retired."

"Oh," I said with a laugh. "I think I might disagree with you there, sir. Every day I wake up with some new pain or ache."

Twenty-seven years I worked for Mr. Trump. First as food and beverage manager at the Trump Magnifica, in Wetminster,

New Jersey. Then as assistant general manager at the Trump Farrago-sur-Mer. That led to my promotion as the first general manager of the Trump Bloody Run Golf Club in Little Hot Pepper, Virginia. My time there was not dull. Indeed, it included some controversy.

Mr. Trump was of the opinion that a major, decisive Civil War battle had been fought on the property. Most historians disagreed. (Actually, every historian.) But that wasn't going to deter Mr. Trump. It takes more than historians to deter Mr. Trump. So a second decisive battle was fought.*

We prevailed, after some heated litigation with the local authorities. Mr. Trump's personal attorney, Mr. Cohen, finally overwhelmed the various commissions by means of what I believe is called force majeure. In this particular case, he told the head of the Virginia Historical Commission that he "might want to hire someone to turn on the ignition in your car when you leave for work in the morning."

We got our historical marker. A statue was erected on the seventeenth green to the Confederate colonel who (according to Mr. Trump) had "kicked Union ass." Later, Mr. Trump tried to persuade Senator Squigg Lee Biskitt of South Carolina to dedicate the statue, but the senator demurred.

Mr. Trump then expressed his confidence in me by making me part of his effort to realize his long-cherished dream of building a Trump Tower Kremlin in Moscow. That process made getting approval for the statue of Col. Robert E. Bigly seem like small potatoes. Meanwhile, to return to Mr. Trump's fateful phone call that day.

I knew that whatever he had in mind for me would not sit well with Hetta. For over a quarter century, Hetta had yearned for our post-Trump life. She never felt comfortable with what

* Second, that is, assuming one believed in the first.

4

she called the "meretricious glamour" of Trump World. I misunderstood. All those years she'd been saying that, I thought she meant *meritorious* glamour, as in glamour that you earn. I'm no Mr. Dictionary. One day, years later, after one of her eruptions, I looked it up, and learned that in fact she meant something quite different. The word means seemingly attractive, but actually cheap, or, if you will, fake.

"Listen," the president said. I braced, because whenever Mr. Trump tells you "Listen," you know something not wonderful is coming. "I need you back."

Given the brouhaha over the Trump Tower Kremlin, I figured that the project had been put on the back burner. So I assumed he was about to offer me the general manager job at Trump Farrago. He had hinted once or twice someday that might be mine. Five years ago, I might have leapt at it.

"Sir," I said, "you deserve the best." He loved hearing that. "I'm no longer at the top of my game, though. Running Trump Farrago-sur-Mer is a job for a younger man. But I'm honored to be asked."

He laughed. Mr. Trump rarely laughs, unless, say, he's just been informed that someone he despises has been diagnosed with malignant tumors or has experienced some other calamity. It's not that he lacks a sense of humor. I believe it derives from his German extraction. Who but the Germans would have such a precise word as "schadenfreude," meaning "a gleeful satisfaction from the misfortune of others."* Just think: at some point in German history, it occurred to someone to make up that word. No wonder they came up the with the V-1 and V-2 rockets that terrorized the civilian population of London

---

* The German language is like a pipe organ, combining as it does so many elements. It even has a word for "a face crying out for a fist to be smashed into it": *Backpfeifengesicht*. Imagine coming across that in a book of useful German phrases.

during World War II. Those Vs stand for the German word for vengeance. By contrast, we gave our first nuclear bombs cute names like Fat Man and Little Boy.

"Herb," Mr. Trump said. "Fuck the Farrago. I want you to come work for me at the White House."

This I was not expecting. I stammered. In Mr. Trump's employ, stammering happens.

"But, but, *sir*," I said, head spinning. "My understanding is that the White House Mess is run by the US Navy. Surely the person in charge should be an admiral or commodore or some such personage."

"*Herb*," he said, annoyed. Mr. Trump hates dithering by his subordinates. "I'm not asking you to run the fucking kitchen. I want you to be my chief of staff."

Well, believe me, to this I had no answer. Now, it was no secret that Mr. Trump was unhappy with his current chief of staff. In his tweets and comments he was calling him things like "bozo" and "that idiot."

"Sir," I said. "I've had no experience in government."

"Yeah you have," he said.

"I have?" Really, I was at a loss.

"You dealt with that asshole commissioner in Virginia over the Confederate thing. That's experience with government."

This seemed a stretch. I said, "It was really Mr. Cohen who did the heavy lifting."

"Herb. Did *I* have any experience in government? Look at the job I'm doing. I'm crushing it. They're comparing me to Lincoln. [Mr. Trump did not specify who exactly was comparing him to Lincoln.] Look, I've had a political chief of staff. He was a disaster. I had a four-star general. He was worse. How many chiefs of staff have I had now? I've lost count. Terrible, all of them. I need someone I can trust. I need a manager. I need my favorite Jew."

"That's, uh, very generous of you, sir," I stammered. "But . . ."

"Have you been following the news? I'm in the middle of a shit storm. It's all fake, what they're saying. They're disgusting people, the media. Really, really disgusting. MBS, the guy runs Saudi Arabia? He had it right. The only way to deal with those assholes is to smother them and dismember them with bone saws. I'm telling you."

"Well, sir," I said, clearing my throat, "I *had* gotten the general impression that things were"—I was careful not to mention I-words like "impeachment" and "indictment"—"a bit of a roller coaster. But your base is with you one hundred percent." (This was not technically accurate at this point, his support having fallen to 89 percent among Republicans. Still, not bad, all things considered.)

"It's true," he said. "They love me. But that's not the problem, Herb. The problem is I'm surrounded by fucking incompetents. You've never seen incompetence like this, Herb. These people wouldn't last one *week* in the Trump Organization. It's very disappointing, Herb. So I need you. Okay?"

What could I say? *No, thank you, Mr. President. I'd love to help you run the country, but it might interfere with my Wednesday night poker game?*

"Well," I said, flailing. "I'd have to run it by Hetta."

"Who?"

"My wife, sir," I said with a touch of impatience. I was tempted to add, "Of thirty-two years. Whom you've met on maybe five hundred occasions."

"Yeah, yeah," he said. "She's great. Hetta is going to be very, very happy about this. What an honor, right? How many people get to be Trump's White House chief of staff?" (Seven in not quite four years, actually.)

I cannot truthfully describe Hetta's reaction as "very, very happy." As I stood there in the kitchen trying to rationalize with her, she said nothing. She just went on peeling beets. I stressed the theme of "duty." Still nothing. She continued peeling, more and more aggressively. To this day, even in the kitchen here at Federal Correctional Institute Wingdale, I have never seen beets—or for that matter any vegetable or legume—peeled with such vehemence. It actually crossed my mind that it was just as well she was able to work out her frustration on the beets, inasmuch as she was wielding a knife. It would be weeks before we had anything like a normal married-couple conversation, much less married-couple "relations."

As it happened, Mr. Trump didn't wait for me to call him back with my decision. Within five minutes, he'd tweeted that Herbert K. Nutterman, "A great, TRUMP-TRAINED MANIGER," would be replacing Mack Mulkinson as White House chief of staff.

For the record, I was dismayed when I learned that Mr. Mulkinson heard of his dismissal from his driver. He was on his way back to the White House from a meeting on Capitol Hill with the House Aryan Caucus.* The driver received a text instructing him to pull over and tell Mr. Mulkinson to "exit the vehicle immediately." Mr. Mulkinson did, apparently under the impression that a terrorist act was imminent, whereupon the driver drove off and left him on the sidewalk. The photograph of him standing there with a *What the . . . ?* look on his face was not, I stipulate, one of the Trump administration's proudest moments. It became a meme and went viral.

Hetta never made the borscht. She finished peeling the beets, took off her apron, folded it neatly, went to the bedroom, and closed the door. I wondered: is she committing suicide?

I stared forlornly at the pile of purple peelings. There is something inherently forlorn about a pile of pointless beet

---

* A group of congresspeople who generally, but not exclusively, focus on matters dealing with immigration.

shavings on a kitchen floor. Here, I suppose, was *our* meme. I certainly wasn't about to take a picture and post it on Instagram. But I can tell you that it did go viral throughout the Herbert K. Nutterman central nervous system. It forever ruined borscht for me. Ever since, the mere thought of beets makes me queasy.

In ancient Rome, they would slice birds open and study their entrails to see what the future held. Disgusting, I agree, and scientifically speaking, nuts. But looking back, I've sometimes wondered if perhaps I should have studied those purple beet peelings more closely. I might have, but now the phone was ringing and life hasn't been quite the same since.

2

News of my appointment was greeted—if "greeted" is the appropriate word—with surprise and, Washington being Washington, a heaping helping of snark.

The *Washington Post* made it sound as though my duties would consist of making sure everyone got a mint on their pillow along with the daily turndown service. And of course it couldn't resist a cheap sideswipe at Mr. Trump: "Doubtless, Mr. Nutterman will ensure a reliable supply chain of McDonald's Quarter Pounders with Cheese Deluxe and keep the Oval Office minibar stocked with Diet Cokes."

It took the *New York Times* less than an hour to post an indignant—and highly exaggerated—account of my role as "Trump's resident fake Civil War historian." I was beginning to understand why Mr. Trump yearned to have the media suffocated and dismembered. But I understood that character assassination went with my new job.

Fox News was gracious, though I wished they hadn't compared me to Mussolini. ("By all accounts, Mr. Nutterman made the Trump trains run on time.") There are no trains at any of the Trump properties, but as the younger generation would say, whatever.

One of the first congratulatory phone calls I got was from Mr. Seamus Colonnity, Fox News's number-one personality. I was a great admirer of his, so I'll admit to feeling flattered. To me, Mr. Colonnity is the news version of Phil Spector, the music producer who developed the so-called Wall of Sound. (Mr. Spector, alas, would come to grief by shooting his girlfriend in the mouth. The music business is certainly not for the faint of heart.) Mr. Colonnity's genius was to devise a Wall of Talk. His monologues were marathons. He could go on for what seemed like hours without even pausing for breath. His liberal detractors may have disparaged his defenses of Mr. Trump as "steroid-driven drool" and "extended bar rants," but to me, Mr. Colonnity was a modern-day Cicero.

I had met him on numerous occasions, at Trump Magnifica, Farrago-sur-Mer, and Bloody Run. He and Mr. Trump golfed together and swapped off-color stories. A frequent theme was Ukraine. One I remember was: "How many Ukrainians does it take to change a lightbulb?" Answer: "Twelve, because Ukrainians are so fucking stupid. Plus Biden's son, to charge a fifty-thousand-dollar consulting fee."

Over the years, I watched many people fawn over Mr. Trump. I mean "fawn" in a positive way, that is, expressing effusive admiration. I felt that Mr. Colonnity truly enjoyed fawning over Mr. Trump, whereas others fawned out of fear.

Mr. Trump thought very highly of Mr. Colonnity. He frequently looked to him for guidance. While listening to Mr. Colonnity's nightly Wall of Talk, Mr. Trump would hit the pause button on the remote control and tell his tweet-wallah, "What he just said about Nancy Pelosi having bad breath—write that down. I can use that." He'd then compose a tweet on the theme of Mrs. Pelosi's

"HORRIBLE halitosis" and share it with the fifty-three million people in his tweetersphere. Mr. Trump channeled so many of Mr. Colonnity's insights that Mr. Colonnity came to be called "the shadow White House chief of staff." And even "the real chief of staff." (Sometimes snarkily followed by "God save us.")

It was this very thing that Mr. Colonnity wished to discuss with me in that call.

"Herb," he said, "don't buy into that 'Colonnity is the real power behind the throne' bullcrap. They only say that to drive a wedge between me and the president."

"Thank you for sharing that, sir," I said.

"Herb," he said, "you don't have to call *me* sir. You're the White House chief of staff. You can call me anything you want, including shithead."

I sensed he was being mirthful, so I laughed. I had to pinch myself. Here was Mr. Seamus Colonnity himself, inviting me to call him a shithead. I wanted to say, *Well, that's awfully white of you, shithead.* But I couldn't make the words come out of my mouth. A quarter century in the hospitality business had installed a profanity dam in my mouth.

"Herb," he said in an intimate tone. "As you know, the boss has been expressing some dissatisfaction with Fox."

I reassured him that so far as I knew, Mr. Trump's admiration for Fox was undimmed.

"I dunno," Mr. Colonnity said. "He wasn't pleased about that poll we ran showing the two-point drop in his approval rating among World War II veterans."

I agreed that he wasn't happy, but said that he hadn't been dwelling on it.

"I hope he understands that I had nothing to do with that," Mr. Colonnity said.

I thought it prudent not to comment, so I made an ambiguous *hmpf* sound.

Mr. Colonnity continued: "I don't know what's going on with those people on *Fox and Fiends* lately. They used to be team players. Frankly, I'm starting to wonder whose team they're on."

I wasn't sure where this was going, so I made another *hmpf*.

"What *really* pissed me off," Mr. Colonnity went on, "was that idiot they had on who said the FBI was only following 'established procedure' when they sent in that SWAT team to arrest Mitch McConnell's sister-in-law."

Anjelica "Empress" Chong was the sister of the wife of Senate Majority Leader Mitch McConnell and part owner of her family's Flying Junk Shipping of Shanghai. The company had been transporting great quantities of soil from the mainland as part of China's program of building artificial islands in the South China Sea. This apparently violated some obscure treaty, exposing "Empress" to legal action.

"I mean, come on. Why was that necessary? She's not El Chapo, for Chrissake. What did they think, the sister-in-law of the Senate majority leader was going to open fire on them? She'd have turned herself in peacefully. And by the way, the *fuck* is going on with Barr? Why would he sign off on a raid like that?"

Careful, Herb, I told myself, for here was thin ice. I could hardly reveal to Mr. Colonnity—however close he was to the president—the real reason behind it.

I suggested that perhaps the attorney general had intended the arrest, which involved some two dozen FBI agents, a helicopter, and two armored riot-control vehicles, to "send a message" to other sisters-in-law of the majority leader not to violate international embargoes. But Mr. Colonnity's Wall of Talk was up and running and there was no penetrating it.

"I'll tell you why he did it," he continued. "Barr's just falling for this *judgment of history* bullshit that's going around like Wuhan coronavirus. Everyone's going, '*Oh no! George Will says we're all going to look bad a hundred years from now!'* Talk about summer soldiers and sunshine patriots! These people make me sick, Herb. They make me want to vomit."

I was truly flattered at how quickly Mr. Colonnity had taken me into his confidence. Only five minutes into our first conversation together, and here he was sharing details of his gastric system with me. It made me want to share with him the background behind "Empress" Chong's arrest. But I couldn't reveal that the president had instructed AG Barr to "take the bitch down hard," as payback to Senator McConnell for allowing the impeachment trial to proceed in the Senate.

"I'll be sure to convey your concern to the president," I said.

Apparently this sounded bland, or evasive, for Mr. Colonnity's tone suddenly cooled by several degrees. Double-digit degrees.

After a silence he said, in a brusque sort of way, "Yeah, well, you *do* that, Herb." And hung up.

I rebuked myself. *Well done, Herb. Not yet noon on your first day and already you have offended Mr. Trump's chief media champion.*

I made a mental note to be more—I don't want to say "sycophantic"—proactive when it came to massaging the egos of the larger personalities in Mr. Trump's inner circle. It goes with the job. A quarter century in the hospitality business would be good training.

A bit after noon, Greta Fibberson, our chief of communications, came into my office. Greta was a highly attractive female person: tall, dark haired, cheekbones like knives, great gams, high heels, and as the older generation would say, "A balcony you could play Shakespeare from."*

---

* I stipulate that in the #MeToo era, one would never use such a description. Still.

Greta's default expression was one of anxiety verging on panic, not uncommon in the Trump White House, where staff were expected to function at peak efficiency or be fired by tweet.

"Herb," she said, favoring me with one of her three-second smiles. "Welcome aboard. Surviving so far? That's great. Herb, we need to talk."

"Of course," I said. "What's up?"

"Why does Seamus Colonnity hate you?"

Bit of a jolt.

"I have no idea. Why do you say this?"

"He just called you a bellhop on his radio show."

"Well, I . . . we had a perfectly agreeable talk, just now. *He* called me. To congratulate me on the job."

"Uh-huh. And?"

"He said not to take seriously what people say about him being the real White House chief of staff."

"Was that *all*?"

"No. He expressed dismay, I'd call it, over the arrest of Senator McConnell's sister-in-law. Specifically, about the somewhat dramatic manner in which it was conducted."

I didn't know if the president had looped Greta in on his reason for treating Senator McConnell's sister-in-law like the head of a Mexican drug cartel.

I added, "He referred to the *Fox and Fiends* hosts by an unflattering name."

"For the veterans poll?"

"Yes."

Greta sniffed.

"Okay. But why has Seamus got it in for you? You did kiss his ring, I hope."

A quarter century in the hospitality business may have

instilled a desire to please, but it hadn't quite turned me into Uriah Heep.*

"If by 'kiss his ring' you mean was I polite, the answer is yes, Greta. But I had the distinct impression that Mr. Colonnity had called to kiss *my* ring. Not that I actually wear a ring."

She crossed her arms over her Shakespearean mezzanine and made a bemused snort.

"It's my fault," she said. "I should have given you a heads-up. Seamus always calls new chiefs on their first day. To show them who's really chief. It's his way of letting you know you're on probation."

"Oh," I said. "And how does one get off probation?"

"By feeding him."

"I was under the impression the president fed him. But thank you for the advice."

"Look, Herb. The boss thinks the sun rises and sets on Seamus's ass. If Seamus shot someone on Fifth Avenue in broad daylight, he'd pardon him before they got the handcuffs on him. Bear that in mind going forward. Okay? Gotta go. Hey—everyone is *thrilled* you're here. The boss needs a comfort zone, and you are it. Mulkinson was a total disaster. Meanwhile, don't worry about Seamus. I'll give him a hand job. But the next one's on you."

I understand that in White House communications— "commo," in the parlance—folks like Greta were required to perform glad-handing and ego-stroking on the media. Still. I was willing to kiss Mr. Colonnity's ring if that was the price of getting him to stop referring to me as a bellhop; but there would be no "hand job" for him from Herb Nutterman.

It was no time for brooding. Mr. Trump was not exaggerating when he told me he was in the middle of a "shit storm." Indeed, the feces were incoming from every direction: impeachment

* An unpleasantly servile Dickens character.

proceedings; terrorist attacks by the newly formed Kurdish "Death to America" Brigade; the nomination of Roy Moore* to replace Ruth Bader Ginsburg on the Supreme Court; the court-ordered release of Mr. Trump's tax returns (a veritable Pandora's box of horrors); plus the news that presidential son-in-law Jored Kushner had refinanced the family company's trouble-plagued luxury apartment complex in Puerto Vaya con Dios, Mexico, with a loan from the sultan of Brunei. It was one thing after another. The liberal mainstream media, whose motto is "America Last," was feasting.

Mr. Colonnity's valiant colleague, Mr. Corky Fartmartin, was joining in Fox's defense of the president. So we had on our side twin Galahads tilting lances. But Mr. Fartmartin's efforts to link Hillary Clinton to all of Mr. Trump's calamities weren't quite getting traction. Still, one had to applaud the passion with which these two "Lions of Fox" defended their president.† If only more members of the media were as patriotic. Mr. Trump returned the favor by inviting them frequently to golf with him, and told me to comp them whenever they stayed at Trump properties. Naturally, the media even managed to make these friendly gestures by Mr. Trump seem criminal.

It was all enough to keep a dozen White House chiefs of staff busy. I sometimes had a cot brought in to my office so I could work through the night, catching occasional fifteen-minute power naps between incoming rounds of feces. Yet it was also exhilarating. Here I was at ground zero, doing my part to Make America Great Again. I hadn't worked this hard since the reverse-flow sewage disaster at Farrago.

---

* Former chief justice of the Alabama Supreme Court, alleged by some to have had a perhaps overzealous interest in fourteen-year-old girls.

† The term "Lions of Fox" seems incongruent, but the promotional department at Fox made good use of it.

3

No need to go into too much detail. You'd have to have been living on Mars—or Pluto—not to know that on that fateful day the world awoke to the arresting news that Vladimir Putin, president of the Russian Federation, had been defeated by the candidate of the Communist Party of the Russian Federation. Many a cup of coffee cooled before being drunk that morning.

Mr. Putin had proposed the bold idea of moving the 2024 presidential election up by four years, so as to make him president for life, thus eliminating the need for endless periodic elections. This would result in considerable budget savings as well as eliminating the inevitable disruptions that elections cause.

Mr. Putin and his newly renamed Putin Forever Party— formerly United Russia—had been comfortably ahead of the others. Vladimir Zhirinovsky's Russia for Russians Only Party was twenty points behind. Anatoli Zitkin's Communist Party trailed by almost fifty points. No one expected him to win, even the nincompoops at the *New York Times* who gave Hillary Clinton a 97 percent chance of winning in 2016.

Then—cue the kettle drums in Tchaikovsky's 1812 Overture—
ba-boom: Putin came in second, *behind* Zitkin. Around the
globe could be heard a collective "What? That *can't* be right."

Because Zitkin's margin of victory was less than 2 percent,
Russian law mandated a second, runoff election.

Now it's no secret that Mr. Trump was a huge admirer of
Mr. Putin. But I stress, this was not, as his detractors have so
malevolently suggested, because he owed his presidency to
him. No. Not at all.

Yes, some alleged that Russia had interfered in the 2016
election on Mr. Trump's behalf. Specifically, all seventeen of the
US intelligence agencies, giving rise to suspicion in the Trump
camp that the "deep state" was determined to make his victory
appear illegitimate. But there was never any hard evidence or
smoking gun. No ballots were found in Michigan with "Trump"
written in Cyrillic.

Mr. Trump was understandably aggrieved by allegations
that he owed his presidency to Russian military intelligence and
so-called troll farms and "bots." And yes, technically, Hillary
Clinton got three million more votes, but as Mr. Trump said,
most of those were fraudulent, cast by Mexican drug gangs and
agents of George Soros. Anyway, presidents are elected by the
Electoral College, not by actual people.*

The plain truth is that Mr. Trump "clicked" with Mr. Putin.
Mr. Trump has always admired strong personalities. This is
why he got along so well with such world leaders as Mr. Kim
of North Korea; President Attajurk of Turkey; Mr. Orban of
Hungary; Mr. Duterte of the Philippines; Mr. Goerring, the
new chancellor of Germany; and the new boy on the block, the
frisky, bellicose Emperor Hirohito II of Japan.

---

* The origins of the Electoral College are obscure, but some scholars hold
that it was intended to annoy the more populous states.

So when the astonishing news broke that Mr. Putin had lost to a *Communist*, the general reaction was "No way."

Mr. Trump typically lost interest in his daily intelligence briefing after about thirty seconds. Not this morning.

"How could this have *happened*?" he demanded of DNI Miriam "Mother" Jones.*

I liked and respected Miriam.† She struck me as a no-nonsense sort, which is what you want in a director of national intelligence. I'm sure that as the first female DNI she was aware that she was on probation. If she didn't know the answer to a question, she would say honestly, "I don't know, sir."

"Hadda be a hack," Mr. Trump insisted. "Putin was fifty points ahead of the other guy, whatshisname?"

"Zitkin," Miriam said, since she did know the answer to this question. "Anatoli Zitkin."

"Whatever. Well what do you know?"

"I have a briefing paper on him for you," Miriam said, handing the president a thick folder.

"I don't have time to read that crap. What's he look like? Do you have a picture of him?"

Miriam had come prepared.

Mr. Trump stared at the photo before him of a stout, balding, bespectacled man in his early sixties. He was smiling, which struck me as unusual. In most photos I've seen of Communists, they're scowling and grim, as though someone's just insulted their mother or told them that *Das Kapital* was so boring they never made it past page three. Smiling might give them away

---

* The director of national intelligence is ostensibly the head of America's collective seventeen intelligence agencies.

† For some reason, I have always been attracted to women who wear their hair in tight buns.

for having a sneaky bourgeois thought, or deviating from true Marxist-Leninism, or putting out capitalist attitude.

Comrade Zitkin didn't look scary enough to be a Russian Commie. I couldn't imagine him ordering the czar and his entire family to be shot, or sending millions of people off to Siberia, or signing a nonaggression pact with Hitler. I could see him standing on Lenin's mausoleum in Red Square with his fellow Commies, waving at tanks and missiles and the goose-stepping soldiers. But he'd probably still be smiling, unlike the old Soviet sourpusses who as the parade went past seemed to be thinking, *When is this fucking parade going to be over? I'm freezing. Who's got the vodka?*

Mr. Trump tossed the photo back at Miriam.

"That's not a winner," he said. "That's a loser. What's his story? Not that I care. Twenty-five words or less."

"A brief brief?" Miriam said. "Okay. Sixty-three. From Tbilisi. Like Stalin. But not a Stalinist himself. Probably as a result of his father and three uncles dying in the Gulag."

"The what?"

"The old Soviet network of political prisons. Slave labor camps."

"He didn't fuck around, Stalin. You gotta give him that."

Sensing that Mr. Trump's attention was already wandering, Miriam finished her brief with: "Came up through the trade unions. Organizer. Married the boss's daughter. Two grown children. This is the third time he's run for president. Apparently against the wishes of his wife. She calls him Comrade Quixote."

"Comrade what?"

"I take it as a reference to Don Quixote. The muddleheaded Spanish knight. *Man of La Mancha*?"

"Yeah, yeah. So what's his thing?"

"Thing?"

"Why is he a *Communist*?"

"Ah. He only became one after Putin came to power. His principal theme is"—Miriam seemed to be mentally editing—"that Putin is running a kleptocracy."

"That he's a thief?"

"Essentially. That he runs the country much as a mafia don would run his empire. Got the oligarchs organized and functioning as the underbosses, the capos, if you will."

"He hates rich people, in other words. He's Bernie Sanders."

Miriam smiled. "I imagine he and Senator Sanders might agree on a few things."

"Okay. Got it. And you and the however many *intelligence* agencies we have didn't see this coming?"

"We were as surprised by the result as everyone else, sir."

"What's the intelligence budget these days? Trillions?"

"Fifty-four billion."

"How could this *loser* pull off something like this?"

Miriam said she would rather wait until she had "actionable humint," a phrase that probably meant as little to the president as it did to me. (It turned out to mean "human intelligence," as opposed to "siginit," which means "signals intelligence.")

The moment Miriam left the Oval Office, tightly clutching her presidential daily briefing tablet, Mr. Trump picked up the phone and told the operator to get Mr. Putin on the line.

"Sir," I said, "do you want me to get Mr. Wootten?" Judd Wootten was director of the National Security Council. I thought it would be prudent to have him in on a conversation between the president and the leader of Russia. While speaking with world leaders on the phone, Mr. Trump had a tendency to improvise. The fallout from his "perfect" call with the leader of Ukraine had been rather considerable.

Mr. Trump grunted dismissively, which I took to mean "no." He seemed extremely agitated, fiddling with the bejeweled-dagger letter opener the Saudi leader had given him, tapping it on his desk like a drumstick as he waited for Mr. Putin to come on the line.

He said to me with a worried look, "What if he thinks *we* had something to do with it?"

"Why would he think that, sir?" I said. "He knows you have the warmest feelings for him."

"He's Russian. They're all paranoid, Russians. And what if we *did* have something to do with it?"

"Surely not, sir. You'd have to authorize something like that."

"They hate me, the intelligence people. You know why? Because I called bullshit on them when they claimed Putin put me in office. You don't think the deep state would pull some stunt like this? To make Putin think *I* was behind it? Vladimir? Is that you? Jesus fucking Christ, what's going *on* over there? Are you okay, my friend? Is this some kind of coup? What can we do to help? Name it, you got it. Anything. I asked our intelligence numbnuts what was going on, but . . . what? Numbnuts . . ."

There was a pause. Perhaps the translator was struggling with "numbnuts." "Idiots, all of them. The same people who say you elected me president. By the way, if you did, thank you. Very nice of you. Now they're telling me they don't know diddly-squat." (Another pause indicated this was presenting challenges to the translator.) "They've got a big surprise coming. Uh-huh. I'm gonna cut their fucking budgets by *half*. They're gonna be out on the street, rattling cups. So what the hell? What happened? How did this asshole Zipkin hijack your election?"*

The call went on for some time. I wasn't listening in on an extension, so it wasn't until later, when I got the transcript of their "private" conversation, that I gathered Mr. Putin was

---

* The president never could get Zitkin's name right, possibly owing to his having known a New York socialite in the 1980s named (Jerome) Zipkin.

keeping an open mind as to who might have stolen his election. As a former KGB officer, Mr. Putin was, you might say, a professional paranoid. He thanked Mr. Trump for the call and seemed faintly amused by Mr. Trump's repeated suggestion to "Lock him up!"

Judd was beside himself when he learned of the call. He demanded to know why I hadn't summoned him "in real time." I didn't have the heart to tell him, "Because, Judd, the president doesn't like you."

It was no secret that Mr. Trump's relations with his National Security Council directors had been less than smooth. Judd was his ninth in three and a half years, and Mr. Trump was far from pleased with him. Judd was an academic, and perhaps as a consequence, a bit of what Mr. Trump called a "yapper."

An NSC director with a PhD isn't necessarily a handicap. Henry Kissinger was an academic, and that turned out well, except maybe for the Vietnam part. But Mr. Trump wasn't Richard Nixon. Which is to say, the kind of president who's read a great deal about national security and discussed it with intellectuals, grilling them for hours, exploring every aspect of this or that policy. That sort of thing Mr. Trump called "yada yada."

If Judd wanted us to go to war, or lob a few Tomahawk missiles at someone, he'd come to the meeting with a forty-five-minute PowerPoint, explaining why he wanted the war, or the Tomahawks. Mr. Trump simply had no patience for that. He liked his briefings short, crisp, and to the point, and above all, without briefing books or even short memos. Mr. Trump's eyes had some sort of membrane that caused them to glaze over. He attributed this to his "lightning-fast brain," not to attention deficit disorder. The one exception was if someone was praising him. He had inexhaustible patience when it came to encomia, such as when Kanye West would drop by and deliver a soliloquy comparing Mr. Trump to Napoleon, or God.

I liked Judd, and he liked me, if for no other reason than that I protected him. I thought the optics of replacing him with a tenth NSC director would be unfavorable.*

But three times now Mr. Trump had told me, "Get rid of that bug-eyed prick." I pretended not to have heard him, and as often was the case, Mr. Trump forgot about it, his lightning mind having moved on. He juggled so many balls, Mr. Trump, that he sometimes lost track of just how many were in the air. I don't mean this as a criticism.

"Herb," Judd said nervously, "this could be a minefield."

I briefed him on the president's call with Mr. Putin, telling him that the president expressed hearty support for Mr. Putin.

"He more or less told Putin he should line Zitkin and his fellow Commies up against the Kremlin wall and shoot them," I said. "Putin is fully aware of Mr. Trump's support."

Judd sighed in that way PhDs do, to convey that only they, with their advanced degrees, can fully comprehend the "parameters," as they call them.

"I'm saying it could be a problem, Herb," Judd insisted mysteriously. He wore thick glasses, presumably from the strain of all that PhD-related reading. They magnified his eyes, like the ones of the locomotive cartoon character Thomas the Tank Engine in the children's TV program. It could be distracting at times, and it annoyed Mr. Trump, who preferred the optics (as it were) of being surrounded by people who, as he put it, "look good."

"What kind of problem, Judd?" I said a bit impatiently. I wasn't in the mood for Twenty Questions.

"A *cyberwar*-type problem, Herb," he replied, lowering his voice even though there was no one else in the room. "I had

---

* "Optics" is Washington parlance for "appearances." I don't know how optometry crept into the lingo, but whatever.

a call from Flipper Murphy at CyberCom. I'm on my way to Meade.* I'll give you a fill when I get back. But"—another sigh— "this could be a bit of a clusterfuck."

Not to split hairs, but I wondered how can one have a bit of a clusterfuck? "Clusterfuck" seems to me a comprehensive term, denoting total disaster. A bit of a total disaster?

But Judd had gotten my attention. It was difficult to concentrate on Air Force One seating assignments for the upcoming big Trump rally in Testicle, Ohio.

* Fort Meade, Maryland, headquarters of the National Security Agency and the United States Cyber Command, headed by Adm. Phillip "Flipper" Murphy.

4

"So that's the sitrep," Judd said as he finished briefing me. Sitrep is a contraction of "situation report."

It's my experience that people who have never worn a uniform are the ones who most love military parlance. As sitreps went, this was a lulu; or as they say in the military, a clusterfuck.

"I'm not sure I understand," I said. "Flipper—Admiral Murphy—did he say that this computer program—"

"Platform."

"Whatever. That one of his computers hacked the Russian election—on its *own*? Without authorization?"

Judd sighed at my obtuseness.

"Herb, we're talking about an autonomous retaliatory protocol. The whole point of a platform like Placid Reflux is that it self-activates. That's what AI is all about—outsourcing."

"But can't that lead to blowing up the world?"

"Herb," he said as though he were explaining all this to an imbecile, "Placid Reflux doesn't launch nuclear weapons. Its mission parameters are limited. It will only retaliate symmetrically against foreign interference in a US election."

"Judd," I said, "I have no idea what you are talking about. But never mind explaining. Why did it see fit to activate on its *own*?"

"Well . . ." Judd now seemed to be choosing his words carefully. He and I disagreed about the alleged Russian interference in the 2016 election. "It *appears* to have determined that the Russians *did*, in fact, interfere in the 2016 election."

"Who asked it to determine anything?"

"Look, Herb, you are aware that all seventeen of our intelligence agencies agree that the Russians interfered. Point is, this computer also agrees. So when the president *didn't* retaliate after the 2016 election, Placid Reflux concluded that he'd been neutralized."

"Neutralized?"

"Killed. Incapacitated. In war theory, they call it 'decapitation.' Unable to retaliate."

"Well, Judd, the president is *not* decapitated. And I still don't understand how something like this could have happened. Are you telling me that no one at US Cyber Command noticed that one of its computers had gone rogue and attacked a foreign power?"

"No, they noticed."

"Then why didn't they hit the off button?"

"Autonomous protocol platforms don't have off buttons, Herb. It's a safeguard against infiltration. So the enemy can't shut them down."

"Safeguard? Brilliant. Can't they turn off the electricity?"

"The batteries would only kick in. And they're good for years. Look, Flipper's aware that it puts the president in an awkward position." Judd arched an eyebrow. "Given his extraordinary *warmth* toward Putin."

Judd himself felt no warmth toward the Russian leader. Whenever Mr. Putin allegedly had someone murdered or took over another portion of Ukraine, Judd was always the first to say *I told you so*. I finally had to tell him not to do this in front of Mr. Trump. It annoyed him.

"Awkward?" I said. "Not nearly as awkward as the position Admiral Flipper is going to find himself in at his court-martial!"

Judd took off his owl glasses and rubbed the bridge of his nose.

"Herb, we need to have a come-to-Jesus."

"I'm Jewish. I don't do come-to-Jesus, as you put it. With all due respect to the Christian faith. Jesus *Christ*, Judd, can you *imagine* how this is going to sit with the president?"

"Herb. Walk with me."

"Where, backward?"

"I'm saying let's just look at it."

"You know the president's feelings about the deep state. This is only going to confirm his worst suspicions."

"I appreciate that, Herb. I read you five by five.* I'm suggesting that we put on our big-girl panties and deal with the situation."

I listened as Judd made his case, mercifully without Power-Point:

First, he said, aside from himself and me, only a handful of personnel at US Cyber Command knew that this accursed Placid Reflux had activated. Second, it was designed to be virtually untraceable, so the Russians would be highly unlikely to determine its origin. Third, if President Trump learned about it, he would "go bananas" and shut down not only US Cyber Command, but probably *all* US intelligence agencies, which he already despised for asserting that Mr. Putin had gotten him elected president. This, Judd emphasized, would be catastrophic to national security. And last, if Putin learned about it, which he

---

* Presumably another military term for "I understand." Honestly . . .

29

surely would if the president did, he would retaliate by—Judd chose his words carefully here—"going public with whatever he *might* have on Mr. Trump. And that," Judd said gravely, "would be game over." He concluded, "Knowing of your devotion to Mr. Trump, Herb, I'm sure that you'd find that a bad outcome."

There was the sitrep, in all its beauty. I felt physically ill.

"Herb?"

"What?"

"You okay? You look a little green around the gills."

"No, Judd, I am not 'okay.' You've just informed me that the United States has grossly—grotesquely—interfered in a foreign election. And not just any foreign election. We have essentially undertaken a coup d'état against the president of Russia."

He grinned. "Pretty slick, huh? Who knew we had this kind of capability."

"Capability? *Capability?*"

"Calm down, Herb."

I stammered. "And why did this, this, this *machine* elect a Communist? Was that one of its *parameters?*"

"Placid's algorithm would have incorporated historical precedent." (Judd was apparently now on a first-name basis with the beast.) "Being aware that the US defeated Russian Communism before, it would likely predicate another future victory. Eventually."

"What, after another seventy-four-year golden age of Gulag, Berlin Wall, and Iron Curtain? Who programmed this Pandora's box? Mr. Trump will doubtless want to give him a Presidential Medal of Freedom."

"*Herb,*" Judd said, "you're overworking the problem. Look, here's how this thing's going to play out. Vladimir Putin will win the runoff election by the biggest landslide in Russian history. In *any* history. And Anatoli Zitkin, poor son of a bitch, will curse the day he won the first round. I wouldn't predict longevity for

Comrade Zitkin. The GRU is probably whipping up a fresh batch of Novichok to smear on his doorknobs." (GRU is the rather grim-sounding acronym for Russian military intelligence. More on Novichok in due course.)

I hadn't felt such weight on my shoulders since Mr. and Mrs. Trump's wedding reception at Farrago-sur-Mer.

"So," I sighed, "you're proposing that we *don't* tell the president?"

"If he doesn't know about it, he doesn't have to deny knowing about it."

This sounded eerily Rumsfeldian.

"It's called 'plausible deniability,' Herb. Most presidents would kill to have it."

"But isn't it our duty to tell him?"

"I'd say that depends on your definition of 'duty.'"

"Judd," I said, "we're not talking about playing hide the cigar with the intern."

"I understand. But isn't our highest duty to *protect* the president?"

This was hard to disagree with.

"You do understand," he said, "that if the president learns about it, it won't remain secret."

I had to agree with this assessment.

"He'll tell Putin. And Putin will retaliate. How? Again, I'm not saying Putin *has* something on the president. However . . ."

He let that sink in and said, "The question you have to ask yourself is: *Do I tell the president,* knowing *that it would lead to yet* another *impeachment? And* this *time, conviction by the Senate.* Even Squiggly Biskitt would have a hard time defending him."

Judd seemed pleased with himself for having thought it all through so neatly. I suppose that's what PhDs do.

"Your call, Chief," he said. "Way above my pay grade."

Chief? He'd never called me Chief before. And that *way above my pay grade* mumbo jumbo was slicing the salami a bit thin. Looking back, it's clear that Judd was in effect handing me ownership of this odious enchilada.

As the reader is probably aware, Judd's blithe prediction as to how it would play out would prove as accurate as the prediction by the nincompoop "experts" who gave Mr. Trump a 3 percent chance of beating Hillary Clinton in 2016.

5

Naturally, the media feasted on the Zitkin victory. Commentators who'd previously denounced Mr. Trump's "bromance" with Putin were now in a bind, scratching their heads and wondering if he'd come to his senses and ordered the US to retaliate and interfere in *his* election.

Chip Holleran of *Eightball*—who'd spent the last three and a half years comparing Mr. Trump to Caligula, Nero, Genghis Khan, Tsar Nicholas II, Antichrist, and Porky Pig—opened his show with "Is the Trump-Putin wedding *off*?"

The stunning Zitkin victory was even giving pause to the more staid element of the Never Trump punditariat. George Will, dean of the paleoconservatives,* wrote with characteristic hauteur, "One can continue to find Donald Trump repugnant at every level while nonetheless wondering if all along he has been in a subtle pas de deux with Putin."

* So called because of their dietary habits.

Needless to say, all this made Mr. Trump exceedingly nervous that the Kremlin might conclude he *had* ordered the cyberattack. I reassured him that Mr. Putin had better things to do than watch Chip Holleran or read George Will, but the poor man's stomach was in knots. He issued a tweetnado, expressing solidarity with Mr. Putin and denouncing Comrade Zitkin in the harshest terms, including "Grand Larceny" and attempting to "Make Russia Red Again."

One particularly barbed tweet declared that locking up Mr. Zitkin was inadequate punishment for what he had done. Mr. Trump proposed he should be "wrapped in chains and lowered into a Pit full of Starving Dogs. DASVIDANYA!!!" Whether Mr. Putin was persuaded of Mr. Trump's innocence by these somewhat overheated protestations was unclear.

Our stalwart communications director, Greta Fibberson, swatted away media questions about US involvement in the hack, calling the reporters who posed them "human filth" and "execrable swine."

But with all due respect to Greta's high standards of professionalism, it was Katie Borgia-O'Reilly who "fixed bayonet" and charged out of the trench at the enemy. Love her or hate her, you had to admit that Katie took the art of going low to new heights. Really, she was dazzling.

Katie was sexy in a—I don't want to say "creepy"—certain kind of way, as if you might discover after sleeping with her that she was in fact an android or an Albanian assassin sent to murder your grandmother for no clear reason. She had no specific function at the White House other than to seek out the nearest camera or microphone and declaim defiantly in support of whatever the president had said or done.

Katie had been with Mr. Trump from the start of the 2016 campaign. She'd earned her chops defending Mr. Trump's attack on Sen. John McCain as a bogus war hero and doing pushback on the uproar over the *Hollywood Access* tape.*

Now, almost four years later, her ardor for Mr. Trump was undiminished, as was her disdain for factual niceties. There was a magnificence—an indomitability, if you will—in the gleeful way in which she went mano a mano with the "enemies of the people."

The first time I saw Katie up close in action was shortly after I got to the White House. Mr. Trump had been displeased by a remark made by visiting German chancellor Angela Merkel, to the effect that "not all immigrants are vermin." The president later referred to her—humorously, I'm sure—as "an old hag." He said this in front of fifty or so TV cameras, and his subsequent claim that he'd said "old bag" didn't convince everyone. (No one, actually.) The media, always quick to criticize Mr. Trump, went into full outrage mode.

From the West Wing door leapt Katie, like a lioness attacking a herd of water buffalo.

"The president respects Mrs. Merkel," she said in her raspy voice. (One commentator described it as "meth-lab Lauren Bacall.") "He thinks she's terrific. They have a very warm relationship. And frankly, allegations like this one aren't helpful. You people in the media are always going on about how important NATO is? Well, trying to drive a wedge between the president and the German leader is unhelpful. It doesn't help. It doesn't. No. I'm sorry. You should all be ashamed of yourselves. You should all go home and die."

Again, not to gush, but: "You go, girl!" Katie was to Mr. Trump World what Joan of Arc was to whatever part of France she was

---

* I myself thought McCain was a genuine war hero, despite having gotten shot down. As for Mr. Trump's remark about "grab 'em by the pussy," Katie's audacious assertion he was talking about cats never quite gained traction. But one had to admire her creativity and energy.

from. I murmured my admiration to a staffer standing next to me. "Yeah," he said. "Katie sure tells it like it ain't."

Mr. Trump adored her, to the extent that he was capable of adoration for other people. His affection was evident in his nickname for her: "My blond tarantula." Katie was flattered, knowing that with Mr. Trump, the more disparaging the nickname, the higher you stood in his estimation. He called Mr. Fangschwaller, his top adviser on immigration, "My German shepherd." There was no higher compliment.

Katie's job was not made any easier by her husband, Jerome "Romy" O'Reilly. Romy was a partner in the prestigious Washington law firm of Baggot, Bain, Bakely, Blaster, and Botz.* When he wasn't billing a thousand dollars an hour, he was dissing Mr. Trump. His disparagement had become increasingly ad hominem, to use a legal term. He'd even called the president "a head case." Not much respect for the office there. We at the White House could only wonder what it must be like around the Borgia-O'Reilly dinner table, what with the four little Borgia-O'Reillys sitting there spooning up their porridge. What strange bedfellows Washingtonians make.†

Katie had initially signed up with the Trump campaign "as a lark." No one—Mr. Trump himself included—expected him to win. Back then Romy seemed not to care, though he'd already gone on the record declaring that Mr. Trump was "not recognizably human." As we say in Washington, "We'll put you down as undecided, leaning against."

---

* The alliteration of the firm's name is, I'm told, accidental.

† I confess that we also wondered what the Borgia-O'Reilly boudoir scene must be like. One staffer said it put her in mind of the poster for that movie *Fatal Instinct*, with Sharon Stone embracing her partner in joy and brandishing an ice pick behind his back. In reply, another staffer said that Katie did resemble Sharon Stone—"after being run through a car wash a half dozen times." Rather unkind, though the image does stick in the mind.

Then, the dream became reality. Mr. Trump was elected. Romy was now moaning to the press about Katie's "transformation from my sweet darling to blond tarantula." He likened his wife's championing of Mr. Trump to another bad remake of *Invasion of the Body Snatchers.** It's not for me to say, but really.

As Katie's notoriety as a Trump defender increased, Romy felt compelled, pari passu,† to provide real-time counterpoint. In the process, he became the president's numero-uno Twitter tormentor. He denounced him in harshest terms, including the above-mentioned questioning of Mr. Trump's sanity. Far be it from me to suggest that Jerome O'Reilly, esquire, reveled in all this self-generated publicity. Naturally, the enemies of the people lapped it up. Before long, Romy had accumulated 842,000 Twitter followers and *People* magazine–level name recognition.

Out of respect, I never asked poor Katie what it was like at home. Did Romy return home, having spent the day tweeting that the president suffered from "malignant narcissistic personality disorder," tussle the cowlicks of the four wee Borgia-O'Reillys, sit down to the table, tuck his napkin into his collar, and ask, "And how was *your* day, dear?" Talk about the proverbial pulling the pin on a hand grenade and tossing it into the tureen.

Mixed political marriages are not uncommon in Washington. James Carville, who helped elect Bill Clinton, was famously married to Mary Matalin, who did what she could to reelect George Herbert Walker Bush. For this quaint, bipartisan connubiality they were feted and lionized by The Swamp. They wrote a best-selling book for a big pile of money and raked in

---

* Horror movie in which human beings are bodily invaded by unpleasant aliens.

† Latin phrase for something. Used a lot by the late William F. Buckley, Jr.

more piles in speaking fees and product endorsements. I often wondered why American Express would run commercials featuring these two. Why on earth the Carville-Matalin ménage should make American Express cardholders want to shop more or upgrade from green to platinum is anyone's guess. Whatever their charms, James and Mary wouldn't be confused with, say, George and Amal Clooney. Mr. Carville was always referring to himself as "the product of the love scene in *Deliverance*."

At any rate, there was none of this *wink-wink, aren't we adorable?* vibe with Katie and Romy. The only company likely to hire them for its commercials was Ultimate Fighting Championship.

At the risk of speaking "out of school," I can't resist recounting a scene I accidentally witnessed one day.

I'd gone to see Katie in her closet-sized West Wing office about my notion of forming a special inner donor circle called "Ever Trumpers."

I knocked. Katie waved me in and gestured for me to sit in the one chair squeezed into the space. Barely a minute into our conversation her iPhone rang. A blaze of fury came into her eyes as she recognized the caller ID.

"My husband. I have to take this."

I got up to leave, but she firmly motioned me to sit and proceeded to conduct a most intimate conversation on speaker.

"You *cocksucker*," she said.

"Hi, sweetie," came Romy's voice, all sunbeams and sugarplums. "How's my best girl?"

"Don't *sweetie* me, Jerome O'Reilly," she seethed. "You did that on purpose, you prick."

"This would be in reference to . . . ?"

"No. No, no, no. Don't bother with that horseshit. You know perfectly fucking well what it's *in reference to!*"

"Hmmm," Romy said. "Would it be the tweet in which I expressed concern about the president's sanity? Or lack thereof?"

"*Yes*, Jerome. And it was uncalled for."

"Um, afraid I disagree, sweetie. Your boss makes Captain Queeg look sane. Any minute now, he's going to start ranting that someone's eaten his strawberries."

"Jerome. This has *got. To. Stop!*"

"I couldn't agree more, sweetie. This presidency needs to be stopped. And the sooner the better."

"Jerome! You cannot go around calling the president of the United States a mental case!"

"Why?"

"Because he's the *fucking president!*"

"Umm, there's a bit of undistributed middle in there, sweetie. Tsk-tsk. And you a Loyola graduate. Did we not attend Logic 101 the day they discussed the fallacy of the undistributed middle?"

Katie's face was turning seven shades of red. She'd been educated by the Jesuits of Loyola, Jesuits being the Catholic order of priests from which we get the term "jesuitical."

The *Washington Post* had by this point tallied Mr. Trump's alleged false statements, prevarications, and outright lies at more than sixteen thousand since taking office. Since Katie had defended practically each one, the *Post* had dubbed her Mr. Trump's "vice prevaricator," and suggested that she title her future memoir *The Audacity of Mendacity.**

Romy said with what sounded like genuine tenderness: "Sweetie, it's your mental health, not his, that concerns me more at this point."

Well. Katie looked about to unleash her inner dragon and scorch the earth. I actually leaned back in my tiny chair to avoid collateral immolation. But instead she said in a tone of disappointment, "I think that's *sad*, Jerome. Sad."

---

* Her eventual memoir is in fact titled: *Always Wear Pearls Before Swine: Briefing the Press in the Trump Era.*

"Listen to yourself, sweetie. You're even starting to talk like him. It really is *Invasion of the Body Snatchers*. Remember how that turned out?"

"Jerome!" she said. "Do you *realize* how *fucking insulting that is*?"

"It's not meant as an insult, sweetie. It's intended as an expression of love."

"The only reason anyone pays *any* attention to your dumb tweets is you're my husband!"

"Stipulated. Nolo contendere.* And the only reason that *I* tweet is you're my wife."

"What the fuck is *that* supposed to mean?" Katie demanded hotly.

"I'll tell you. It's not very nice, but you need to hear it. Years from now, when our children are old enough to learn about Mommy's role in what historians will probably be calling The Dark Time, they'll ask, 'Daddy, what did *you* do while Mommy was working for the bad man? And I'll be able to say, 'I did what I could to salvage the honor of our good family name. I tweeted.'"

Katie shook her head. She, who always had words at the ready, seemed to have run out. Finally she said, "That is just . . . I don't even *know* how to respond to that."

There was an excruciatingly awkward—for me, anyway— silence. I averted my eyes, pretending to read a policy paper on her desk about immigrant Mexican rapists.

After an eternity, Romy said, "So . . . what time do we have to be at this thing tonight?"

The "thing," I learned, was dinner with Trump's daughter and son-in-law.

---

* Legal Latin for "I shrug" or "Whatever."

Romy pronounced the president's son-in-law's name "Jor-*ed*." I wondered, was this a sly taunt suggesting that Mr. Kushner came from the same planet as Superman?

Katie said icily, "Under the circumstances, Jerome, do you really think your presence would be appropriate? At an intimate dinner with Ivunka and Jored? At their residence, for God's sake?"

I may be reading more into Romy's tone of voice than was actually there, but I could swear I detected a note of joy as he said, "Well . . . maybe not." Pause. "Your call, sweetie."

A bit of background: presidential daughter Ivunka and son-in-law Jored had been problematic for Katie, as indeed they had been for many, indeed, more or less, the entire nation. Candidly, I cannot say that they made *my* job any easier. Certainly, they did not make the president's easier.

The president began to have second thoughts early on about having his daughter and son-in-law in the White House as "counselors" with vague portfolios. Then there was the kerfuffle over Jored's security clearance; specifically, the reluctance of the entire US security community to provide him with one.*

To be honest, everyone wanted them gone from the White House—chief among them Mr. Trump himself. But, poor man, he could never bring himself to say to them, "Please, just *go!*" So he tasked his faithful blond tarantula with the role of exterminator. Awkward.

---

* It didn't help that Jored was constantly "misplacing" his secure cell phone, and conducting what sounded like real estate deals with people named Achmed and Azbinababdullabab during cabinet meetings. Mr. Trump himself was constantly having to take away his phone, saying, "Gimme that. What are you doing? Sit there and shut up." Jored would look at his father-in-law with a bland, faintly evil expression, as if to say, "You can't get rid of me. I married your daughter."

Katie had gone out of her way to have a good relationship with Ivunka. They called each other "girlfriend" and were always discussing girlfriend-type topics like leg razors, mascara, and such. They were constantly going on about the merits and demerits of the controversial "vaginal lozenges" marketed by Gwyneth Paltrow's company, Gunk. I had little to offer on that subject.

After the president tasked Katie with getting his daughter to go away, she tried dropping casual hints along the lines of, "You and Jored must really miss New York, huh? All those fabulous parties!"

But Ivunka had now become accustomed to an entirely new level of cosseting and deference. She was in no hurry to return to New York, ground zero of glamour.

Katie changed tactics. Her signaling now took the form of: "Isn't Washington just the worst, most vicious, horrible town? Do you ever wish you were back in Manhattan? Or anywhere? Even like North Korea? Boy, I do!"

Alas, again: Ivunka and Jored weren't going anywhere. Katie confided to me, "It's like waiting for Brexit." The golden couple had no thought to depart the odious Swamp. Here they would remain, mixing it up with world leaders who frankly didn't care about their views on anything, including vaginal lozenges, though they politely nodded and pretended. "Jovunka"—to use the portmanteau—were determined to play their part in making America great again.

Katie had a fleeting moment of hope when Ivunka's brand of clothing failed to achieve "synergistic branding potential." Jor-ed,* meanwhile, had managed to leverage his presidential son-in-law-ness into a fat, greasy wad of sheik money with

---

* At this point I will not conceal from the reader that I had formed a disliking for this entitled young man.

which to bail out his disastrous purchase of the satanically addressed 666 Fifth Avenue.

"Maybe it *would* be better if you didn't come tonight," Katie said.

I now detected a note of ecstasy as Romy said, "Well, sweetie, if you think that would be for the best . . ."

Katie sighed.

"What am I supposed to say to Ivunka? 'I'm sorry my husband called your father a head case'?"

"No," Romy replied in a thoughtful tone. "But you could say, 'I'm sorry that your father is destroying long-standing norms of decency and civility, and in the process, our country.'"

Katie's trademark look of ferret defiance returned. Her eyes narrowed. Her lower jaw protruded, as if preparing to fasten onto her opponent's jugular. (She had a bit of an underbite, Katie.)

"I'm not going to have this conversation with you right now, Jerome. I'm just not. I'll make some excuse."

"Want me to wait up for you?"

"*No!*"

"Well, I've got an early deposition tomorrow. Give Jor-ed and Ivunka my—"

"I'm hanging up, Jerome."

"Bye, sweetie. Love you." He made a *smoochie-smoochie* sound.

Katie threw the phone onto her desk and shook her head.

"He's *such* an asshole. So what's up?"

I'd forgotten. I improvised an excuse and made my exit.

But despite what I'd just inadvertently witnessed, despite Katie's icy look of contempt as she called the father of her four children an asshole, I sensed that deep down, beneath it all, she still loved her "Romy-Oh." (Her term for him in happier times.)

What a complicated organ is the human heart. But the Borgia-O'Reilly marriage had yet to experience its most trying stress test.

6

A few days after the Moscow election shocker, I was in my office going over the menu for the state visit by Turkish president Attajurk, triple-checking to make sure there were no pork items or alcohol-based sauces.

At my direction, the chicken pot pies were crescent shaped, which I thought would please our Ottoman guests. Alas, this turned out to be a serious diplomatic faux pas: the "croissant" in fact originated in Vienna in 1683. The owner of a bakery near the city wall heard Ottoman sappers digging a tunnel. He alerted the authorities, who foiled the attack. To commemorate his role in the event, he was given permission to devise a pastry in the shape of the thwarted Turk. Oy.

NSC director Judd Wootten came into my office.

"We have a problem."

He was always saying this. At times Judd seemed to be a frustrated astronaut who'd seen *Apollo 13* twelve too many times. But as he'd recently informed me that a US Cyber Command computer had autonomously declared war on Russia, today's channeling of Cdr. James Lovell got my attention.

"Mom stopped by my office after briefing the president."

I groaned inwardly. How many times had I asked Judd not to refer to the director of national intelligence by that name? Her nickname might be Mother Jones, but for my taste, "Mom" was too informal by half, never mind the Freudian connotations. Miriam was a highly regarded female professional. I doubt Judd would enjoy being referred to in the corridors of power as "Scooter."

"She had some pretty hot stuff for him on Iran and Syria," Judd said, "but he didn't want to hear it. All he wants these days is what the fuck happened in Moscow."

"Understandably," I said.

"So, Herb . . ."

"Yes, Judd?"

"She says our CIA people in Moscow scored something by way of a coup."

"I wish you'd use another term, given what's happened. What *kind* of coup?"

"An asset they recruited. Just prior to the election. At the time, it didn't seem like a big fish. You know, nothing you'd mount over your mantelpiece."

"Judd," I interrupted, "could you please just get on with it?"

"Right. So the asset is like the number-two or -three guy in the Communist Party."

"So?"

Judd looked at me.

"Herb, the CP just won the election. With a little help from Placid Reflux."

"What does that have to—oh my *God* . . ." The import of this now dawned on me unpleasantly.

"How about that?" Judd said in a way I found inappropriately admiring. "Two weeks ago, this guy was just a tired old Bolshevik looking to supplement his income by getting on the CIA tit. Now? Fucker could be in line to be the next prime minister of Russia."

"Hold on," I said. "Aren't you getting ahead of the curve here? You told me Putin's going to win the runoff in a landslide. And send Zitkin and his fellow Reds to the Gulag. How is it this 'tired old Bolshevik,' as you call him, stands to become prime minister?"

Judd nodded and shrugged.

"Well, theoretically. Amazing synchronicity, wouldn't you say? We recruit the guy and next thing you know, bingo, he's a contendah."

"No, Judd. I do not find it 'amazing synchronicity,' whatever that means. I find it very, very unfortunate."

"Thing is, the asset—his code name's Huggybear—he's the problem."

"How, specifically?"

"If they find out he's on our payroll, how's *that* going to look? Given what's happened."

I stared. "Why would they find out?"

"Mom—Miriam—says the Kremlin's gone rip shit. Putin's demanding heads on spikes. They're doing CAT scans on everyone in the CP leadership trying to find out how they pulled this off."

"CAT scans? Why are they performing medical tests on them?"

"It's a figure of speech, Herb. Should I put it more plainly?"

"Please do."

"The Kremlin is intensely scrutinizing everyone in the Communist Party. Top to bottom, three sixty degrees. Huggybear is the number-two or -three guy in the CP politburo. So—if you'll allow me just one more medical metaphor—they're probably doing a colonoscopy on him. So it's therefore not beyond the realm of possibility that they might find out he's on our payroll. The optics of that,* alongside the fact that the CP won, are less than wonderful."

To use a medical metaphor, I felt like throwing up. The optics were indeed less than wonderful.

Judd continued: "Miriam thought it would be best *not* to share news of the CIA's recruitment of Huggybear with the president. For the time being. She felt it might make him a little anxious."

"The president is already anxious, Judd. I've never seen him this anxious. Even when they released his tax returns."

"Yeah, he's definitely nonphlegmatic. Miriam thinks it's best not to tell him about Placid Reflux. Or more technically, to remind him."

"What do you mean?"

"He was briefed on it right after taking office. He never read the briefing paper. He doesn't read."

"Hold on. Did you just say *Miriam* knows about the cyber-attack?"

"Of course she knows, Herb. She's the DNI."

"Yes, I suppose. But my God, Judd. Who else knows?"

"Not Putin. Which is what matters most. Meanwhile, we're not going to tell the president about Huggybear. We're going to keep calm and carry on, like the English poster says. Pretend nothing happened. Let Mr. Putin arrange for his landslide in the runoff. Russia will resume being great again. The dogs bark, the caravan moves on."

Looking back on that morning, I recognize that this was my "Rubicon Moment," as they said in ancient Rome. Many times

---

* Optometry, again. Why?

since, I've asked myself: should I have marched into the Oval Office and told Mr. Trump everything and thrown myself on his mercy?

Before I answer my own question, a few points:

1 Mercy is not really Mr. Trump's thing. Nor is forgiveness. He demanded perfection. And why shouldn't he? It was this very quality that made him a giant in the hospitality world.

2 The "I'm only the messenger here" defense doesn't work with Mr. Trump. In Trump World, the messenger was generally the first to die. Over the years, I'd had seen many a messenger hurled into the alligator-filled moat at Farrago-sur-Mer.

3 As result of the relentless attacks on him by the enemies of the people—the Democrat witch-hunter-impeachers, the "Never Trumpers," the college-educated portion of the electorate, the migrant huggers, Kurd lovers, the whole Trump-detesting kit and caboodle—the poor president was by this point just plain worn out. Why trouble him with this? Putin was going to win. The caravan would move on.

His presidency had been a nonstop conveyor belt of unpleasantness: the chorus line of tramps clamoring for hush money; the devastating release of the tax returns; the Senate trial; the rumors about Vice President Pants trying to get the cabinet members to invoke the Twenty-Fifth Amendment; all of it.

Mr. Trump's mental state was—I don't want to say "precarious"—fragile. (This is not to say I agreed with Romy that he was "a head case.") But for me to go into the Oval (as we call the Oval Office) and say, "Oh, by the way, sir, seems one of our computers hacked the Russian election. And did I mention that the CIA put the number-two Commie on our payroll? Whaddya think Mr. Putin will make of *them* apples? Ready for your second Double Whopper with Bacon?"

It might just put Mr. Trump over the edge. Call me squeamish, but it is my firm belief that one should think twice before inducing a nervous breakdown in someone with a finger on the nuclear button.

Finally,

4 By now I had come to the regretful conclusion that Mr. Putin probably did, in fact, "have something" on Mr. Trump.

Why did I come to this conclusion? Call it intuition. Call it what you will. But as I assembled the various pieces of the jigsaw puzzle, it began to make sense: the heroic (if that's quite the right word) lengths Mr. Trump had gone to in order to keep Putin happy; calling his own intelligence people bozos for saying Russia interfered in 2016; holding up military assistance to Ukraine; pooh-poohing the fact that Mr. Putin routinely murdered journalists and dissidents, often very unpleasantly; and generally never missing an opportunity to say something positive about "my beautiful friend Vladimir."

But there would be no keeping beautiful Vladimir happy if he learned about Placid Reflux.

For his many virtues, Mr. Trump was not always "tidy" when it came to keeping a lid on classified matters. He was constantly doing things like telling the Russian ambassador about some Israeli intelligence operation, thus blowing some very hush-hush operation years in the works. At dinner, he'd regale people with the positions of our nuclear subs. I could easily imagine this Placid Reflux thing spiraling out of control. Wars have started over less.

So, no, Herbert K. Nutterman did not march into the Oval Office and inform the president that his own government was keeping him in the dark.

That said, how many times did Herbert K. Nutterman look himself in the mirror and ask, "Herb, are you *sure* you're doing the right thing?"

Answer: a number of times. But each time, the mirror replied, "Well, Herb, I guess it all depends on your definition of 'right,' doesn't it?"

How could I argue with that?

Yes, I "get" that a federal judge and jury arrived at a definition of "wrong" (after what seemed to me a rather brisk deliberation). As a result of which Herbert K. Nutterman—or as he is currently known, #107-3374-34-8*—is writing this in the library at FCI Wingdale, between napkin-folding classes in the vocational center.

And I'm okay with that. Because at the end of the day I can look into that mirror and say, "It didn't end in nuclear war."

How many White House chiefs of staff can say the same? Well, all of them, I grant, but I'm making a larger point here.

A few days later Judd came to see me. He had a "get a load of this" look that reminded me of the bemused—or sometimes revolted—expressions on the faces of the housekeeping staff when they found certain items that guests left behind in the room. Items used by consenting adults for . . . well, you get the picture. In one instance, the item was quite expensive. Our diligent head of housekeeping looked it up on the Internet and reported that it cost over two thousand dollars. The guest was a

---

* I sometimes tell visitors, "We're informal here. Call me 107," but it rarely gets a laugh.

valued repeat customer. I had to make the decision: do we send it to her with a note, "Dear Mrs. So-and-So, Enclosed please find your Shiri Zinn Double-Ended Limited Edition Glass Dildo, valued at $2,095. We very much hope you enjoyed your stay with us, and we look forward to your next"? The hospitality business can be a minefield.

He handed me a folder marked "Eyes Only."

"What's this?"

"Transcript of an intercept of a phone call between Comrade Zitkin and Mrs. Comrade Zitkin. The morning after he won the election."

I looked at him.

"Judd, is this . . . *kosher*?"

"Why not?"

"I'm asking if this is . . . what's the word Miriam is always using . . ."

"Actionable."

"Or just prurient? If it's the latter, I'm not going to read it, and shame on you for suggesting I do."

"It's an intimate, nonprurient conversation between a potential future prime minister of the Russian government and his wife. I'd say it qualifies as legitimately of interest."

I frowned and read:

OKSANA ZITKIN: I've been trying to reach you all morning.

ANATOLI ZITKIN: It's been a bit busy here. I was about to call you. Can you believe—"

O. Z.: What have you done? Are you trying to ruin us?

A. Z.: But haven't you seen the news? I won! That is, the people won.

O. Z.: The devil take the people! Yes I have seen the news! And it's making me sick! I'm having hot flashes, and it's not menopause, I'll tell you.

A. Z.: Why do you say this, Little Mink?

O. Z.: Don't call me that! You stole the election!

A. Z.: But why do you say that? It's not true.

O. Z.: Of course you stole it! You were so far behind Putin in the polls you couldn't see the rear fender of his limousine with a telescope. So, please, tell me how is it that you won?

A. Z.: Well, truthfully, we're not altogether sure. But—

O. Z.: You listen to me, Anatoli Ivanovich. Something is very wrong here. And it's not going to be pleasant for any of us when the truth gets out. Shame on you! [*Negodyay!*]

[HANGS UP.]

UNIDENTIFIED VOICE: Was that Oksana, Comrade?

A. Z.: Yes.

U. V.: She must be beside herself, eh?

A. Z.: You could put it that way.

I handed it back to Judd.

"Thanks," I said. "There's nothing actionable in it. You've made me feel like a Peeping Tom."

It also made me feel guilty. I hardly knew this Anatoli Zitkin person, and I'm no fan of Communism, but the poor man was getting pummeled by his wife—who sounded like a real handful—and accused of something he didn't do. It was all well and fine for Placid Reflux to punish Russia for election interfering, but the only one taking a beating was Comrade Zitkin. I felt bad. I wanted to pick up the phone and call Mrs. Zitkin and tell her to lay off Anatoli. But it was a bit late in the game for that. Well, Mr. Putin would win the runoff election and things would settle down.

7

In an attempt to keep calm and carry on, I kept a calendar in my desk with the date of the Russian runoff election marked in red. At the end of every day, I drew an X through it, relieved that we were one day closer to Mr. Putin's triumph over the neo-Bolsheviks and Placid Reflux.

The White House medical office supplied me with anxiety-reducing beta-blockers. I didn't tell them the cause of my anxiety, and they didn't press. I inferred that I was not the first White House chief of staff to seek pharmaceutical assistance for stress reduction.

It didn't help my stress level when the president summoned me the day after Judd dropped his "We have a problem" stink bomb on my lap.

"Our old friend Oleg is reaching out," he said.

This unhappy news blew through the beta-blockers like Mexicans swarming the border wall.

"You *spoke* to Oleg, sir?"

"Herb, do I look like an idiot?"

"Never, sir. But how is it you're aware that Oleg is reaching out?"

"Paul told me."

Another swarm of migrants charged the wall, shoving aside beta-blockers.

"You spoke to *Paul*? Oh, sir."

"What's the problem?"

"Sir, your former campaign manager is serving a seven-year sentence in federal prison. Greta or Katie is better suited than I am to judge the optics of a phone call between the president of the United States and a convicted felon. But—"

"Trump does not abandon his friends. You should know that. I'm disappointed in you, Herb. Very disappointed."

"I apologize, sir."

"Point is, we need to make Oleg happy again. So you need to do that."

This was a broad remit, to say the least.

"I'll do whatever I can, sir, but—"

"Just do it." The president shook his head. "This fucking job. All I do is make people happy."

"You are a river to your people, sir."

"You know what would be nice?"

"What's that, sir?"

"If every now and then someone wanted to make *me* happy." The president mimed: "*So what can I do for you? And you? What about you? What do* you *need? Sure. Fine. You want fries with that?* It never stops. I never should have run for president. What were we talking about?"

"Oleg."

"Right. Make him happy. But keep him away from me."

Keeping Oleg physically away was not a problem, inasmuch as he'd be arrested if he tried to enter the United States. The

Glebnikov Act, named for the deceased Moscow bureau chief of a Washington newspaper, had frozen Oleg's US assets and barred him from entering the United States.

The billionaire publisher of the *Washington Examinator* had declared war on Oleg for (allegedly) murdering his Moscow bureau chief, Peter Glebnikov, after he published a highly unflattering five-part series on Oleg. The US Congress, always eager to please a media baron, swiftly passed the bill. President Obama signed it into law.*

It didn't take much wondering as to what would Make Oleg Happy Again. I could see him now, his meaty Slavic face, grinning at me beneath a red sable fur hat embossed in glittering gold letters: MOHA.

Mr. Trump and I first met Oleg Pishinsky in Moscow in 2013. He was then ranked number seventeen on *Forbes* magazine's annual "Deplorable Billionaires" list; and number four in the "Deplorable Russian Oligarchs" subcategory.

Oleg had had come a long way from his days as a garage mechanic in St. Petersburg. There he had befriended the young KGB lieutenant Vladimir Putin. Oleg's subsequent rise from that modest station to chairman, CEO, and majority stockholder of GluboNasti Industries is a case studied both at the Harvard Business School and at Interpol.

Say what you will about Oleg—and a great deal has been said: he had charisma by the bucketful, and magnetism by however you measure magnetism. Big chested, red haired—he was especially proud of his "Why-kink" (Viking) heritage—hearty,

---

* One could speculate whether President Trump would have signed a bill punishing a Russian oligarch friend of Putin for assassinating an "enemy of the people." But it would be a short speculation.

grinning, teeth like keys on a grand piano, Oleg was in ways a Russian version of Mr. Trump. Both had presence—and then some. Charismatic people turn heads when they enter a room. Hypercharismatics like Mr. Trump and Oleg make the chandeliers rattle. (I intend no reference to their weight.)

I vividly recall our first glimpse of him as he welcomed us aboard his 376-foot megayacht in the Crimean harbor of Sochi, which Mr. Putin had not yet annexed. He stood there at the top of the gangway, arms outstretched like a proverbial Russian bear, beaming, *"Doh-nald! Wel-come to my hamble boat!"*

Welcome Mr. Trump and I indeed felt. The opulence of Oleg's "humble" boat was blinding. Literally. I had to put on sunglasses in some of the rooms to counter the bling glare. The yacht's decor was of the "Gold, more gold!" type that appeals to Mr. Trump. Oleg was clearly proud of it, and Mr. Trump was duly impressed. He whispered to me, "We need one of these. Remind me to buy one when we get back to New York."

Oleg had named it *Maria Ivanovna*, in honor of Mr. Putin's mother. Apparently, no fewer than fourteen oligarchs also named their megayachts after her. When they all anchored off Sochi during the summer Olympics, they made the Russian naval fleet look shabby. Awkward. President Putin put word out among the oligarchiate please to stop honoring his dear mama.

Oleg's other "ownings"—as he called them in his imperfect but endearing English—included a considerable tract of the Amazon rain forest, currently being "repurposed." The *Financial Times* estimated his share of London real estate market at between 3 and 6 percent. Following our visit in 2013, he purchased a triplex in the Trump Tower in New York, a gesture that greatly touched Mr. Trump, especially when he insisted on paying one-third *over* the asking price. (There is no better way to impress Mr. Trump than overpaying.)

Many of Oleg's "second homes"—as he jocularly called them—shared an amusing theme: they'd all belonged to dictators. Mr. Trump was very impressed.

The villa in Cap d'Antibes had belonged to "Baby Doc" Duvalier, former ruler of Haiti. The palazzo in Umbria had been the summer residence of Benito Mussolini. Mr. Trump wanted to know if it was where "they strung him upside down with whatshername,"* and was disappointed to hear *nyet*. At Oleg's hunting lodge in Argentina, Presidente Juan Perón had once annihilated flights of duck and other avians of game persuasion.

"That's great," Mr. Trump remarked. "I'm not into hunting. But it's great."

Oleg beamed. His principal lady friend—there were a number of highly attractive lady friends aboard—remarked, "Oleg have thing for palatzos what are belongink to strong mans."

Mr. Trump nodded, again impressed.

Oleg and Mr. Putin were close friends. When the Russian media made a big thing over what it called Putin's "billion-dollar palace on the Black Sea"—the Kremlin preferred the term "modest seaside cabin"—Oleg stepped up to the plate and bought it outright. Then generously leased it back to the state for a hundred rubles per year.†

"*That's* friendship," Mr. Trump observed. "Beautiful gesture."

It was in fact this episode that finally persuaded Mr. Putin to rethink the whole post-Soviet "freedom of the press" thing. As one Kremlin spokesman wryly paraphrased Janis Joplin's song, "Freedom's just another word for disrespecting the state with impunity."

Oleg himself was certainly no fan of the media. Oh no. Years later, when now-President Trump was calling the media

---

* Claretta Petacci.

† $1.55.

"enemies of the people," "scum," "filth," "disgusting, depraved animals," and other colorful terms, Oleg cheered. His own difficulties with the media seemed only to increase, even after Mr. Putin issued his celebrated "Don't make me come and fire-bomb your offices" warning to the Russian media.

Another of Oleg's "ownings" was his clinic in Tajikistan that supplied human organs for transplanting. You'd think people would applaud such a humanitarian enterprise. But "bravo" was not the universal opinion, perhaps owing to the rather stunning efficiency with which the clinic supplied organs on demand.

The Moscow newspaper *Novy Smir* ran a snarky article dubbing Oleg "*korlo' pochka*" ("King Kidney"), and alleging that some of the organs had not been donated voluntarily. Ouch.

Oleg brought a libel action against the paper. And who'd blame him? As luck would have it, the Kremlin simultaneously promulgated yet another "media reform" law, this one prohibiting *plokhoye otnospheniye* ("bad attitude"). The newspaper was duly shut down, sparing Oleg further legal fees.

Unfortunately for Oleg, this only stimulated interest in him by the foreign media.

As a general rule, Russian oligarchs prefer not to be taken interest in by the media. Like mushrooms, they thrive in darkness and well-manured soil. So when Peter Glebnikov, Moscow bureau chief of the *Washington Examinator*, published his five-part series about how Oleg, with a little help from his friend Vladimir Putin, built GluboNasti Industries into the world's leading producer of molybdenum, Oleg was neither flattered nor pleased. *Nyet*.

He was particularly incensed by the part about GluboNasti's pharmacology division. Among its other products, GluboNasti had won the government contract to produce the nerve agent Novichok. The name translates as "new boy," which is the only cute thing about this highly unpleasant substance. The agent is—correction: is *said* to be—what the Kremlin uses to "disincentivize" former KGB agents, diplomats, dissidents, and others who oppose Mr. Putin. Getting smeared with Novichok is no picnic. As the old Brylcreem hair tonic ads used to say, "A little dab'll do ya." (I certainly don't mean to make light of nerve agents.) The *Examinator* article revealed yet another of Oleg's titles: "Putin's Pharmacist." Neither Mr. Putin nor his pharmacist was flattered.

A month after the series concluded, Mr. Glebnikov was taken ill. Photos showed doctors and nurses attending him dressed in hazmat-type clothing associated with toxic or radio-active materials. The postmortem toxicology report indicated that the unfortunate journalist had indeed somehow absorbed Novichok.

Fingers pointed at Oleg. He stoutly denied culpability, and as a "gesture of good will," offered to have Mr. Glebnikov's organs serially replaced as they failed, with organs from his clinic. Gra-tis. Alas, the new organs couldn't keep pace with the failing ones and Mr. Glebnikov expired, but not before writing a fiery *j'accuse!** charging Oleg with his demise.

Oleg continued to proclaim his innocence, even to strike a note of self-pity—no mean feat, under the circumstances—pointing out that no one had expressed thanks to him for donat-ing all those expensive organs.

An unfortunate business all around, but again, the dogs bark and the caravan moves on.

Mr. Trump and Oleg hit it off "bigly" in 2013 when they convened for the Miss Universe pageant.

Alas, Herb Nutterman hadn't come to Moscow to drink vodka and eat caviar and gawp at the truly jaw-dropping, heart-attack-inducing pageant of pulchritude. My role in

---

* French for "This is really a bit much."

Moscow was a tad less "glam" than Mr. Trump's, namely undertaking the negotiations for the Trump Tower Kremlin.

It didn't take long to realize that like Rome, Mr. Trump's tower wasn't going to be built in a day. *Nyet* again. Doing business in Russia is a subject for an entire book, but not this one. As I write, years later, Trump Tower Kremlin remains a dream. Among the frustrating factors was Mr. Trump's insistence that the hotel be physically attached to the actual Kremlin. He also at one point became enamored of the idea of having Lenin's mausoleum, where Mr. Lenin's embalmed body is on display, in the hotel's lobby. Then there was his reluctance to—I don't want to say "bribe"—contribute to the "charitable funds" administered by the myriad licensing authorities. And I thought dealing with the Virginia Historical Marker Commission was a challenge.

As I busied myself with all this, Mr. Trump and Oleg concentrated on the Miss Universe pageant. Mr. Trump declared it a "yuuge" success. When we boarded the plane to come home, I'd never seen him so physically drained. He slept the entire way back and practically had to be carried off the plane. (It required four strong men.) I remember thinking at the time admiringly, *How that man drives himself.*

It was only now, seven years later, when "our old friend Oleg" reached out, that I was able to get a more detailed view of the big picture. As it turned out, Mr. Trump's post–Miss Universe fatigue was not entirely due to meetings and marathon networking. Depending, of course, on one's definition of "meeting" and "networking." More on this in due course.

Meanwhile, in the years since our pleasant cruise aboard the *Maria Ivanovna* and the "*Kaval-kada iz plot*" ("Cavalcade of Flesh," Russian for "Miss Universe pageant") a lot had happened. For one thing, Mr. Trump had been elected president of the United States.

Oleg, too, had prospered, if not quite as spectacularly. The price of molybdenum was at an all-time high. (He controlled the world's reserves of this interestingly spelled metal.) His mercenary army division was going great guns in Africa, Syria, Venezuela, and other eternally vexed hot spots. The keel had been laid for an even bigger megayacht, this one to be named *Katerina Tikhonova*, in honor of Mr. Putin's daughter, an accomplished acrobatic dancer. The organ farm in Tajikistan was thriving, and had established satellite branches in China, India, South America, and Cincinnati.

But as Oleg strode this yellow brick road of prosperity, he'd stepped on a few toes. On entire feet, really. The tally of people who'd expired from—alleged—Novichok poisoning was now into double digits. Not all of these unfortunates were directly connected to Oleg, mind. Many were—I don't want to say "legitimate targets"—people who'd done something to annoy Mr. Putin: defect, say, or report on his overseas bank accounts, disagree with his management policies, that sort of thing.

But there were enough among the heap of bodies—the so-called *neschastnyy Ublyudok Novichoked**—who *did* have connections with Oleg, and that raised eyebrows. In a grim homage, the CIA had now taken to calling Novichok "Oil of Oleg." When an intelligence agency nicknames a lethal nerve agent after you, it could be a sign that you've been overdoing it.

At any rate, my portfolio now included Make Oleg Happy Again. Not an assignment for which I had great relish, but in the spirit of *Theirs-not-to-question-why*, I "embraced the suck," as our military people say when posted to far-off, unpleasant places. Again, a vision of Hetta's pile of purple beet peelings swam before me as I gulped another fistful of beta-blockers.

---

* Roughly: Russian for "poor bastards who have been smeared with Novichok."

8

WH CHIEF OF STAFF HERB NUTTERMAN AND
"PUTIN'S PHARMACIST" HOLD SECRET TALKS

A headline like that would be suboptimal, so I resolved to
"approach with caution" as the wine vintage charts warn.

We'd just come off the Senate impeachment trial. Mr. Trump
had triumphed, receiving acquittal of bribery, extortion, blackmail, and assorted other baseless "hoax" Democrat charges.
He was of course displeased by the two Republican senators
who voted to allow witnesses and evidence. But as he tweeted,
he looked forward to "destroying their lives." All in all, he was
feeling pretty upbeat.

But now we had an election to win in November, so this was
no time for complacency.

Boyd Crampon, our pollster, was telling us that the general
mood in the country was a little frazzled. He said we were not
doing great among suburban women, the college educated, and
"people who drink wine." Boyd was particularly concerned that

Russian troll activity was down in key precincts in Wisconsin, Michigan, and Pennsylvania.

Mr. Trump summoned Sergei Kropotnik, the Russian ambassador, to the Oval and demanded an explanation. Kropotnik apologized, explaining that the GRU—Russian military intelligence—had had to divert resources to ensure Mr. Putin's own victory in the runoff election against the Communists. But he assured Mr. Trump that President Putin was "all in" for a second Trump term, and hinted that "we have big surprise for whoever is Democrat nominee." It was just what Mr. Trump needed to hear. In return, he told Kropotnik about an ongoing CIA operation in Ukraine.

Mr. Trump very much wanted to keep Russia—as well as Oleg—happy. The liberal mainstream media, frustrated by his triumph in the Senate trial, was looking for anything to attack him with; if they got wind his chief of staff was having chats with Oleg Pishinsky—well, I didn't even want to think about that.

I consulted with Judd, and swore him to secrecy.

Judd's Thomas the Tank Engine eyes popped when I told him that the president had tasked me with Oleg happiness maintenance. He made a pensive clucking noise with his tongue.

"Tricky, Herb," he said. "Very tricky."

"I'm aware of that, Judd. That's why I'm asking you for advice."

"*Why* exactly do we want to keep Oleg happy?"

"I can't go into that." I was hedging, for in fact I myself did not know the precise reason.

"That bad, huh?"

Judd now warmed to the task. He loved knowing things other people didn't. Not that I had told him what I knew—or rather didn't know. But I wasn't about to tell him what I didn't know. For now it was enough that he knew that I knew something, even if I didn't. Something that was presumably known only to the president and a—I don't want to say "shady"—problematical Russian oligarch.

Naturally, he tried to wheedle it out of me.

"What *can* you tell me about whatever it is?"

"Nothing."

"I'm asking for a reason."

"*Judd.*"

"Okay, okay. Got it."

I asked him if I could call Oleg directly.

Judd found this highly amusing.

"Sure. If you don't mind the whole IC [intelligence community] reading a transcript of your call. *And* the Kremlin."

"So what do you recommend? How do I communicate with Oleg? Carrier pigeons?"

"Pablo Escobar actually resorted to those when he was in that jail. Look, Herb, is it absolutely necessary you communicate with this guy? He's radioactive."

"Judd. Hear me. The president has asked me to make him happy. How am I supposed to accomplish felicity for him without communicating with him?"

"Back up a sec. How did the president learn that Pishinsky was 'reaching out'?"

"I'd rather not go into that, either."

"*Paul?*"

I reluctantly nodded.

"*Jesus,*" he muttered. "Let's hope *that* doesn't get out."

I've long envied the Christian ability of invoking the deity on a first-name basis. We don't have that. You don't hear us going, "Yahweh!" or "Hashem!" or "Adonai on a pogo stick!" and other variations.

"It's that important, is it?" he asked.

"The president asked me to do it. So yes, Judd, I'd say that qualifies it as important."

"In the early days, staff just ignored him when he wanted to do something stupid. People used to steal documents from his outbox and shred them."

I groaned.

"Judd. Are you advising me to ignore a direct order from the president of the United States?"

"Couldn't you just, I dunno, let it cool? Maybe he'll forget about it."

"A Russian oligarch who *may* have something on the president has sent a message that he wants to talk. I'm not saying this is a quote-unquote blackmail situation. But in blackmail situations, does the blackmailed party typically just 'forget about it'?"

"Okay. Lemme talk to Miriam."

"Please do."

9

A person Miriam sent—I assumed he was CIA—said it would be a better cover for my trip if I were accompanied by Hetta. Just another American couple on vacation.

"What if I'm recognized?" I asked. I'm not by nature vain, but when your picture appears with regularity in the news, recognition ensues, and in the case of Trump White House staff, not always favorable recognition. Hetta and I had by now pretty much given up dining out, after a few unpleasant heckling episodes. The decline of civility in this country is truly worrisome.

The CIA person looked me over and paid me the compliment of telling me that my features were "unremarkable." He suggested that I not shave, wear different eyeglasses, and part my hair on the other side. Also avoid eye contact and walk with a limp.

I announced to Hetta in an upbeat tone the "fun news" that we were going to San Marino for a little romantic getaway. I was uncomfortable dissembling, but it was a matter of national security.

"California?" she said. "What, are you nuts? They're having more fires. It's all they do out there these days, is have fires. I'm not going to California. I don't want to be burned alive."

"Silly girl," I rejoined. "San Marino, Europe. Do you really think my idea of a romantic getaway is being burned alive?"

"Where in Europe?"

"It's sort of in the middle of Italy. But it's its own country. It's an 'enclaved microstate.'" (I'd done some brushing up on San Marino.) "How about that? Pretty exotic, eh?"

"Enslaved micro-what?"

"I'll tell you all about it on the plane. We don't have to—" I stopped myself from saying "stay long." I said, "I can only get away for two days, so pack lightly."

"We're going to a place I've never heard of in Europe—for two days?"

"Yes. Isn't it wonderful that I could get away for that long?"

"Why don't we just go to the beach?"

The honest answer would have been: "Because the beach is US soil, and the person I'm meeting with isn't allowed on US soil, because they say he assassinates people with nerve agent."

A longer answer would have been: "The Republic of San Marino is one of few counties—including North Korea, the Solomon Islands, Kiribati, and the Vatican—that is not a member of Interpol. The person I'm meeting, the aforementioned assassin, can go there without fear of being arrested."

"You go," she said.

"Sweetheart. It'll be great. Just the two of us." And Putin's Pharmacist. What could be more romantic?

"I'm not going."

"They say the food is sensational. Seafood. You love seafood. It's fresh. From . . . right there, whatever the sea is called. Adriatic. That's it. Were you aware that the best seafood in the world is from the Adriatic?"

"We can get seafood at the beach."

"Sweetheart."

"I don't care how good the seafood is. I'm not going to sit on a plane for two days to spend ten minutes in a place I don't even want to go."

"But you're always telling me you want to go on a trip."

"Yeah. So you took me to a Trump rally in Alabama. Still I'm having nightmares. No wonder they call those people his base."

I love my Hetta but she can be—I don't want to say "snobbish"—particular. That said, Mr. Trump's audience in Mobile was a bit—I don't want to say "barbaric"—earthy. Biting off the CNN reporter's ear was uncalled for. I did at least try to get the president to tweet about it.

"Hetta, dear, I'm not taking you to a Trump rally in San Marino. You couldn't *fit* a Trump rally in it."

"So why are we going, Herb?"

"To San Marino? Aren't you the least bit curious to see one of the"—I was improvising here—"undiscovered gems of the Adriatic?"

"No, Herb. I'm not. And stop lying. What's this all about?"

Thirty-two years later and you realize you married a polygraph machine.

"We need to go to San Marino, Hetta. For our country. That's all I can tell you."

"No. *You* need to go to San Marino. And I love my country, so don't try any of that crap with me."

Much as I wanted to, how could I explain to her about Oleg? Hetta was bound to have views about people who smear lethal nerve agent on other people.

I told her it was "a diplomatic thing." A lunch. In, out. Done—in plenty of time for the two of us to do some "serious shopping." She perked up at that. She likes a bit of shopping, my Hetta. We still have the crockery and plates we got there, though these days I'm eating my meals off tin.

There are no airports in San Marino. This is a disadvantage of being an "enclaved microstate": no room for things like runways. If you're going to San Marino—and you should, it's very nice, very pleasant—you fly into the Federico Fellini International Airport in nearby Rimini.

Was that going to complicate things for Oleg? I wondered. Italy *is* a member of Interpol. How was he going to get around that? Land in his private jet and leave the crew to shoot it out with Immigration and Customs while he legged it for San Marino? But that was Oleg's problem, not mine. I was just grateful I wasn't schlepping Hetta off for a romantic getaway in Pyongyang or Kiribati, wherever the hell it is.

I was not looking forward to lunch with Oleg, for this reason:

The day before I left, Judd came to my office with another folder marked "Eyes Only." He pulled out a CIA document, a list of a dozen or more names, all Russian sounding.

"What's this?"

"A list."

"I *see* that."

"The so-called *Novichokkiy*. People who've died from Novichok poisoning. Courtesy of your pal Oleg."

"Please don't call him that." The list felt heavy in my hand.

"This one here?" Judd pointed. "Katya Anasimova. That's the interesting one."

"Why?"

"She was one of the contestants in the 2013 Miss Universe pageant."

I groaned.

"Sorry," Judd said, "but I thought you might find that useful, going in. Now, none of the autopsies for these poor sumbitches specifically state, 'Death by Novichok poisoning.' Langley says there's a reason for that. Russian hospitals stopped putting that down as cause of death after the third incident. The Kremlin sent out a memo saying ix-nay on the ovichok-nay autopsy reports."

I stared at the name on the list.

"Why would Oleg do that to a beauty pageant contestant?"

"No idea. Maybe it'll come up during lunch."

So after a tiring flight—three flights, actually—in the company of a very sullen wife, my mood was not at my hospitality-professional best.

Oleg was already there on the rooftop of La Terrazza, with its—I must say—fabulous view of what must be most of San Marino, there not being much of San Marino. Befitting his oligarch status, the entourage of scowling bodyguards was impressive. Federico Fellini's entire immigration department would have been no match for them in a firefight.

Oleg rose to greet me with a bear hug.

"Errrbert!"

"Hello, Oleg," I said without reciprocal warmth.

"Sit. We will have wine."

"No, thank you."

"Yes, we will have wine."

He stared at my "unremarkable" face. A broad Slavic smile spread across his meaty one. He chuckled and wagged a finger the size of a salami at me.

"You look different."

"It's been a while."

"You don't look happy to see me."

"I'm here, aren't I?"

"How is Paul? I like Paul."

"Do you?"

"Oh yes. Is wery good fellow."

"How much did you pay him to lobby against the Glebnikov bill?"

"Not enough, it sims!" he said with discrepant amusement.

"I've come a long way, Oleg. Shall we get down to—"

"How is Donald?"

"The president of the United States, you mean? Rather busy."

"Am wery glad about Senate vote. I sent flowers. They arrive?"

"I'm sure. Yes, we were all gratified. The impeachment was a disgrace from beginning to end. It seems there is nothing to which the Democrats will not stoop."

"Why they allow such thing? President on trial? What kind of system is this?"

"A very poor system," I replied. "Now, Oleg, why don't you tell me whatever it is I've come all this very long way to hear?"

But there was no hurrying Oleg along. *Nyet.* He stared out at the medieval cityscape of towers and churches.

"It's nice, San Marino, eh?"

"Charming," I said. "And how nice they don't belong to Interpol."

He laughed. "This I wery much like about San Marino. Errbert, we must make a finish of this silly Glebnikov Act."

"How do you mean?"

"Make go away, of course."

If you have not had the experience of explaining US constitutional procedure to a Russian oligarch, all I can say is, you haven't missed a thing. After half an hour spent mostly repeating myself, I managed to penetrate into Oleg's skull the fact that the president cannot—I threw in an "alas," though I don't know why—simply nullify acts of Congress. Oleg found this a) wery disappointing and b) "stupit."

"So," he said, "what's solution?"

"How do you mean?"

"How do we fix?"

The next half hour was spent in much the way as the previous, this time explaining how you have to introduce a bill to—sorry, but I simply can't bring myself to type the rest of this sentence without screaming. And they don't like us to scream here in the library at FCI Wingdale.

By now I wanted to reach across the table, yank him by the tie, and smash his Why-kink face into his scampi, the way they do in the movies. But as I am a person of peaceable nature and had no desire to annoy seven Uzi-armed bodyguards, I refrained. I waited for the other shoe, as it were, to drop.

"Errburt. Have ever I told you about Miss Universe contest 2013?"

"No, Oleg."

"The girls? *Fan-tastic*. But it's Miss Universe contest, so yes of course they are beautifool. You want to eat them."

"I'm sure."

"Donald was wery happy, I tell you."

"The president is known to enjoy the company of beautiful women. Of beautiful people, generally. Women and men."

"Donald also like *men*?"

"No, no, no. I meant—never mind. He admires beautiful people. It's an expression. Glamorous people. You know . . ."

My left leg chose this moment for some reason to go numb. My brain had been numb for an hour.

"As you were saying, Oleg?"

"Donald, he want to"—Oleg mimed coition—"with *all* the girls."

"Well," I said, "it's only natural that as chief judge of the pageant he would exercise due diligence."

I explained the concept of due diligence. Oleg found it wery mirthful.

"Yes, Errbert. He make doo dilly-chintz with every girl in contest. Eighteen girls."

"That *is* due diligence," I observed.

"The girls, they are not wanting"—Oleg re-mimed coition—"make boom-boom with Donald. So he tell them: 'Okay, make boom-boom, you win contest. Guarantee.'"

When I say that I was beginning to have a bad feeling, I mean: a bad feeling like the one you get when the doctor tells you, *I'm sorry, but there's nothing more we can do.* Or when the pilot comes on the PA system and says, *Brace for impact.* That kind.

Oleg continued: "So Donald have wery good time with eighteen girls. But of course only one girl is winnink. Because there only can be one Miss Universe."

"That is, yes, how these things work. Generally."

"So after winner is announce, now we have seventeen not-happy girls."

"Well, that's life, I'm afraid."

"Maybe. But girls are not saying 'that's life.' Some are saying, *We will make a noise.* Big *noise. Noisy noise.* So Donald say to his good friend Oleg, 'Oleg, make girls to understand, yes?' And because Oleg is good friend, he tell Donald, 'Okay. Oleg take care of.'"

"Well, that's what friends are for. Isn't it?"

"*So!*" he boomed with a vertebra-snapping, adverbial exclamation. "*What* shall we have for dessert?"

10

Judd listened in silence to my account of lunch with Oleg. I had to tell someone. His comments consisted mostly of serial first-name invocations of the Christian deity. I left out the detail of the thumb drive.

"Maybe you should come with me," I said, "when I brief the president."

"I think he'd be more comfortable if it was just you. You two have history."

Yes. And doubtless, more "history" in our future.

Walking to the Oval felt like an inversion of being sent to the principal's office. I would be telling the principal that *he* was in big trouble.

"So?" Mr. Trump said.

"Oleg sends his warmest wishes, sir. He especially asked me to congratulate you on the Senate acquittal."

"Uh-huh."

"Well, our, uh,* conversation was largely focused on the 2013 Miss Universe pageant . . ."

The president frowned, his lips forming a tight moue, the labial equivalent of crossed arms over the chest. It's his default expression when hearing something that displeases him.

"He told me that prior to the voting, you . . . canvassed the eighteen contestants individually. And further suggested that you provided each of them with . . . incentive."

The presidential moue tightened.

"And that after the winner was announced, some of the contestants felt that the incentives they had given were not reciprocated. And that they expressed disappointment. And that you asked Oleg—as a friend—to ameliorate the situation."

"So? That's *it*?"

"Essentially. There was one further detail. Namely that one of the contestants in particular felt aggrieved."

"So?"

"Well, she . . . died."

The president stared.

"Died? Of what? Drug overdose? All those girls take drugs. To keep the weight off. Backstage was like Central Park after it snows. Coke, everywhere. Disgusting. It's a very bad drug, cocaine."

"Well, no. Not coke. The precise cause of her death remains a bit vague. The difficulty is . . . once again it comes down to optics."

"What *optics*?"

"Well, sir, Oleg *is* associated with a number of incidents involving—you've heard of Novichok?"

---

* For editorial reasons, I have removed seventy-four instances of "uh" from this conversation. The reader will be able to fill them back in.

"No."

"The nerve agent. His company makes it for the Russian government. Unpleasant stuff."

"What's this got to do with me?"

"Well, sir, you see, Oleg *asserts* that you asked him to 'take care' of the problem. So it could be inferred . . . well, you see the difficulty."

"No, I don't. Are you telling me Oleg says I asked him to rub out some disgruntled bimbo? What a bunch of crap."

"I couldn't agree more, sir. Disgraceful."

"Is that *it*?" Mr. Trump seemed eager to return to watching Mr. Colonnity. Which I thought—and think still—bespoke his innocence in the matter. A guilty person would hardly have shrugged at such an odious accusation.

"He asked me to give you this." I handed Mr. Trump the thumb drive.

"What's this?"

"Well, sir, he *claims* it's a recording. Of the two of you discussing the situation. At the time."

"Fucker was taping me?"

"So he alleges, sir."

"What's it say?"

"I don't know, sir."

"What do you mean you don't know?"

"I mean that I don't know what's on it."

"You didn't listen to it?"

"I didn't think it polite to, sir."

Mr. Trump picked up the thumb drive, stared at it, and placed it at arm's length on his desk, as if concerned it might explode.

"Oleg did mention that it contains, in addition to the aforementioned alleged recording of your conversation, films."

"Of what?"

"Of yourself. And the eighteen contestants. He complimented you on your extraordinary vitality."

Mr. Trump considered.

"It *was* a great Miss Universe," he said. "Maybe the best. But they're all great."

I felt a weight lift off my shoulders. And here I'd been a near nervous wreck headed into the Oval. I felt a surge of "Vitamin T" in my veins. Mr. Trump can have that effect on you.

"You haven't seen these movies?"

"No, sir." I silently prayed that he wasn't about to insert the thumb drive in his computer.

"Okay," Mr. Trump said, unmuting the TV. Mr. Colonnity was shouting at the camera, angrily pointing his finger. "Good job, Herb. Thanks."

Good job, Herb. Thanks! I could count on one hand the number of times I'd heard that in twenty-seven years. My feet barely touched the ground as I exited the Oval.

"How did it go?" Judd asked anxiously.

"I'll tell you, Judd. It reminded me yet again why people love and admire that man."

Judd seemed confused. But given Mr. Trump's obvious innocence, I made the spot decision that I could safely tell Judd about the thumb drive. Ever since the ridiculous Stormy Daniels business, Mr. Trump's extracurricular activities in the Casanova Department had ceased to matter, insofar as his approval ratings went. No one cared. Not even his evangelical supporters. As one of them preached from the pulpit of his megachurch, "Did our Lord not instruct us to love one another as we do ourselves?"

Instead of looking relieved, Judd looked—I don't want to say "aghast"—concerned.

My elation turned out to be short-lived, for the next day, Mr. Trump called me in and ordered me to work closely with Senator Biskitt of South Carolina on repealing the Glebnikov

Act; and with Treasury Secretary Minutian on unfreezing Oleg's US assets.

I must have stared at Mr. Trump rather too long.

"Do you have a problem, Herb?"

"No, sir," I stammered. "Might I ask—is this in connection with what we discussed yesterday?"

He shook his head.

"Nothing at all. Nothing. Zero. We're doing this because it's the right thing to do. Obama should never have signed this fucking Glebnikov Act into law. It's a disgrace."

I didn't know how to respond. Say what you will, Mr. Trump was being consistent with his agenda, namely nullifying the Obama legacy. The fact that he was willing to nullify this in particular, despite very suboptimal optics, speaks volumes about his integrity.

11

Sen. Squigg Lee Biskitt of South Carolina was an unlikely Trump champion. He certainly didn't start out as one. Prior to the 2016 campaign, he was calling Mr. Trump just about every unpleasant name under the sun, from "kook" to "damn lunatic" and "lower than alligator poo." Strong words, indeed.

Then, when it appeared Mr. Trump was going to be the nominee of the Republican Party, "Squiggly" had a classic "road to Damascus" moment.

The expression derives from the story of the future Saint Paul, at the time known as "Better Call Saul." While on his way to Damascus to persecute Christians, Saul was knocked off his horse and blinded by God—who else? God said to him, "Schmuck! Enough with the persecuting!" Saul got the point.

So did Squiggly, who now declared that Mr. Trump was "the Second Coming—maybe even the Third and Fourth." Squiggly's ability to adapt was beyond even Darwin's imagination. This made him either laudable or despicable, depending on your point of view. He attached himself to Mr. Trump like a remora fish. Mr. Trump was not unsusceptible to flattery, but in Squiggly's case, he knew the score, as they say in Queens. That is, he knew perfectly well that the chipmunk squeaks of praise were motivated solely by shameless, unapologetic, "slap yo mamma" level ambition to get reelected to a fourth term. Mr. Trump's true feeling for Senator Biskitt was evident in his private nickname for him: "Buttplug." As previously noted, normally the more debasing the nickname, the higher you stood with Mr. Trump. Buttplug was the exception.

South Carolina was Trump Country, God bless it. You couldn't throw a stone in the Palmetto State without hitting someone wearing a MAGA hat. And then God save you, because that person was almost certainly armed.

In his own small way, Squiggly was consequential. His folksy rhetoric earned him titles like "Li'l Cicero" and "Tiny Titan of the Senate." He cultivated an aura of down-home aw-shuck-siness, of bourbon and balderdash: "Seems to me we oughta be talking about locking up the *criminals* instead of making it harder for decent folks who just wanna shoot raccoons with AR-15s and high-capacity magazines. But I could be wrong."

He was adept at "making nice" with the liberal mainstream media, whom he knew loathed him. He always made himself available for an on-the-fly interview, scampering on little feet across the polished floor of the Capitol Rotunda. One observer likened his gait to "a penguin on an ice floe trying to escape a sea lion." He'd pause in midscamper to greet politely the enemy of the people from CNN or MSNBC; never mind that the night before, someone on those networks had denounced him as "an invertebrate" or "a Vichy Republican." (See "civility, decline of.")

With his native southern courtesy, he'd cheerfully provide a nice, chewy sound bite, and even tease the correspondent: "Now don't y'all choke on that aroo-gula y'all like to eat. Back home we call 'em collard greens." Then he'd look at his wristwatch in mock horror and say, "Uh-oh, time to get this loco in motion," and scamper off, one step ahead of the sea lion. If it hadn't been for his—I don't want to say "sycophancy"—allegiance to Mr. Trump, Squigg Lee Biskitt might have been an admired, even beloved, US politician.*

I watched the senator's face as Mr. Trump told him that he wanted him to take the lead in overturning the Glebnikov Act. I thought: This *will be the test.*

His round, boyish face remained impassive. He always had a bad haircut. I decided that this must be deliberate, part of his faux-naïf non-arugula-ness, so he could boast he'd never spent more than ten bucks on a haircut.

"It's very important we do this," the president said.

Squiggly's Adam's apple bobbed as he swallowed.

"Why, exactly, sir? I'm not saying I disagree. But we are—both of us—in the middle of a reelection campaign. And something like this is—"

"Squigg," the president cut him off, "people *want* this."

"They do?"

"Are you kidding?" Mr. Trump said. "We're getting flooded with calls about it. Isn't that right, Herb?"

"Yes, sir," I said dutifully.

"How many this week?" the president prodded.

"Hard to say. Certainly . . . a number."

The president turned his attention back to the senator, who looked like he'd just seen another sea lion, away from which there was no scampering.

"The armed services are very concerned, Squigg."

"They are? I'm on the Armed Services Committee and I haven't heard a—"

---

* I don't mean this critically.

"Squigg. Wakey-wakey. The military runs on moly . . . nemmin . . ."

"Molybdenum," I interjected.

"Right. They need it. Our military says they can't make anything without it. Bombs, tanks, missiles. Ships. This guy Pishinsky is sitting on the world's biggest reserves of the stuff. And we're making his life miserable because of some asshole journalist? Whose death, by the way, he had nothing to do with. Okay? It's nuts. Completely nuts. Another bullshit Obama move to cripple the military and make us vulnerable."

Squiggly was perspiring.

"I certainly don't want to sound in any way contrary," he said. "But I'm not sure five people in the whole country even know about the Glebnikov Act."

"You come with me tomorrow on Air Force One to Testicle, Ohio, to my rally and you'll hear more than five people chanting, 'Free Oleg!'"

I made a note to get with the speechwriters to come up with a chant that sounded less Russian. Something more generic. Making a chant out of "molybdenum" was probably a bad idea.

Squiggly took in another deep breath of rarefied Oval air.

"Overturning a law is a complex business, sir. We'd need fifty-one votes in the Senate. That's not necessarily a problem. But we also need 51 percent of the House. And . . . well, I don't need to tell you that's a tall order."

"I have tremendous faith in your abilities, Squigg. You're an amazing parliamentarian. The way you walked out of the Senate trial—how many times?"

"Three."

"You know what Colonnity said about that, right? He said it was the most principled thing he'd ever seen in the United States Senate. Ever."

"He's very generous, Seamus."

"Generous? Fuck generous! He understated! You were fucking magnificent. I'll never forget it. I'll tell you who else won't forget it. My base. Come with me to Testicle, Squiggly. I'll give you a shout-out like you've never had."

Yet again I marveled at the president's powers of persuasion. *Come with me to Testicle, Squiggly,* is up there with "I have seen the promised land." I got goose bumps.

"Let me get with the leadership and get back to you."

"You're a great man, Squigg Lee Biskitt. Very great." Squiggly blushed. Mr. Trump added, "Don't let anyone tell you different," which I thought somewhat undercut the first part. Mr. Trump turned to me and said, "Herb, anything Senator Biskitt asks for, he gets. Got it? Anything."

"Yes, sir."

"Herb, could we talk for just a moment?" Squiggly whispered to me outside the Oval.

In my office with the door closed, he said, "With all due respect, what the hell was that about?"

Careful Herb, I cautioned myself. It's a fine line between loyalty and perfidy.

"Well, Senator," I said, "seems to me the president is genuinely concerned about the molybdenum situation."

"Well, this is the first *I've* heard anything about that," he said. "I sit on that committee and no one's said word one about molyb—however the heck you pronounce it."

"Senator," I said, "I don't pretend to understand the complexities of it. I come from the hospitality world, not the military industrial complex. But I can tell you that the president deeply, deeply cares that our men—and women—have the tools they need to protect the country. And if the generals tell the president, 'We need this Pishinsky fellow's molybdenum,' the president's reply is going to be, 'How much do you need and when do you need it by?'"

The senator looked flustered, as well he might. I threw in, "By the way, Senator, we were going over the president's schedule yesterday. Someone in the room—I won't say who—said, '*Two* trips to South Carolina? We're not going to South Carolina twice.' Do you know what the president said?"

"What?"

"He said, 'We're going to South Carolina as many times as Senator Biskitt asks us to go.'"

"He did?"

"Those were his words," I said.

Not exactly a "cue 'The Star-Spangled Banner'" moment, okay. But the commander in chief had tasked me with what he viewed as, well, a task. And if a little dissembling was what it took to close the deal, so be it.

With a bit of on-the-hoof inspiration, I added, "He also wondered if you'd care to go golfing with him this Saturday at Bloody Run. Just you, the president, and President Attajurk."

"He did? Well, yes, I would like that very much." He frowned. "He's not gonna ask me again to dedicate the statue to that nonexistent Confederate colonel is he? I can't *do* that."

"No, sir," I said truthfully.

It had gotten to the point where I felt virtuous merely by not saying something false. As epiphanies go, not a "road to Damascus" level moment. But something.

12

Our chief speechwriter, Stefan Nacht von Nebel, had come to the attention of the president with his thought-provoking essay, "The Final Solution to the Mexican Problem." Mr. Trump, not being a reader himself, had learned of Stefan's essay from Mr. Colonnity's show.

Naturally, the liberal mainstream media did its best to make Stefan out to be the love child of Joseph Goebbels and Leni Riefenstahl. Stefan took it all in stride. "Good thing I don't have a club foot," he quipped.

Communications director Greta had asked him "please"—a word Greta rarely used with staff—to drop the "von" from his name. At first Stefan refused. The "von" apparently signified that he was of *der Adel*—the nobility. He even mentioned it to Mr. Trump, who was proud of his own German ancestry. He told Greta to stop bothering his "word bitch" (as he playfully called Stefan) about his name. Mr. Trump often spoke of his Drumpf family's relations, which apparently included Kaiser Wilhelm, Ludwig II of Bavaria, Frederick the Great, Frederick the Beautiful, and a fearsome, hirsute personage named Teutonicus, who, Mr. Trump proudly averred, "kicked Roman ass." Greta did at least persuade Stefan not to wear his monocle in the presence of reporters and to stop clicking his heels when greeting the president.*

I explained to Stefan about the repeal of the Glebnikov Act initiative and the need for a less Slavic-sounding slogan than "Free Oleg!"

It was a tough sell. Stefan was hardwired against immigration in general. So the idea of rescinding a law that kept just one person from entering the US went against his grain. When I told him that it was personally important to the president, Stefan yielded. He said he'd get to work on a slogan to "arouse the beast in the breast of the base." (He loved alliteration, Stefan.) A few hours later he came up with "Thou shalt not crucify mankind on a cross of molybdenum."

I thought it was a bit of a mouthful, but I was always careful to sugarcoat with Stefan. (Speechwriters are all divas.) He removed his monocle and arched his eyebrow and explained condescendingly that it was a subtle echo of a famous speech by William Jennings Bryan. Whatever, I said. I took it to Mr. Trump, who frowned, then said it "sounded smart" but to run it by Norma.

Pastor Norma Damdiddle was our in-house evangelical. She was a catch. Getting her to come aboard was a major coup. Mr. Trump had seen her TV show and was highly impressed. ("She's almost as good as me," he said.) He called her the next day and asked her to join his "crusade against the left-wing atheists who want to destroy God's kingdom here on earth." To his delight, she accepted.

Norma had rocked the historically male evangelical establishment with her bestseller, *Camels Can Too Pass Through the*

---

* After a highly unpleasant profile in the *Washington Post*, Stefan did drop the "von" and replaced it with a hyphen.

Eye of a Needle—Three Abreast! Her audacious reinterpretation of the gospels as financial seminars proved hugely popular, especially among the less educated and those serving prison sentences. The male evangelical establishment quickly embraced the "Damdiddle Dogma of Enlightened Self-Enrichment."

Norma commuted between Washington and her base in Hosannah City, Georgia, home to her fourteen-thousand-seat megachurch, where she broadcast her regular Sunday TV show, *Are You Investing in Me, Jesus?*

Needless to say, the liberal mainstream media portrayed Norma as a shill, hypocritical, shameless huckster—yada yada yada—for embracing a thrice-married president who employed a full-time lawyer to handle hush payments to porn stars and other assorted jezebels. Yada yada. To which Norma would coolly respond, "Let him who is without stones cast the first sin." That usually shut them up, but inevitably the rending of garments and gnashing of teeth resumed. No matter. Mr. Trump's approval rating among "my evangelicals" was higher than the pope's among American Catholics.*

Norma approved Stefan's "cross of however you pronounce it," so we were good to go.

Prior to the Testicle rally, Greta called Mr. Colonnity at Fox to give him a heads-up. Mr. Colonnity was "all in" on repealing the Glebnikov Act, which he agreed was "another outrageous instance of Obama overreach."

After more than three years of strenuously refuting the notion that Russia had elected Mr. Trump, Mr. Colonnity was now reflexively in favor of *anything* pro-Russian. And reflexively anti anything Ukrainian.

He and Mr. Fartmartin, Fox's number two personality, made

---

* It was this that led the president to make his perhaps ill-advised remark that he was more popular than the pope.

mincemeat of the State Department officials who'd testified at the first impeachment hearing. Who could forget Mr. Fartmartin's reinterpretation of Ambassador Taylor's fifty years of government service as "a half century of feeding at the public trough"? Magnificent. Every night, Mr. Colonnity and Mr. Fartmartin tried to outdo each other with their brilliant put-downs of these self-regarding agents of the deep state as they mounted their odious coup against the democratically elected Mr. Trump.

Mr. Colonnity called Mr. Trump as we were en route to Testicle, to wish him good luck. He urged him to practice saying "molybdenum." The two of them said it to each other over the speakerphone, again and again. It remains one of my most vivid memories, listening to the most powerful man in the world and the most powerful broadcaster in America saying to each other, "Mo-lib-denum . . . mo-libb-denum . . . mo-libbbb-denummmmmm."

"My lips are going numb," Mr. Trump said.

"You're almost there, sir," Mr. Colonnity said. Finally he pronounced Mr. Trump's pronunciation perfect.

"Sir, with your leadership, the name of that metal will be on the lips of every patriotic American." Those of us present aboard Air Force One that day felt our hearts glow.

In the end, the "M-word" did not roll trippingly off the presidential tongue. And the crucifixion metaphor only seemed to confuse the base. The focus group kept asking how nails could be hammered into a cross made of super-hard metal. In the end, Mr. Trump saved the day, brilliantly improvising, leading the crowd, chanting "Olé, Oleg! Olé, Oleg!"

Still too Russian sounding, I thought. But the basic job was done. America was now alert to the looming molybdenum crisis.

As it turned out, that crisis would be a precursor to an even more critical crisis. But as it has been said, it is in the nature of crises to be critical.

13

The state dinner for President Attajurk of Turkey could not in truth be called a complete success.

The fault lay not in my dunderheadedness in the matter of the croissants. The more serious faux pas was the inclusion of the Kardashians.

I myself have never quite understood the extraordinary celebrity of these people, but one bows to public opinion. Mr. Trump was a huge fan of the collagen-lipped, steatopygous-rumped Kim Kardashian, primus inter pares of the clan. He was always saying, "If she wasn't married to Kanye, I'd be in there in a New York minute."

One never quite knew how to react to these mischievous, lubricious remarks by the president, especially when Mrs. Trump was present. But Melania, with her stern, even chilling Slovenian dignity and adamantine runway model poise, never seemed to register emotion. I put it down to the language barrier.

Or *did* she?

Mr. Trump invited Kim and Kanye to the Turkish state dinner for a number of reasons. One, it was a way of thanking Kanye for likening him to Jesus. Two, because—as he put it—"who *wouldn't* want to stare at that ass?" (Ms. K's, that is.)

Normally, Mrs. Trump never involved herself in the seating of state dinners. But this time she did ask for the seating plan, which came back with a few changes, including putting Ms. K on President Attajurk's left, and Mrs. T on his right.

Mr. Trump was delighted that the Turkish president, whom he admired and wanted to please—as he did all authoritarian leaders—would be bookended by such high-quality pulchritude. As he put it, "Atta"—as he called him—"won't know whether to crap or go crazy."

I was curious that she placed Senator Biskitt, whom she detested, at her table. I was at a different one, seated next to the wife of the Turkish minister of fear, who turned out to be not only delightful but also full of fascinating Ankara gossip.

It wasn't until after the dinner that I heard what happened at table one.

Mrs. Trump, speaking across President Attajurk, said to Kim, "Keem, you are Armenian?"

President Attajurk stiffened (as well he might). Kim replied in the affirmative, noting that she was "not Armenian" on her mother's side.

"How many relatives on your father's side were genocided by the Turks?" Mrs. T asked.

That was an icebreaker.

That very afternoon, Senator Biskitt had blocked a vote in the Senate denouncing Turkey for slaughtering 1.5 million Armenians. Not for reasons of principle, which rarely influence Senate votes, but out of courtesy. As he explained to Fox, "How would it look if I was visiting Istanbul and the Turkish senate, or whatever they have over there, denounced me for slavery? A fine welcome that'd be, huh?" Rather good point, I thought.

Senator Biskitt gamely intervened in an attempt to change the topic, complimenting President Attajurk for agreeing to the cease-fire in the (now former) Kurdish border area. But complimenting someone for pausing in the slaughter of one group of people, as a means of changing the topic from the slaughter of another group of people, is slicing the salami pretty thin. The senator was trying to throw him a lifeline.

President Attajurk would not be beguiled from his rage over Mrs. T's mischief-making. The dinner proceeded in what one observer described as "minus-Celsius-degree silence." Mr. Trump was *furious* when he learned what had happened.

President Attajurk canceled the rest of the state visit and left Washington that night, claiming he had to return to supervise lifting the cease-fire and resuming shelling the Kurdish refugee camps.

I've often wondered since: What was Mrs. T's "game" that night? Was it to punish her husband for his quips about how he yearned to disappear into hillocks of Kim-flesh?

Or was she out to spoil a) President Attajurk's relations with the United States, b) dinner, and c) his ogling of the famed Kardashian bazoombas, abundantly on display?

I never asked. Mrs. T remains to me, as she does to many, a Sphinx.

14

As a rule, I did not sit in on the presidential daily briefings, during which the director of national intelligence would bring Mr. Trump up to speed about whatever horror was most pressing at the moment.

I don't mean to sound cynical, but PDBs, as they are called, are almost never cause to make a presidential heart "sing hymns at heaven's gate."

I was only attending the PDBs in order to stay abreast of Russia-related developments, specifically US Cyber Command's rogue Commie-electing computer program, and of course my number-one priority, making Oleg happy again. Judd and I were also concerned about the CIA's new star recruit, Huggybear.

DNI Miriam had told us that CIA's Moscow station reported that their recruited asset was feeling a bit on edge these days, owing to the Communist Party's newfound prominence. The FSB—the Russian not-so-secret police—had been up to its usual tricks, puncturing Comrade Zitkin's tires, rearranging the books in his library, leaving nasty notes on the refrigerator, poisoning his ferrets, and lacing his pipe tobacco with hallucinogens—standard FSB intimidation tactics "to throw you off-balance."

"Good God," I said. "That would certainly throw *me* off-balance. Wouldn't it be best to retire him as an asset? Give him a nice severance package and tell him his services are no longer required?"

"That's not how it works, Herb. He's already asking about exfiltration."

I had no idea what exfiltration was. It sounded like something to do with making coffee. Miriam explained that it is the opposite of infiltration.

"We're doing what we can to calm him down. We don't want him to have a nervous breakdown in the middle of all this."

"I don't mean to sound critical," I said, "but this Huggybear of yours doesn't sound like a nerves-of-steel type. If all they have to do to put him over the edge is poison his ferrets and let the air out of his tires, what happens when they start pulling out his fingernails? And why recruit someone who keeps ferrets in the first place?"

Miriam said that CIA Moscow was considering all options. That made me not want to know what those options were. Meanwhile she agreed that it would be best not to inform Mr. Trump about it, "for now." There was an awful lot of "for now"-ing going on these days. The three of us proceeded to the Oval for the PDB.

"How's Putin doing with the runoff election?" Mr. Trump asked.

Miriam said that polls showed him "more than comfortably ahead" of Mr. Zitkin, the Communist usurper.

"That's what the polls said before the last election." He grunted. "And look what happened."

"Those are the figures, sir. Barring another deus ex machina, Mr. Putin appears to be on a solid track for reelection."

"Barring what?"

"Another cyberattack on the Ministry of Elections, sir."

"Is there anything we can do to help Putin?"

This produced a nearly audible sound of buttock clenching. The president had just asked the head of national intelligence to assist in reelecting Vladimir Putin. Miriam took a deep breath.

"I'm not sure I follow, sir."

"We don't want Russia to be Red again, do we?"

In a normal scenario, this would have been the moment for Miriam triumphantly to reveal that the CIA had recruited the number-two or -three person in the CP. In which case, the answer to the president's question would be, "Actually, sir, we do." Alas.

"I emphasize," Miriam said, "that all the numbers strongly point to a robust Putin victory."

"There's got to be something we can do."

I saw headlines: "Trump Ordered CIA to Reelect Putin" and "Trump Repays Putin for Help in 2016." I was seeing a lot of headlines these days.

Miriam looked like she was walking barefoot on hot coals.

"Did you have something . . . specific in mind, sir?"

"This Zipkin guy, what do we know about him?"

"Far less than Mr. Putin knows, sir. Rest assured, the FSB and GRU have thicker files on him than we do. Frankly, Mr. *Zitkin* (she corrected; Mr. Trump never did get his name right) wasn't really someone of great interest to us. Until . . ." Miriam glanced sideways at Judd and me. I held my breath, thinking she was about to say, *one of our computers elected him president of Russia.* Thankfully she merely said ". . . now."

She added, "There *is* a development." Zitkin had applied to the Kremlin for permission to give a speech from a historic platform in the middle of Red Square.

"So?" said the president.

"What's interesting," she explained, "is that the Kremlin gave permission. The *lobnoye mesto*—the rostrum, or platform—in Red Square is highly symbolic. Ivan the Terrible used to give speeches from it. And then hang half the audience from the Kremlin walls. Numerous proclamations have been announced from it over the centuries. Lenin spoke from it. But it's not a platform for political stumping. For the Kremlin to give Zitkin permission to give a campaign speech—presumably on an anti-Putin theme—would be about the equivalent of you, sir, granting permission to a rival to denounce you from the south lawn of the White House."

"Wouldn't happen."

"No, quite. Indeed, it's so unusual that our people in Moscow think Mr. Putin must be laying a trap for Zitkin."

The president perked up. "Like what?"

"The sound system crashing in the middle of his speech. Heckling. Eggs. Milkshakes. Milkshakes are the current favorite heckler missile. Sometimes packed with rocks."

"What about shooting him?" the president said hopefully.

"We don't have anything about that. Shooting Mr. Zitkin in front of the Kremlin would certainly be a bold act."

"Didn't they shoot that guy on the bridge across from the Kremlin? Whatshisname."

"Boris Nemtsov. Yes, they did. But not during a live broadcast on television."

The president said, "It'd be great TV. Ratings off the chart."

I had a horrible presentiment. What if the Kremlin decided to get rid of him with Oil of Oleg? The president's friend Kim Jong-un had dispatched his half brother with a public smearing of fatal goo. I saw another headline: "Hand of Putin's Pharmacist Seen in Zitkin Death." That would certainly help with repealing the Glebnikov Act.

I wondered if I should convey my concern in my next prison visit with my Oleg go-between, Paul. How would I phrase it? *Paul, would you ask Oleg not to have Mr. Zitkin rubbed with Novichok during his speech in Red Square? Lousy optics.*

So you can imagine my relief when, three days later, Mr. Zitkin did not expire from multiple organ failure in the middle of Red Square as he pounded the pulpit of the *lobnoye mesto*.

But clever old CIA was right: it was a trap. Not three minutes into his speech, Mr. Zitkin succumbed to what one commentator called "the ultimate nightmare of any public speaker." The sound of the tumult in Zitkin's lower GI was audible over the PA system. (The Kremlin had provided concert-quality amplification for the speech.) Moments later—I'll just quote the *New York Times* account: "Mr. Zitkin succumbed to a violent and catastrophic episode of lower GI distress."

Needless to say, the humiliating episode went viral. So viral as to cause servers worldwide to crash. Even Stone Age people in the remotest corners of New Guinea have by now probably viewed Anatoli Zitkin's moment of maximum mortification in—as it was now called—"Brown Square."

The Communist Party accused the Kremlin of adulterating Mr. Zitkin's vodka. Mr. Zitkin was that rarity among Russians: a nondrinker. But it was his custom before speaking to a large audience to take a single swig of vodka from a flask, "for courage."

The Kremlin coolly dismissed the accusation, pointing to a dozen or more emergency room admissions that day for "extreme stomach flu." (CIA Moscow said these were likely cases of "Potemkin stomach bug." That is, staged, to camouflage the Zitkin poisoning. What fun for the stagers.) Mr. Putin, smiling like a Cheshire mountain lion, publicly wished Mr. Zitkin a "full recovery," adding friskily that he looked forward to "hearing the rest of his speech."

Mr. Trump was jubilant. He replayed the tape again and again. Greta begged him, practically on hands and knees, not to tweet about it. He grudgingly consented—and phoned Putin.

Judd learned about the call, as the rest of us did, after the fact. We braced for a transcript of the call to come forth. Thankfully, none did. (I suspect Miriam saw to that.) To this day, it's not known what the president said to Mr. Putin. Probably for the best, all things considered. Me, I was just thankful the Kremlin opted for a less drastic additive to Mr. Zitkin's "courage" vodka than a shot of Oil of Oleg.

Never have I more wanted an election to be over and done with than this one. But we were not there yet. Far from it.

15

Normally, I did not participate in Mr. Trump's golf outings, but since the president had tasked me with "riding herd" on the Glebnikov Act repeal, I joined him and Senator Biskitt for eighteen holes at Bloody Run. President Attajurk did not join, having departed to exterminate another ethnic group.

We flew on Marine One, the presidential helicopter. As we descended, Mr. Trump pointed out to the senator where the supposed battle had taken place.

As a serious Civil War buff, the senator was among those—including the Virginia Historical Marker Commission—who insisted that no battle had ever taken place on Mr. Trump's golf course; or for that matter, anywhere near it. Squiggly would never contradict the president, but I could tell that it was taxing even his protean powers of sycophancy. What could he say as the president insisted that "the outcome of the Civil War was decided right here on the seventeenth fairway"? Not much.

He could do what he had with his other principles, namely throw them under the bus. But as a faithful son of South

Carolina, assenting to Mr. Trump's rewrite of the War of Northern Aggression* caused him near physical pain. He kept trying to change the subject; when that failed, he merely nodded thoughtfully but ambiguously as the president described in detail the particulars of the Battle of Bloody Run. Here and there Squiggly offered anodyne remarks on the order of "Hm," and "Really?" and "Well, that *is* interesting."

The president sliced into the rough.

"Go on, take a mulligan," Squiggly urged.

The second drive curved but landed just inside the fairway.

"Nice shot, sir. I can see you're fixing to beat me like a drum."

"I had Tiger and Nicklaus out here last weekend."

"So I heard. I think I'd have found that kind of intimidating."

"Nicklaus is designing my next course."

"Yeah? Great. Where?"

"Crimea."

A look of horror came over the senator.

"Just fucking with you." The president grinned. He loved teasing his courtiers, the president. He reminded me of the famous Norman Rockwell painting of the boy with a magnifying glass, setting fire to the caterpillar.

"You about gave me a heart attack, sir."

"I could build a golf course in Crimea."

"I don't doubt it. But I hope y'all'll wait until your second term to do that."

The president's next shot went deep into the rough toward the Potomac River. His caddie started off after it but the president said to leave it and dropped another ball onto the fairway.

"I see we're playing Marquis of Queensbury rules," Squiggly said cheekily.

"I don't like to make them go looking for balls down there,"

---

* Also known as "The Civil War."

the president said. "It's snaky. Very snaky. Nasty, snakes. Why would God make snakes? What's the point of snakes? I guess because of Adam and Eve, right?"

The senator did not join the president in theological exploration.

"We got alligators on our courses in South Carolina. Makes poking around for your ball real interesting."

The president seemed to take this as one-upmanship.

"I'm talking rattlesnakes."

"Yeah, we got them, all right. South Carolina has all four types of venomous snakes native to North America."

"Must make you proud, huh?"

"Rattlers, water mocs, cottonmouths, and corals. Corals, they're the little-bitty ones with the colored bands. They're the most venomous. You get bit by one of those rascals, don't even bother dialing 911. If you got a pen and paper on you, make out your will. And write quick."

"I was going to get rid of my snakes," the president said. "But the local Audubon Society or whatever it's called made a thing out of it. Assholes. Audubon's supposed to be about birds. Why would they give a fuck about snakes? Why would anyone want to protect rattlesnakes? Nuts. They're totally nuts. So my caddies have to risk their lives going after the balls. We have to stock the antivenom or whatever it's called. Know what one dose costs? One dose? You don't want to know. Ten fucking grand. I could use my Mexicans. Mexicans love snakes. They grow up with them. They're everywhere in Mexico, snakes. But if I used Mexicans and one got bit? The *Washington Post* would be calling for another impeachment. I'll tell you something. I'm not done with Jeff Bezos yet.* Jeff Bezos has got some major surprises coming his way. You wait."

---

* The owner of the *Washington Post*. Also of Amazon.com.

Squiggly shook his head at the injustice of it all.

"I hate the way they go after you, sir. It's not right."

The president lined up his shot.

"That's why it's important we get the Glebnikov thing done."

As segues go, this was a reach.

"How do you mean, sir?"

"The media needs to learn they can't get away with murder."

An ironic statement, inasmuch as the Glebnikov Act was passed to punish a Russian oligarch for (allegedly) murdering a journalist.

"Well, sir," he said, "there *is* that. But optics-wise, I am convinced it would be better to concentrate on the molybdenum shortage aspect rather than on Mr. Pishinsky's history vis-à-vis the late Mr. Glebnikov."

"Whatever. But we need to get this done, Squigg. This is not a can we can kick down the road. This is not Brexit. My generals and admirals are saying they need molly—this metal to defend our country. This is about national security."

"I am doing what I can, sir. But repealing a law sanctioning a Russian oligarch for—alleged—involvement in the murder of a reporter . . . it's not the kind of initiative that lends itself to momentum-building. It's hard to get people worked up about it."

"It's not about freedom of the fucking press, Squigg. It's about making sure our armed men and women have the tools they need to defend our country. Why is that a hard sell?"

"Right. Right. I do get that. Thing is, most folks have never heard of molybdenum. That said, I hear your rally in Testicle was a great success."

"Colonnity's gonna keep mentioning how great it was. The chanting, 'Olé, Oleg!'"

"It must have been very moving, sir."

"That was very smart on my part. I came up with 'Olé, Oleg' on the spot. That crap line Stefan—and you, Herb—gave me about crucifying mankind on a cross of the stuff, that went over like a fart at a funeral. I'm very disappointed in you, Herb. I asked you and Stefan to come up with something great and you gave me that turd."

"I apologize, Mr. President."

"You're lucky I saved it. 'Olé, Oleg!' is a great line."

Squiggly said, "It is. But I'm thinking the less we make this about someone named Oleg and more about a shortage of strategic matériel, the better off we'll be."

"Whatever. Just get it done."

"I am efforting it, sir. All I'm saying is repeal ain't gonna be a walk in the park."

"That's why I asked you to do it, Squigg. That's how highly I think of you."

I mentally added, *That's why my private nickname for you is Buttplug.* I don't mean to sound bitter, but I was smarting a bit from Mr. Trump's blaming me for Stefan's oratorical "turd."

"I thank you for the compliment of your confidence, sir," Squiggly said.

Senator Biskitt looked as though he'd rather talk about the Battle of Bloody Run.

"Did you see the Commie guy shit himself in Brown Square?" the president asked. "Brown Square. That's what they're calling it. Brown Square. That's great."

"I don't like Communists any more than the next person," Squiggly said, "but I have to say, I kind of felt for the poor guy."

"Why? He's a Communist."

"Well, yeah. But Lordy. Can you imagine?"

"He had it coming."

"He did?"

"He tried to steal the election from Putin."

"Oh. So . . . we know that? For a fact? 'Course you got better sources than I do."

"Sure he did it. Who else could it have been?"

Seldom have I been so happy to hear Mr. Trump assert a falsehood. Though technically, he did not know it to be one.

"Well," Squiggly said, "there's all sorts of speculating. Some people say we had a hand in it. But you'd know more about that than I."

"Bullshit. Not even real bullshit. Fake bullshit."

"If you say."

"We had nothing to do with it. Why would I want to unseat Putin? He's a terrific person. I'm going to invite him to the White House."

Squiggly looked at me. This was the first I'd heard of this—I don't want to say "bizarre"—bold notion.

Mr. Trump's putt overshot the hole by six feet.

"That's a gimme. What do you think? It's great, right? Like Nixon in China. Only Putin in Washington. Big. Very big."

"Have you discussed this with anyone, sir?"

"I'm discussing it with you. You should be flattered."

Squiggly's mouth moved but no words came out. He looked like someone whose dentures had come loose and was trying to reattach them to the gums without using his fingers.

Suddenly Senator Biskitt broke into a grin. He wagged a finger at the president.

"You got me again. You *are* in a devilish mood today, sir. Boy, did you have me, there. Hoo."

"What are you talking about? It's a great idea," the president said sternly. "Herb thinks it's a fabulous idea. Tell him, Herb."

"It is a big idea, sir. One of your biggest."

"See?" the president said to Squiggly. "Herb has very good instincts about this kind of thing."

"This kind of thing?" the senator said.

"Hospitality. He's got twenty-seven years in the hospitality business. He knows something about hospitality."

"Ah. Yes. Well, it is big. But if I might urge you, sir, I would hold off announcing something like that until after the election. Our election, that is."

It was obvious to Mr. Trump that the Tiny Titan of the Senate was not bowled over by his big idea. A rime descended on Bloody Run.

When Mr. Trump felt that one of his ideas was insufficiently praised, his tendency was to withdraw. I don't want to say "pout," but his disappointment conveyed a sense of betrayal.

It was part and parcel, perhaps, of the proverbial "loneliness of command." Churchill was this way. Stalin famously didn't like it when those around him failed to effuse over his ideas. Hitler could get very sulky if he felt that the "*Heil Hitler!*"'s were lacking in *sturm* or *drang*. From what the CIA told us, Kim Jong-un got extremely peevish if he detected diminuendo in the chorus of "Let us eternally glorify the sacred revolutionary careers and immortal feats of the great Comrade Kim Jong-un!" It's a basic human instinct to want those around you to cheer. It goes back to potty training. One can only imagine—not that I care to—what Kim Jong-un's nannies told him when he did his morning BMs. Probably arranged parades.

The flight back to the White House was subdued. Mr. Trump watched *Fox and Fiends* on his iPad. Senator Biskitt stared morosely out the window of Marine One with a look of "What the heck was *that* about?" I chided myself for not being more of a cheerleader to Mr. Trump. You could debate the pros and cons of inviting Putin to the White House, but who could dispute that it was "big"?

Dr. Bernon, our psychiatrist here at FCI Wingdale, tells me I was in a "destructive codependent" relationship with Mr. Trump and that I really shouldn't feel guilty for feeling that I'd failed him. Still.

I was, however, having a continuing case of the guilts about

Comrade Anatoli Zitkin. I couldn't shake the image of the poor son of a gun up there on the *lobnoye mesto*. If we—that is, Placid Reflux—hadn't rigged the election in his favor, he wouldn't have been up there, fouling himself on live TV.

Judd kept bringing me fresh CIA phone intercepts from Communist Party headquarters, but I wasn't in the mood to read them. I did ask him how Anatoli and Oksana were getting on.

"She's refusing to do any campaign events with him," Judd said.

"Can't say I blame her. After what he went through."

"She's still furious with him. She's convinced he and his fellow bolshies did the hack. She wants him to pull out of the race."

"Maybe that would be for the best."

"He's telling her that he can't. He said—sure you don't want to read the transcript?"

"*No*, Judd, I do not. I feel awful about this."

"Herb, he's a Communist. A Russian Communist. Remember them? The Soviets? There is no reason to feel 'awful' for him."

"I'm just saying we've screwed up his life. His wife is furious with him. And Putin may kill him."

"Yeah, well, life's a bitch. Especially when you run against Putin and win. Let me just read you this bit."

"I don't want to hear it, Judd."

ANATOLI ZITKIN: I can't pull out, Oksana. I owe it to the party.

OKSANA ZITKIN: Anatoli Ivanovich! Wake up! The revolution is over! Dead! Which we will be if you don't stop this stupidity.

A.Z.: By "stupidity" do you mean Marxist-Leninist thought, under the ever-vigilant guidance of the party?

O.Z.: On second thought, I may kill you before Putin can.

A.Z.: Little Mink—

O.Z.: Don't call me that!

A.Z.: The very fact that they went to the trouble of silencing me just shows that they fear me. Fear the people, I mean.

O.Z.: I wouldn't say they silenced you. It was very loud. And very embarrassing. As for fearing you—or the people—the Kremlin has an odd way of expressing this fear.

A.Z.: What would you have me do, woman?

O.Z.: Resign!

A.Z.: Resign? Well, there's a fine way to go down in history. What will history say of me: Zitkin, Anatoli Ivanovich, leader of the Communist Party of the Russian Federation, 2004 to 2020. Resigned because his dear wife was afraid he might win the runoff election and lead his country back to greatness. Devoted rest of his life to drinking and smoking heavily and writing pamphlets that no one read. Died in obscurity. Is buried somewhere. No one knows. Or cares.

O.Z.: Would you prefer for history to say: Zitkin, Anatoli Ivanovich, convicted of treason for trying to steal the presidency from Putin, Vladimir Vladimirovich. Died in Lefortovo prison, from beatings. Or tuberculosis. Or both. No one really knows.

[PAUSE.]

A.Z.: Well, either way, I would hope it would also say: "He is mourned by his wife, whom he loved very much."

[PAUSE. SNIFFLING.]

O.Z.: Yes, it would say that. Also that her husband was sometimes so pigheaded that it was necessary for her to throw things at him.

A.Z.: Do you remember when you threw the bust of Engels at me and missed? And destroyed the television? Ooh, you were mad.

o.z.: I am still mad. It was six months before we got another television. The bust you replaced the next day.

[LAUGHTER.]

a.z.: Maybe I should hide the other busts until after the election.

o.z.: I'm scared, Anatoli Ivanovich.

a.z.: Don't be, Little Mink. Truthfully, there is no possibility that I will win.

o.z.: That's what they said about Trump. And look.

a.z.: Well, I'm not running against Hillary Clinton.

o.z.: Anatoli Ivanovich, swear to me that you won't win. Swear that you are not up to monkey business.

a.z.: For the last time, Little Mink. We—the party—did no monkey business. We don't know who was our mysterious angel on the night of the election. Surely it wasn't the Americans. The last thing they want is the hammer and sickle flying over the Kremlin. But whoever it was— Ukraine, who knows?—I assure you they won't succeed again. Putin will build a cyberfortress around the Ministry of Elections. Worry not, Little Mink. The Communist Party of the Russian Federation will go down in glorious defeat. And Russia will remain not great. As Trump would say, Sad!

[LAUGHTER.]

16

Much has been said and written about Mr. Trump and his "cult of personality." Frankly, I've never understood why the term is considered opprobrious, but maybe I'm missing something.

If one has a strong personality, as Mr. Trump certainly does, why is it a bad thing for a "cult" to form around it? And what constitutes a "cult," exactly? Isn't it just a term for "group of insanely devoted admirers"? Why is this sinister?

I am not personally Catholic, but Catholics are always talking about the "Cult of Mary" or the "Cult of Saint So-and-So." Does this mean that Jesus's mom and Saint So-and-So were malignant, attention-demanding narcissists? Really? Then someone ought to tell the pope, and pronto.

That said, most of us at the White House were a tad surprised when the "Ever Trumper" movement folks started volunteering to be shot by Mr. Trump on Fifth Avenue. Here, certainly, was a cult of personality taking it to a whole new level.

In early 2016, as you'll recall, Mr. Trump declared that he could "stand in the middle of Fifth Avenue in New York and shoot somebody and not lose voters."

What a hullabaloo that caused! He meant it as a compliment to the people who believe in him—the "base"—as a tribute to their fidelity and steadfastness.

There are many historical precedents of devoted followers willing to sacrifice themselves for their leaders. It's a very basic human instinct, not some evil, sinister thing. Look at the Japanese in World War II, hurling themselves off cliffs and blowing themselves up for their emperor. Not much fun for the US troops, but you can't deny: they sure loved their emperor.

Mr. Trump never had any intention of opening fire on his fans on Fifth Avenue. Okay, once or twice, in jest, while we were in the limo, he asked the Secret Service guy in the front seat to lend him his pistol so he could "find out if I'm right." (By the way, this totally refutes the idea that Mr. Trump lacks a sense of humor.)

Then the Ever Trumpers started showing up on Fifth Avenue with their bull's-eye shirts saying, "Shoot *me*, Mr. Trump!"

Yes, he was flattered. Who wouldn't be? I don't recall any Obama supporters offering to be shot by their big hero. If any of Hillary Clinton's fans offered themselves as fodder, I missed it.

Mr. Colonnity said on his program that he found the Ever Trumpers "incredibly moving." His follow-up suggestion that Mr. Trump should instead shoot Democrats and the liberal mainstream media was perhaps ill-advised. The handwringers at MSNBC and the failing *New York Times* certainly milked that for all it was worth. Mr. Colonnity lost a few fainthearted advertisers, but they slunk back eventually. Greta was again on her hands and knees, begging Mr. Trump not to fan the flames with a tweet. She even offered to be shot herself as a propitiatory substitute. I think she actually meant it. A real pro, Greta.

To defuse the situation, I did a little discreet outreach with the head of the Ever Trumpers, a former Navy SEAL whom Mr. Trump had pardoned for committing (so-called) "crimes against humanity" in Iraq. I told him that with everything else going on, now was just not a good time for Mr. Trump to be shooting people on Fifth Avenue. Good soldier that he is, he said he understood, but reiterated that the offer to "redeploy" along Fifth Avenue was good "till kingdom come."

Where do we get such men?

Politics is supposed to be a cynical business, but it warmed my heart to see such devotion. Whenever I had doubts about taking the White House job, I thought of some of the people I met and I pinched myself. And when I think about some others, I punch myself.

17

A few days after "Brown Square," President Putin held his annual press conference.

Yevgeny "Yev" Yussupoff, our Russian expert on the NSC staff, had told us that Putin press conferences were actually intended to be boring.

"He doesn't really want people to watch," Yev explained. "The questions are scripted and his answers framed to put everyone to sleep or make them change the channel."

R-1, the state-owned TV network, dutifully broadcast the press conferences, and followed them with thoughtful but equally mind-numbing panel discussions. The panelists would reliably conclude that whatever the problem was, it certainly wasn't the fault of our much-beloved Vladimir Vladimirovich, who, as everyone knows, works like a galley slave. By this time Russia had fallen asleep or switched to *Black Sea Baywatch* or *I Love Ludmilla* or *CSI: Magnitogorsk*.

But this Putin press conference turned out to be "must-see TV."

The Russian president was answering a softball question about the status of some natural gas pipeline from Umpsk to Leipzig. Yes, Mr. Putin admitted with chagrin, it *was* behind schedule. But the delay, as he understood it, was owed to a complexity of factors, among them a difficulty involving blah-blah-blah.

Then, just as viewers were reaching for the remote control (assuming they have those in Russia), the chyron "crawl" at the bottom of the screen started suggesting a rather more aggressive line of questioning.

ASK HIM WHY HE HAS 20 PALACES WHEN 20 MILLION RUSSIANS CAN BARELY MAKE ENDS MEET . . . ASK HIM WHY THERE WERE 10,700 HOSPITALS WHEN HE BECAME PRESIDENT IN 2000 AND NOW THERE ARE ONLY 5,400 . . . HERE'S SOMETHING ELSE TO ASK OUR "GALLEY SLAVE" VLADIMIR VLADIMIROVICH: Mr. PRESIDENT, WHEN YOU TOOK OVER 20 YEARS AGO, THERE WERE 1.2 MILLION BUREAUCRATS. NOW THERE ARE 2.2 MILLION. WHY? WHAT DO THEY DO? DO YOU HAVE THAT MANY BOOTS THAT NEED DAILY POLISHING?

Well. On and on it flippantly continued:

DEAR MR. PRESIDENT, KINDLY EXPLAIN WHY SINCE YOU BECAME PRESIDENT, CHINA'S ECONOMY HAS QUADRUPLED, AMERICA'S HAS DOUBLED, AND OURS HAS SHRUNK . . . WHY DO 35 MILLION RUSSIANS GO WITHOUT INDOOR PLUMBING WHILE YOU CRAP ON A GOLD TOILET SEAT?

The horrified R-1 production staff was unable to stop the fiendish crawl. They frantically pressed buttons and threw kill switches. Finally, in the midst of yet another impertinent question, this one concerning the president's twenty-two-million-ruble collection of wristwatches, they shut off the electricity, plunging Russia's leading network into blackness in the middle of a presidential press conference.

Our embassy in Moscow reported that the president of the Russian Federation was not pleased. (Big surprise.) Also that the red-faced management of R-1 was at a loss to explain what in God's holy name had happened. Their protestations of innocence did not spare them intense questioning by the organs of state security.

President Trump ordered Miriam to find out "what the fuck is going on over there." CIA Moscow reported that Putin's deputy told the head of R-1 he should commit suicide "as a gesture of regret." Putin nixed that, on the grounds that no one would believe it was suicide. Murdering members of the media was currently out of vogue, thanks to our old friend Oleg's handling of Glebnikov and the murder of Mr. Khashoggi at the Saudi embassy in Istanbul.

What a disaster—and with Mr. Putin in the middle of a runoff election! It certainly must have made for lively staff meetings at the Kremlin.

Russian media went into overdrive to refute the "odious insinuations" the rogue chyron had posed. They stoutly averred that Russia was prospering as never before under the inspired and benevolent leadership of President Putin.

What's more, they said, the worthy organs of state security were certain that this latest hack was "yet another undoubted provocation by anti-Russia elements in Ukraine." The Kremlin's patience with Kiev, they said, was "approaching the limits of tolerance." That must have made for lively staff meetings in Kiev.

"Fucking Ukraine," Mr. Trump remarked. He added that Hillary Clinton surely had a hand in it.

Miriam urged him not to accept Russian propaganda at face value. "This wasn't Kiev," she said.

"Who, then? The Commies?"

"We don't know, sir. CIA is looking into it."

"Looking into it." The president snorted. "What does CIA stand for, anyway? Completely Ignorant Agency?"

Judd and I pulled Miriam into my office after we left the Oval. Judd wanted to know if our Moscow "asset" Huggybear could shed any light on what had happened.

"It wasn't the CP," Miriam said, referring to the Communist Party. "They don't have the capability to pull off something like this." She paused, then added with a Mona Lisa half smile, "Any more than they did the *last* time."

"Miriam," Judd said, "what are you saying?"

"Not here," Miriam whispered. Intelligence professionals always assume someone is listening. We followed her to the Situation Room, where, as the name suggests, one goes to discuss situations in a secure environment.

"Flipper didn't call you," she said to Judd, referring to Admiral Murphy of US CyberCom, "because he didn't want to go into it over the phone. Anyway, I told him I'd be seeing you. Placid Reflux reactivated. In response to the attack on Zitkin."

"Jesus Christ," Judd said. "Flipper said he was going to shut it down."

"They tried," Miriam said. "But it's tricky, shutting down these autonomous protocol platforms. Kind of makes you yearn for the good old days of analog."

"Is *that* how you're going to explain it to the president?"

"I'm not suggesting we bother the president with this. For now."

"Excuse me," I said. "So we're also not telling the president about this?"

"For now," Miriam said.

"What if this thing starts launching missiles?" I said.

"Herb. Relax," she said, as though my asking if the world was about to end in thermonuclear holocaust was annoying.

"Placid only retaliates in kind. Its operational parameters are limited to elections."

"Oh, well then," I said in a sarcastic tone. "If it's only a matter of a rogue computer serially attacking one of the most powerful men on earth, no problemo."

I had to sit down and loosen my tie while the director of national intelligence and head of the National Security Council conversed. I pondered what other surprises Placid Reflux might have in its hard drive. The numbers of Mr. Putin's bank accounts in Zurich and the Cayman Islands?

I have an unusual disorder. In moments of great stress, I sometimes go to sleep. It's why I wouldn't have made a good fighter pilot or astronaut. Or policeman, or fireman, or hold any type job where falling asleep at the critical moment is undesirable.

I woke up to Miriam rubbing the top of my head and saying, "Wakey-wakey."

"What did you and Judd decide?"

"We think we're okay. For now."

Another "for now."

"What if this *mishegoss* machine steals the runoff election from Putin?" I asked, using the Yiddish word for nutty.

Miriam nodded. "It's a concern. But let's not throw the baby out with the bathwater."

"What baby?"

"We have an election coming up, too, Herb."

"So?"

"If the Russians interfere—which they're planning to—Placid Reflux could be a very useful countermeasure."

I groaned.

"So you're proposing to subcontract election security to a rogue computer?"

"Would you rather we subcontract it to Russia?"

I suppose Miriam had a point. Still.

"Herb," she said in full Herb-mollifying mode. "If this thing counters Russian interference in our election, wouldn't you call that a desirable outcome? Think of it this way: if the federal government got its act together to be serious about getting the Russians to butt out, something like *this* is what they'd come up with."

I was reasonably sure that Mr. Trump would not consider this a "desirable outcome." But I agreed with Miriam and Judd to leave it alone. For now. Sometimes the best course of action is no action. I'm sure there's a Winston Churchill quote somewhere about that.

18

One of Mr. Trump's great talents is to "suck all the oxygen out of the room," as the saying goes. It was breathtaking to watch, especially if you were in the room.

As the Democratic National Convention in Milwaukee approached, Mr. Trump was determined to inhale every molecule of air in Wisconsin and to dominate the news cycle as the Democrats decided which among their candidates was best suited to make America ungreat again.

Normally, the custom is for the incumbent president to go away while the other side has its convention. But no one ever accused Mr. Trump of being customary.

A number of disruptive ideas were floated: nominating a tenth justice to the Supreme Court; leaking a report that North Korea was fueling a nuclear missile targeting Milwaukee (that might get their attention); urging Mr. Putin to send a few tank divisions into Ukraine ("He would if I asked him," Mr. Trump said); holding an impromptu summit with the Taliban in Afghanistan. Being July, there was always the possibility of a hurricane, an opportunity for Mr. Trump to visit the scene of devastation and throw rolls of paper towels at the survivors.

Of course—though known only to a select few of us—there was also the possibility that Placid Reflux might start World War III. Which would certainly put a firecracker up the donkey's tail.

The idea that most appealed to Mr. Trump was a "megarally"—in Green Bay, Wisconsin, a mere two hours from Milwaukee.

Green Bay's Lambeau Field seats eighty-one thousand people, whereas the Fiserv Forum in Milwaukee seats only seventeen thousand. Mr. Trump loved the idea of holding a bash four times the size of theirs.

Speechwriter Stefan went to work and came up with a brilliant script. In the middle of his speech, Mr. Trump would hold up a finger and shush the crowd.

"Did you hear something? I thought I heard a very small sound. Like a squeak. Hear it? It's coming from Milwaukee. Sounds like . . . *mice.* Wait a minute. Didn't I hear there's a convention of *mice* in Milwaukee? Or is it a convention of *rats*?"

He and Stefan were very excited about it.

To be sure, there were logistical problems, chief among them filling a stadium with eighty-one thousand people. Son-in-law Jored had been given yet another responsibility: campaign manager, adding to his other portfolios: peace in the Middle East; the opioid crisis; climate change denial; getting the wall built; ruining Mitt Romney's life; pulling the US out of NATO; mothballing the USS *John McCain*; moving the US embassy in Paris to Biarritz; and working with Senator Biskitt and me on the Glebnikov Act repeal. Jored certainly had a full plate.

Jored was—I don't want to say "an odd duck"—very much his own person, and not an easy read. He had a way of not answering your questions and staring at you. It could be unsettling. He looked like his own Madame Tussauds waxwork. I wondered if he started every day with a facial. His permanent look of aloofness gave him an otherworldly aspect, like an extraterrestrial being who was mulling whether to annihilate Earth with a death ray that emanated from his eyes—or not. One staff wag said he reminded them of a portrait of a Renaissance prince, "minus the codpiece." That said, Jored and I got along more or less okay. One had to get along with Jored, really.

His Rolodex was now chockablock with more billionaires than an issue of *Forbes* magazine. He was very close to Prince Mohammed Bin Salman, the Saudi ruler. He phoned "Mo"—as he called him—about the rally. Mo offered to write a check on the spot to cover the estimated $40 million cost. And to provide his personal fleet of Boeing 777s to schlepp the base.

"*That's* a pal," Mr. Trump commented. But the Republican National Committee was concerned that it might make the rally "too Araby." Jored was miffed about having to turn down Mo's offer. He pouted for days, refusing to take my calls. But there was no telling Jored, "Look, you little entitled shit, this isn't *about* you."

Then "our old friend" Oleg got wind of the rally and said *he'd* happily write the check. I think he saw it as a way of fast-tracking the Glebnikov Act repeal. I despaired of Oleg's grasp of the US Constitution.

So it fell to White House Russian oligarch wrangler Herb Nutterman to pay yet another visit to Paul at the Metropolitan Correctional Center in Manhattan, and tell him to thank Oleg but *nyet.* Single sponsoring of a Trump rally by a Novichok-dispensing Russian oligarch was optics from hell.

By now I was on a first-name basis with the guards at the MCC, including the ones who'd been a tad negligent about preventing Jeffrey Epstein from hanging himself. They were very nice and asked for my autograph, which I thought was kind of sweet.

By the time Jored emerged from his funk, he'd lost his mojo for the Lambeau rally. (Thanks, Jored—big help.) Meanwhile, the liberal mainstream media had been working overtime to make it sound like we'd summoned Leni Riefenstahl's ghost to produce a "Return to Nuremberg" rally, with everyone wearing cheesehead hats instead of brown shirts. Honestly. I'm all for the First Amendment, but some of these quote-unquote "impartial" reporters had me wanting to call Mo and ask if I could borrow the bone saw.

Fortunately, we had Mr. Colonnity and his Sancho Panza, Mr. Corky Fartmartin, on our side. Mr. Colonnity offered to pay for the rally out of his $35 million annual salary. *That's* friendship. He also offered to emcee the rally. Apparently neither of these very generous offers was appropriate, since he was technically a *news*person. But Mr. Colonnity wasn't one to let technicalities compromise his devotion to Mr. Trump.

Then the sniveling apparatchiks of the Democratic National Committee politburo weighed in and denounced us for "destroying yet another norm of American political tradition." Please.

Whenever Mr. Trump did something original or bold or new, immediately he was accused of destroying some sacred "norm." I never understood what that meant. Did the Founding Fathers destroy a norm with the Declaration of Independence? Did Abraham Lincoln destroy a norm when he freed the slaves? Apparently. Well, shame on them.

Then Mr. Trump decided, as he often did, "Screw it." He tweeted that there had never been a plan to hold a rally in Green Bay, and what's more the DNC could "go fuck themselves." I was never a big fan of Mr. Trump using profanity in his tweets, but this time I cheered.

As it turned out, there was a distraction as the Dems gathered, but not one that we'd cooked up.

19

This time I didn't have to conjure the headline. It was right there in black and white on the front page, "above the fold," as they say in newspaper parlance:

HIGH SCHOOL FRIEND OF PANTS ALLEGES
"YOUTHFUL FLIRTATION" WITH SATANISM

As I read the account in the failing *New York Times*, my first thought was: Some "friend." I didn't know what to make of his story about how he and "Mikey" used to drink goat blood under a full moon and carve satanic-themed crop circles in cornfields with Dad's tractor. It certainly didn't sound like the—I don't want to say "boring"—stolid Mike Pants I'd come to know.

My second thought, as I vomited up breakfast, was: if this is true, how in God's name did the FBI miss this when they did Mike's vice presidential background check? Does their questionnaire not include a box to check if "you have ever participated in satanic or demonic rituals, including, but not limited to, goat sacrifice, blood drinking, carving satanic-themed crop circles in cornfields, etc."? Apparently not.

Mike Pants is not a voluble personality. Far from it. You could slap him on the face with a frozen halibut and he wouldn't blink. Mind you, this doesn't make him a "life of the party" type. He won't even have a drink with a woman unless Mrs. Pants is present. That must make for a fun marriage, but whatever.

Mike never spoke up at cabinet meetings, except in the days when my predecessor, Reince Priebus, would go around the table and make each cabinet member tell Mr. Trump what they most admired about him. On those occasions, Mike could be a real jabberer, going on ad—I don't want to say "nauseam"—infinitum about how great Mr. Trump is. Mr. Trump likes praise, but even he would nod off as the VP got to reason number twenty-eight why Donald Trump is the greatest president in US history.

For once the phlegmatic Mike Pants—who'd once described himself as "Rush Limbaugh on decaf"—registered something resembling actual human emotion. He flushed beet red at the podium in the White House pressroom as he said that he was "profoundly, indeed deeply disappointed with my old friend Bob Krotchmeyer for trotting out this old story."

I was standing next to Katie Borgia-O'Reilly. She tensed and hissed, "*Old* story? Jesus, Mike . . ."

The vice president continued:

"It was never *about* Satan. I sure as heck don't remember drinking goat blood. My recollection is that it was some pretty nasty red wine we found in a cabinet under the sink. Bob's mom used it for drowning garden slugs. We did get up to a bit of mischief with his dad's tractor. I'm not proud of it. But my memory is that we were trying to carve the McDonald's Golden Arches logo in the cornfield, not the Sigil of Baphomet.* I wouldn't even know where to *start*, carving that."

Katie was now hyperventilating and muttering, "Shut *up*, Mike. Shut the fuck *up*."

Here Mike deftly pirouetted: "But speaking of the devil . . ." and launched into an impassioned denunciation of the *New York Times* and the news media in general, suggesting that maybe they were the ones who were doing "Satan's work here on earth." Bravo, Mike.

It didn't land well with the media. Oh no. They're way better dishing it out than taking it. The warriors of the First Amendment didn't much like being told they were "in the employ of the cloven-hoofed one."

Our friends at Fox News were valiant as ever. Mr. Colonnity had our resident evangelical, Pastor Norma Damdiddle, on his show three nights running, bless him. She said that it just went to show that Mr. Trump and Mr. Pants were doing God's work, and "It's driving Satan *cuckoo*."

The VP's old "friend" Bob Krotchmeyer stuck by his story. He seemed oblivious to the furor he'd created, but then he had been diagnosed as being in the early stages of dementia. He said he'd voted for Trump and "Mikey" in 2016 and was looking forward to voting for them again in the fall. It was "nothing personal," he said. "Mikey remembers it a bit different than me, but hey, whatever." He added that the alleged youthful flirtation with satanism remained "among my happiest memories." Thanks, Bob.

Happily, our pollster, Boyd Crampon, reported that the incident caused our support among evangelicals to spike, from the

---

* The official emblem of the Church of Satan, consisting of the head of a goat transfixed on a reversed pentagram flanked by the Hebrew letters of the word "Leviathan." Bit of a mouthful, that.

mid nineties to the high nineties. Hallelujah, as they would say. Moreover, Republican voters now "despised the Jewish-controlled media even more than before." Great.

In other good news, ratings for the opening night of the Democratic convention were down by a third over their convention four years ago. Whaddya know: viewers seemed to care more about whether their vice president was a practicing demon worshipper than listening to Dems read aloud from the podium their favorite selections from *Das Kapital* and *Lenin's Greatest Hits.* Maybe it's true, as they say, that God works in mysterious ways.

20

Mr. Trump himself certainly works in mysterious ways. No sooner had "Satan-gate" faded from the news cycle than he began dropping hints that "maybe it's time to freshen up the ticket."

As a hospitality professional, I'm all about freshening. But dumping a loyal vice president is different than providing clean towels and tuning the bedside-table clock radio to the easy-listening music channel.

I asked the president if the "Pants Satan thing" had gotten him thinking. No, he said, he was just "bored out of my gourd by Mike." I agreed that I, too, was bored. Still.

"We're going into our fifth season, Herb. You gotta have fresh material."

At first I didn't get the reference to "our fifth season." Then it dawned on me—duh, Herb—he meant the first year of his second four-year term. Mr. Trump viewed himself not as president but as the host of TV's top-rated show. Still, I worried that dumping a loyal, if mind-numbingly boring—and possibly Satan-worshipping—vice president might be viewed as throwing him under the bus.

"But, sir, isn't Mike vital to our evangelical support?"

"What are they gonna do?" he snorted. "Vote for Goldibucks?"

"Goldibucks" was Mr. Trump's disparaging nickname for Morris Goldberg, the billionaire nonevangelical former mayor of New York, whose evil plan was to wait until the other candidates had spent all their money and then swoop in.

Biden had shot himself in the foot yet again, this time before the Iowa Caucuses, with his remark about how "Caucasians are the best!" Tabitha Cramp's proposal to ban all fossil fuels "on day one" had not won over shivering voters in New Hampshire. Karl Handpuppetz's barking about how "We'll find the money somehow, quit *worrying* about it!" was wearing thin. And coming off his big win in New Hampshire, Randy Rhodes had stumbled in South Carolina with his suggestion the issue of Confederate statues could be solved by covering them with "white hoods and robes."

Meanwhile, every time you turned on the TV, there was "Hizzoner" Morrie Goldberg, offering to personally fund everyone's college tuition and medical bills *and* pay for defense, out of his own pocket. He seemed quite blithe about giving away all his money. "What am I gonna do? Take it with me? I'm not a pharaoh, for crying out loud."

Goldberg called Mr. Trump "Richie Not-So-Rich." It got under his skin. The one thing that reliably drove him up a wall was being accused of not being as rich as he claimed to be. Unfortunately, the Supreme Court—or as Mr. Trump now called it, "those dirtbags"—had ordered him to release his tax returns, which showed his actual worth to be quite significantly lower than advertised. He instructed White House counsel Blyster Forkmorgan to appeal. It fell to Blyster to point

out that the "dirtbags" were the last stop on the judicial elevator. The next blow came when *Forbes* magazine dropped
him from its 400 Top Millionaires issue. That hurt. Goldberg
seized on a new slogan: "Isn't it time we had a president who's
actually rich?"

Goldberg was also dropping hints about how he was going
to appoint Bill Gates head of the Office of Management and
Budget.

"Bill loves giving away his money," he said in speeches. "And
I have no doubt he'd love giving some of it to you." This was
well received by the so-called Millennial Pinks.

As if to twist the knife, Goldberg also started dropping hints
that he was going to nominate Jeff Bezos, the richest man on
earth *and* publisher of the Trump-loathing *Washington Post*,
to be secretary of treasury.

So Mr. Trump was not in the best of moods. He responded
to my question about the danger of alienating evangelicals a
bit snappishly.

"Herb, you're missing it. Sometimes you're very stupid, you
know. It's me the evangelicals love, not Pants."

"Quite right, sir. Who'd you have in mind as a possible
replacement?"

The president shrugged.

"I don't know. A woman, maybe. Crampon is very depressed
about the suburban women. If we had a woman on the ticket . . .
the twats would have to vote for her. What are they gonna do?
Not vote for a woman? I can understand women not voting for
Hillary. But this would be totally different."

"Who?"

"What about Ivunka?"

Oh dear.

"Two Trumps on one ticket?" the president said. "Talk about
wow factor, huh? The base would shit itself."

I didn't know what to say. There had been concern about this. Mr. Trump had brought it up on a number of occasions. Each time, the reaction was the same: blank stares and averted eye contact. It wasn't that people didn't like Ivunka. Still.

Mr. Trump said, "Seamus thinks it's too soon. He thinks we should wait until 2024."

I mentally dropped to my knees and thanked Mr. Colonnity.

"I was thinking—Cricket," Mr. Trump said.

I can't say I was surprised. Cricket Singh, the former governor of South Carolina, had served as Mr. Trump's first ambassador to the United Nations. She had not pleased Mr. Trump by making a big scene over Russia supplying Syria with chemical weapons to spray on its people. Then the weasel White House staffer, aka "Anonymous," wrote a ridiculous book about the so-called Resistance movement in the Trump White House. Anonymous praised Singh for "refusing to go along with Trump's more lunatic instincts." That went over well.

But then Cricket published her own Trump memoir, *What An Incredible Honor: Helping Donald Trump Restore America's Standing in the World.* The book was an extended ode to Mr. Trump, praising him for "his deep knowledge of complicated issues," "always putting country first," "standing up to authoritarian leaders," and "his superhuman work ethic."

Washington being Washington—namely a pestilential, crocodile- and piranha-infested swamp—some regarded this as "dog whistling" calculated to seduce Mr. Trump into throwing Pants under the proverbial Greyhound and nominating Cricket in his stead.

I felt this critique of Cricket missed the larger picture. As president, Mr. Trump's highest loyalty had to be to himself. By his own candid admission, he hadn't yet completed the job of making American great again. As he told the base at the rally in Testicle, "To make America totally, one hundred percent great again, I need another four years. Maybe even more."* If this meant that Mike Pants would have to "suck it up" and lie down under the bus, well, so be it. The point is: the election wasn't about Mike. It was about Mr. Trump. And so far no one had accused Mrs. Singh of Satan worship.†

Mr. Trump looked pensive. "I don't know," he said. "Putin hates her. I gotta factor that in."

True enough. In addition to making a big deal out of Russia helping Syria gas its own people, Cricket had made a number of unfriendly statements about Mr. Putin himself. Such as: "We don't trust Putin. We never will."

When Mr. Trump heard that, I actually thought he might physically explode. He composed a tweet calling her "very rude" and "menstrual." Fortunately, Greta threatened to kill herself if he posted it, so he didn't.

We left it there for the time being. Meanwhile, I undertook some discreet due diligence and sounded out Pastor Norma. I wanted her take on how the evangelicals might react to Mike getting bus tire tracks all over his body.

"Say, Norma," I said casually, "did you happen to see that item suggesting the president drop Mike from the ticket?" (There hadn't actually been any item.)

"What, on account of that devil-worshipping stuff?" she replied. "Why heck, we all do things as kids that we shouldn'ta. I used to drop my panties behind the barn and let boys stare at my foofie for a quarter. I was a millionaire by the time I was eleven."

I didn't know how to respond to that. Evangelicals always seem eager to tell you the most appalling things about their

---

* The comment provoked all sorts of hand-wringing about whether he was planning to run for a third term, despite the Twenty-Second Amendment. Mr. Trump certainly knew how to make everyone dance to his tune.

† Though she was half Indian, and Hindus have some pretty fruity gods.

presaved selves: how they drank and beat their wives; stole the church collection money; set fire to Mexicans; blew up outhouses with Gramps inside; all manner of wickedness. I finally concluded that this "unholier than thou" shtick allowed them to advertise how great they felt about themselves now. I thought Norma's refusal to join in the carping about Mike's Satan worship was admirably Christian.

"No," I said, "the item about how Cricket Singh would make a good replacement for Mike. What do you think?"

Norma looked at me as though I'd suggested she should ask Stormy Daniels to give the guest sermon at her megachurch.

"Cricket Singh?" She harrumphed. "The very *idea* . . ."

My takeaway was that both Norma and Mr. Putin were of the same mind about Cricket, but presumably for different reasons.

21

Judd came to my office one morning, eyes a-popping.

"Just got off the phone with McTight," he said, referring to the chairman of the Joint Chiefs of Staff. Judd had the annoying habit of announcing that he had something of great import to tell you, then going silent and making you wait for it.

"Judd," I said impatiently, "I'm very busy. If the country is under attack, just tell me."

"He and the chiefs are not happy about your molybdenum crisis."

I was tempted to tell him, "There is no 'Y' in 'O-U-R.'" The molybdenum crisis had been a hard sell on the chiefs from the get-go. I'd gone out of my way to bring them on board, explaining as earnestly as I could that the president was "highly concerned about the potential"—I was careful to phrase it that way—"that the US might find its access to the molybdenum supply chain jeopardized by a few shortsighted, politically motivated members of Congress eager to score cheap PR points with a media baron."

This was met with steely looks. Over the course of my career, I've gotten the proverbial "evil eye" from a number of people: guests who'd found pubic hairs on their bed; who'd been erroneously charged for minibar items; who resented the two-hundred-dollar fee for opening their room safe after they forgot the combination (that *they* had programmed). But getting it from seven scowling generals and admirals with an aggregate acre of decorations for valor on their chests does make you squirm.

"Mr. Nutterman," General McTight said in a tone of ill-concealed disdain. "We all share the president's concern about strategic matériel. But we've seen absolutely no indications of any interruption in molybdenum acquisition. Frank?" he said to a general who, I gathered, had something to do with molybdenum acquisition. "Any difficulties there?"

"No, sir. We're good. More than good. We're swimming in molybdenum."

I was tempted to ask him how one swam in molybdenum.

Chairman McTight turned his death-ray gaze back on me, as if to say, *Was there any other pointless bullshit you wanted to waste our valuable time with?*

"I'm glad to hear it," I said. "But the president feels that this is no time for complacency. He doesn't want us to be caught short if there's another—God forbid—9/11, or Benghazi. To that end, therefore, he feels it would be helpful if you and the other chiefs—and by the way, thank you all for your service—shared his concern in the course of your testifying on Capitol Hill."

Fourteen icy eyeballs. End of meeting.

I'd been hoping for the headline:

PENTAGON EXPRESSES "GRAVE CONCERN"
OVER MOLYBDENUM SUPPLY

When one finally did appear, it was somewhat different:

PENTAGON "PUZZLED" BY WHITE HOUSE
CONCERN OVER MOLYBDENUM

So much for civilian leadership of the military. We ought to try it someday.

President Putin had conveyed to Mr. Trump his unhappiness over US military aid to Ukraine. There's a rule in the hospitality business: "If the lady is not happy, the gentleman is not happy." If Mr. Putin was not happy, Mr. Trump was not happy.

But the president couldn't just cut off military aid to Ukraine, not after getting impeached for (allegedly) threatening to withhold it unless Ukraine announced that it would not rest until Hunter Biden was in handcuffs. Instead, he came up with a rather deft solution that would satisfy Ukraine (up to a point) and make Mr. Putin happy: rendering the military aid useless.

"This is so brilliant," Mr. Trump said. "Only I could come up with something like this." He was just glowing, and not from the spray-on tan.

He explained: "We tell the Pentagon to remove parts from the Javelin antitank missiles and the other stuff. Firing pins, fuses, whatever. So when the Ukies go to use them—*pffft*—nothing happens."

"Brilliant, sir," I affirmed. "But won't the Ukies complain?"

The president shrugged.

"Fuck 'em. We'll tell them, 'I guess you people aren't sophisticated enough to handle this kind of hardware. It is very technical. Maybe you should stick to pitchforks and clubs.'"

Clever as it was, I wasn't 100 percent comfortable. After one staring contest with the Joint Chiefs, I didn't relish ordering them to sabotage $400 million worth of antitank missiles and what-not. They'd probably have views about that.

Fortunately, Mr. Trump forgot about it. An upside to his stable genius was that he had so many brilliant ideas, he simply couldn't keep track of them all.

But if he did remember this one, I feared the chiefs would already be in a foul mood over being asked to testify to the Congress about the coming molybdenum Pearl Harbor. So I didn't press them further about it. You have to be careful with the military. In the end, they're the ones with the guns.

Mr. Trump was constantly fretting about the possibility of a coup. His—I don't want to say "paranoia"—concern about it always seemed worse after he'd spent time with leaders like President Attajurk of Turkey, or Mohammed Bin Salman of Saudi Arabia, or Kim Jong-un. They filled his head with visions of conniving generals. I suppose leaders of countries like that have to "stay sharp" about their militaries. Mr. Trump kept sharp by increasing the defense budgets and pardoning over-enthusiastic soldiers.

One time we were in Marine One, flying over the Bosporus, after watching a Graeco-Roman wrestling tournament with President Attajurk. The Turkish president had regaled Mr. Trump with details of the attempted coup against him.

The president turned to Mike Keller, head of his Secret Service detail, and said, "Mike, if it came to a coup, you guys would be on my side, right?"

Awkward. Poor Mike shot me a glance that said, "*Help.*" I tried to change the subject by pointing out the Hagia Sophia, but Mr. Trump was more concerned with obtaining a guarantee of loyalty from his chief bodyguard. Mike finally said, "Sir, all of us would take a bullet for you." But that wasn't enough to reassure Mr. Trump.

"The Pentagon has a lot of bullets, Mike."

Mike looked about ready to unlatch the door and leap into the waters of the Bosporus. Fortunately, the president got an alert on his iPhone that there'd been an episode of mass food poisoning at the Trump Hotel on Pennsylvania Avenue. He began furiously tweeting. Mike was spared having to pledge a blood oath of loyalty.

22

Rudy Giuliani, the president's former personal attorney, was now living in the Julian Assange suite at the Ecuadorean embassy in London.

While changing planes at Heathrow, Rudy was tipped off that the Justice Department had issued a warrant for his arrest for injurious punditry and pernicious legal representation. Knowing that the British authorities would have no choice but to extradite him to the US, Rudy did the smart thing—"for once," as one commentator said—and sought asylum from the famously fugitive-welcoming Ecuadoreans, whose motto is: "*Nuestra embajada es tu embajada.*"

Mr. Trump was hugely relieved. He'd sent Rudy back to Ukraine just to get him out of the US and away from the cable TV shows.

"Better he should be in an asylum than seeking asylum," he said.

The president had had enough of Rudy's shenanigans. Mr. Trump was never one to admit that he himself might have erred, but he was now openly saying, "What the fuck was I thinking when I asked that idiot to be my lawyer? Whose idea was that? Was that Jored's idea? Hadda be. It couldn't have been me. I would never do something so stupid."

But it was no time for complacency. Mr. Trump was nervous that Rudy would step out onto the balcony—the very one Julian Assange had used as his bully pulpit—and start ranting.

"Italians and balconies—very bad combination," Mr. Trump said, alluding to Mussolini, who spent a lot of time declaiming from balconies. "If that idiot goes out there and starts spewing . . . I don't even want to think about that. Get Jones in here. They handle stuff like this, right?"

I didn't much like the sound of that.

"How do you mean 'stuff,' sir?"

"Never mind. Just get her in here."

I called Miriam and told her to arrive "with an open mind." She didn't much like the sound of that. Meanwhile, I tried to calm the president, telling him that by now everyone considered Giuliani to be a mental case. It didn't matter what he might say.

From the look on the president's face, I realized that this was not necessarily true. Rudy might be unhinged, but he was also a hoarder of documents. He stashed documents like hamsters stuff food into their cheeks. God knows what he had in there. In one of his more notorious instances of "butt-dialing," the dialee (a *Washington Post* reporter) listened as Rudy offered a Ukrainian mob boss a weekend at Farrago-sur-Mer, "everything comped—coke, hookers, minibar—everything," if he would sign an affidavit swearing that Hunter Biden had tried to hire him to assassinate Marie Yovanovitch, then US ambassador to Ukraine. Not much lawyer-client confidentiality there.

I was not asked to sit in on the president's meeting with Miriam; nor was Judd. Miriam emerged from the Oval looking as though she'd just donated a pint too much blood and was in dire need of a cookie and juice.

"How did it go?" I asked.

"Can't discuss it," she said, heading out the door, followed by her bodyguards. Years later an unusually well-sourced book on the CIA came out with the arresting revelation that "Trump inquired into the feasibility of stationing a CIA sniper on the roof of Harrods department store, to shoot Giuliani if he stepped out onto the Assange balcony." No wonder Miriam couldn't discuss it.

I myself preferred to know less, rather than more, about whatever Mr. Trump and Mr. Giuliani had been up to in Ukraine. Public service is an honor and a duty, and I'm not complaining, but I didn't relish the prospect of retaining a legal team in the event *United States v. Rudolph Giuliani* came to trial.

Not—I emphasize—because I knew anything incriminating. But these legal cases are financial sinkholes. One minute you're on the golf course minding your own business, thinking, *Gosh, what a nice day.* The next, the earth has gone out from under you and you're in a conference room being deposed with three lawyers in attendance at a thousand dollars an hour each. Every time Mr. Trump mentioned Mr. Giuliani's name, I wanted to cover my ears and shout, "La-la-la-la I can't *hear* you, sir." But that's not a protocol available to White House chiefs of staff. Fortunately, Mr. Trump had been fairly tight-lipped about his dealings with Rudy.

Imagine my joy then when my secretary, Caramella, told me that Mr. Giuliani was holding on line one.

"For God's sake, Caramella," I said. "He's a fugitive from justice. I can't talk to him."

"You visit Paul in jail all the time," she said. "He's a convicted felon."

"There's a difference," I said. "Tell him I'm unavailable."

She buzzed me back.

"I think you better talk to him. He sounds weird."

"He is weird. Just hang up."

She came back on again a minute later.

"He says if you don't talk to him, someone in Kiev will hack your credit cards and bank accounts. And Mrs. Nutterman's."

I considered.

"Put him through to Mr. Forkmorgan's office." Blyster Forkmorgan. Let Blyster deal with Rudy, lawyer to lawyer. They could hurl Latin at each other.

Still, I was curious: Why was the man formerly known as "America's Mayor" reaching out to me? Could it be because his client, the president, wasn't talking his calls? Oy.

Blyster called me ten minutes later.

"Thanks a bunch, Herb."

"Anytime. Did he threaten to have someone in Kiev hack your wife's bank account?"

"He's saying unless the indictment is dropped, he'll—"

"Whoa right there, Counselor," I said. "Why do I need to hear this?"

"Because you're chief of staff, Herb."

"As I am woefully aware, Blyster. But unless you fix me up with a six-lawyer team who'll represent me pro bono, I don't want to hear one more word. And now I'm going to hang up. Let's do lunch. Say, in the post-Giuliani era."

And that was that. Or so I'd hoped.

Judd came into my office looking like Thomas the Tank Engine careening down the tracks toward the washed-out bridge with no brakes.

"What the fuck just happened in there between him and Miriam?"

"I don't know, Judd. I wasn't asked to join. Thank God."

"Well, I just spent fifteen minutes talking her out of resigning."

"What?"

"She wouldn't tell me why. Just kept saying she didn't think she could continue. 'In good conscience.'"

In my experience, it is never a good sign when staff start talking about their consciences. One time at Farrago-sur-Mer I had to go mano a mano with the head of housekeeping. To cut down on costs, I'd issued a directive that bed linen didn't need to be changed between occupancies, unless it was "visibly soiled."

Rosa Maria told me this was unhygienic and that her conscience would not allow her to "spread diseases." I told her that this was a bit much, coming from someone who'd never slept between sheets until she dog-paddled across the Rio Grande. But she wasn't cowed, even by a pointed reference about her current immigration status. I have to say, I admired Rosa Maria for sticking to her guns. In the end, we compromised. I can report that no Farrago-sur-Mer guests died of Ebola or other unspeakable diseases after their stay with us.

I called Miriam and told her that the president had phoned me after she left. I said that he had expressed "the greatest admiration" for her for "sticking to her guns." I was groping in the dark, since I had no idea what was said in the meeting, or what guns she was sticking to. (CIA sniper guns, as I learned years later.)

Miriam was no fool. I suspect that as a trained intelligence professional, she saw my call for what it was—a bald-faced lie in the service of damage control. Nevertheless, I laid it on thick, telling her that the president thought she was "just aces," and how he was "really starting to come around about the value of the intelligence community," despite never missing an opportunity to call them "imbeciles" and "traitors" in public.

There was a longish silence on the line. Then Miriam thanked me for the call, "Even though everything you just told me is horseshit."

Another day in the White House. But as they say in the Mafia, this is the life we chose.

23

When those of the Cosa Nostra persuasion wish to send a message, it comes in the form of a fish wrapped in newspaper, or a horse head in your bed. (For the record, the latter would qualify as "obviously soiled," per my Farrago-sur-Mer directive.)

When Oleg Pishinsky wishes to send a message that he's impatient with the pace with which you're repealing the law freezing his US assets and banning him from entering the country, it arrives in the form of a video on Facebook. The message showed in high resolution the future president of the United States performing due diligence on a Miss Universe contestant. It went very, very viral.

Fortunately, we now lived—thanks in no small part to Mr. Trump—in the age of fake news, where, as they say in Moscow, "Nothing is real and everything is possible." Still.

It's not exaggerating to say that Mr. Trump's anger was about as volcanic as Mt. Vesuvius, circa AD 79. I was not the only one in the Oval that morning who felt like a resident of unhappy Pompeii as hot ash descended and toxic gases filled the lungs.

After ten or fifteen minutes of violent excoriation, Mr. Trump finally slumped his great shoulders, his voice hoarse from bellowing.

No one wanted to be the first to say something. Doing so risked triggering aftershocks and new issuance of scalding lava. I remained silent, knowing that my abasement would take place in private, after the staff meeting.

Katie—brave, valiant Katie—was the first to speak.

"I just think it's disgusting that the Democrats would resort to something like this. They probably got their Hollywood friends to help with the CGI." (That is, computer generated imaging. Katie was boldly asserting that the film shown of Mr. Trump ravishing Miss Sri Lanka was fake.)

I could have kissed her. It was as if fresh oxygen was being pumped into the room. People breathed. Color returned to cheeks.

Picking up her cue, Greta said, "And we're asking the FBI to look into it."

"*No!*" Mr. Trump said. "No FBI! They'll say it's real. Which it isn't."

"Right," Greta self-corrected. "*Normally* we would ask the FBI. But as we learned during the impeachment hoax and the farce Senate trial, the FBI has tried again and again to mount a coup against the president. So—"

"We can no longer rely on the FBI," Jored said. "And how sad is that?" Jored loved to finish other people's sentences so their ideas would appear to be his.

Mr. Trump nodded, hunched forward in his chair, his little thumbs tapping a tweet fandango on the keys of his iPhone. I could almost see the words flying up into the ethersphere or

whatever it's called: DISGUSTING! SAD! DESPERATE! DEMO-
CRATIC NATIONAL COMMITTEE, AUTHOR OF THIS HOR-
RIBLE FRAUD, OWES AMERICA AN APOLOGY!!!!

The TV, sound muted, showed the hosts of *Fox and Fiends* shaking their heads in collective revulsion. The crawl at the bottom of the screen was a conveyor belt:

**FACEBOOK, INSTAGRAM REFUSE TO REMOVE OFFENSIVE POST . . .
WHITE HOUSE: VIDEO ORIGINATED IN UKRAINE . . . GIULIANI
COMPLAINING OF "WAY TOO SPICY FOOD" AT ECUADOREAN
EMBASSY . . . WILL HAVE FUTURE MEALS CATERED BY FORTNUM &
MASON, SUPPLIERS TO BUCKINGHAM PALACE . . .**

The president finished tapping and said, "Everyone except Herb—*out*." The Oval briskly cleared.

"What the fuck, Herb?"

Yet again, Herb Nutterman found himself between the old rock and hard place. On the one hand, I had a pretty good idea that the video of Mr. Trump—I don't want to say "boning"—partnering in joy with Miss Sri Lanka was authentic. And to think that this was but the first of eighteen such videos on the thumb drive that our old friend Oleg had gifted me in San Marino.

On the other hand, I had deliberately not viewed it before regifting it to Mr. Trump, for precisely this reason. I knew then that the day might come when I would be called upon to denounce the videos as patent fakes. In that event, I wanted to be able to do it with a semblance of a straight face.

"I spoke with Admiral Murphy at US CyberCom," I said. "He, like all of us, is appalled. CyberCom is doing everything it can to identify the source."

"We *know* who the fucking source is, Herb."

"Yes, I suppose. But I didn't want to say as much to Admiral Murphy. For obvious reasons."

"You and Buttplug were supposed to make Oleg happy. Clearly Oleg is *not* happy. This is very disappointing, Herb. Very."

"I apologize, sir. We are making what progress we can. But alas, the Constitution requires fifty-one percent in both the House and Senate to repeal. And creating a national panic over a theoretical shortage of molybdenum is proving to be more challenging than Senator Biskitt and I had envisioned."

Mr. Trump scowled at a squirrel in the Rose Garden.

"You need to talk to Oleg. Ask him what the fuck."

"That is at the top of my agenda, sir."

"This is completely unsatisfactory, Herb."

"I feel your disappointment acutely, sir. If my resignation would help, you have only to ask for it." I felt a little buzz of elation at the prospect of resigning. That should have told me something.

"What would *help*, Herb, is for you to make Oleg happy again. There are eighteen women on that thumb drive. How many days until the election?"

"Two months and three days, sir."

"Is Oleg's plan to post a fucking video every three or four days? Miss Albania on Monday. Miss South Korea on Thursday. Miss Bolivia on Saturday. Miss Tuvalu . . . Jesus, Herb. Damn fine job by you and Buttplug. By the way, you can tell him I won't be doing any rallies in North Carolina. Not until this is fixed."

"South Carolina."

"Whatever."

"Sir, in Butt—in Senator Biskitt's defense, sir, I do think he, too, is doing his best, as am I. But the Constitution—"

"Fuck the Constitution! Putin or Attajurk wouldn't put up with this shit for one minute."

"Again, if you'd like my resignation—"

"Herb. Shut up about your resignation! When it's time for you to go, you'll know. Trust me."

The president shook his head at the unfairness of it all.

"Sir," I said, "wouldn't it make sense for you to have a chat with Mr. Putin? After all you've done for him, it seems to me the least he could do is ask Oleg to . . . cool it with the porn show."

The president stared.

"Porn? This is not porn, Herb. This is Donald Trump making it with the most beautiful women on earth. And by the way, performing like a fucking stallion. How is that 'porn'?"

"A deplorable choice of words, sir. Forgive me."

For a moment I thought I saw the ax descending. Then he said, "Herb. You just don't get it, do you?"

"It, sir?"

"Who do you think took these fucking movies? Oleg? You think Oleg is the Cecil B. DeMille, here? No, Herb. It was the FSB, or whatever the fuck the KGB is calling itself these days."

"You're saying that Mr. Putin is behind this?"

"Herb. You're being very slow today. Yes. Putin is the head of Russia. It's his country. He's knows everything. A mouse doesn't fart in Vladivostok without Vlad knowing about it."

"Well," I said, swelling with indignation. "In that case all I can say is, it's certainly shabby treatment after everything you've done for him."

"Herb, Herb, Herb. You're missing it. Did you sleep through all your classes at Trump University?"

When I retired, Mr. Trump kindly gave me a discount on a semester of online classes at his Trump University. Before the class-action suit that forced Mr. Trump to shut it down and pay large fines.

"I'm sorry if I'm being obtuse, sir."

"Okay. Okay. Let me explain what's happening here. Putin

likes me, okay? He loves me. We have this amazing relationship. He and Oleg, they're old buddies. They go way back. Maybe they go back so far that Oleg knows things about Putin that Putin would not want posted on Facebook. Whatever. Putin likes Oleg. He indulges him. He gives him space.

"So Oleg gets himself in this situation, this fucking Glebnikov thing. He asks Putin to fix it. Putin calls me, says could you do me a favor? I say sure. He asks me to get the act, the law, whatever, repealed. I tell him, 'Done.'

"So I call Forkmorgan. And what do I find out? I find out what I find out every fucking day in this fucking job, namely that even though I'm the president of the fucking United States, I can't do it.

"I tell Forkmorgan, 'Yo, Perry Mason. We need to repeal the Glebnikov Act. Just do it. It's very important. And by the way, I'm the fucking *president*.

"Answer: 'Sorry, Mr. President, but the Constitution blah-blah-blah.' Great. Thank you, White House legal counsel. What a big fucking help you've been. Remind me not to nominate you to the dirtbag Supreme Court.

"So I call Putin. I say, 'Vlad, you *know* how much I like you, right? You know what a great relationship we have. I would *so* love to do this favor for you. But guess what? I can't. Why? Because the morons who designed our system of government were afraid that two hundred and whatever years later the president of the United States might want to do a favor for the president of Russia. We can't allow that. Noo. Idiots.

"They designed the Constitution specifically to castrate presidents. Great system, huh?

"'*However*,' I tell Putin, 'we're gonna get it done one way or the other. My consiglieres, Herb and Senator Buttplug, tell me there's some process whereby you kiss fifty-one percent of the asses in the House, then you kiss fifty-one percent of the asses in the Senate. And bingo, it's repealed. So we're going to work it that way. Okay?

"But it's going to take some time. It may even have to wait until my second term, which I am trying very hard to achieve, despite the astounding amount of bullshit I have to put up with, including being fucking impeached. Which was a total hoax. And very insulting. But we'll get it done. Okay? Relax. It's all good. It's all going to be great. Everyone is going to be very happy.

"Putin is completely fine with this. He tells me, 'Donald, you are fantastic. You are amazing. Thank you.'

"But now with this fucked election of his, he's having to deal with that. He's gotta find out who screwed him. Ukraine, probably. Assholes. Anyway, at the moment he's a little distracted.

"Meanwhile, Oleg is sending me messages saying, 'Donald, come on, hurry up and get this fucking Glebnikov monkey off my back so I can come to US and party down with you.'

"I told him, 'Oleg, please. Chill. We're working on it. Day and fucking night. We're doing our best here.

"But Oleg isn't chilling. Why? I'll tell you why. Because he's worried I might not *get* another four years. So he's saying, 'You must fix *before* election.'

"And now this. He releases *Episode One: Trump Does Sri Lanka*. Oleg's thinking, *This will light fire under Donald's ass.*

"The problem is if Oleg releases one of these movies every other day between now and November 3, *Donald* is not going to *have* another four years. Even my evangelicals are gonna be going, *Jesus fucking Christ!*

"So, Herb, what we—that is, *you*—are going to do is explain to our old friend Oleg that this is completely counterproductive. Not helpful. Not at all helpful. In fact, it's very unhelpful. So—quit it. No more episodes of Trump *shtupping* Miss Whoever."

The president paused. He said in a reflective tone, "Miss Sri Lanka. Very talented lady. You saw the movie?"

"No, sir. As I said earlier, I didn't think it would be polite."

He shrugged.

"Too bad. She does this . . . 360-degree rotating thing. While you're still attached. Like a crab, rotating, 360 degrees. I tell you Herb, I'd have given her the Miss Universe title there and then. But they were all pretty amazing. Really, it was a very good Miss Universe. Possibly the best."

It was a lot to absorb, but it was clarifying.

24

As anyone who watched the Senate impeachment trial knows, Senator Biskitt was a Trump Galahad. Three times he walked out of the chamber—technically risking "imprisonment"—declaring that he would "not be party to the most shameful episode in US history since the Salem witch trials." Goose bumpy.

So imagine how I felt, telling him that the president would not after all be going to South Carolina to campaign with him unless he got the Glebnikov Act repealed.

His little face crumpled. I thought he might burst into tears.

"Doesn't the president realize I'm busting my *ass* on this?" he said pitiably. "I can't just wave some magic wand over the US Congress."

"I'm just the messenger here, Senator." I love saying that. It's so liberating.

"Well, I got to tell you, Herb, frankly I find this real disappointing."

"Those were his own exact words, sir. And if it makes you

feel any better, he told me the same thing. Our president is not happy with either of us."

"I've been a team player. Short of actually kissing his ass in public, there isn't a thing I haven't done for him."

"Except this."

"Darn it, Herb, what am I supposed to *do*?"

"You're on the Armed Services Committee. You might suggest to Chairman McTight and those other generalissimos that the president feels they're being rather complacent about the imminent molybdenum cri—"

"Aw, *shee-it*," Squiggly exploded. Strong language for a Baptist. "This molybdenum crisis is a dog that just ain't gonna hunt."

I took this southern expression to denote "nonstarter."

Senator Biskitt said, "Have I not disgraced myself sufficiently in the service of Donald Trump? I have done so many 180-degree turns—in policy, principle, and everything else I once held sacred—that my dang head is spinning. How low must a man go to rise in his estimation?"

"It's a valid question, Senator," I replied. "But one we must all answer individually. I myself am getting on a plane this afternoon to fly to the Vatican. When I tell you this is a trip I would much rather not be making, believe me. But I'm going. Because it's what the president of the United States wants."

Squiggly stared.

"The Vatican? What the hell are you gonna do about this at the Vatican?"

"Vatican City is one of the few sovereign countries that is not a member of Interpol. As it is closer to Washington than Tuvalu or Samoa or North Korea and the others, it's a—I don't want to say 'convenient'—suitable venue for my *second* meeting with Oleg. The highly sensitive nature of my mission requires that I travel in mufti. So you'll appreciate that I'm doing my part here.

"My aim is to persuade Oleg that releasing seventeen more compromising videos of the president would only be counterproductive. If I succeed in persuading him of this, then you and I can relax. And we can revisit Glebnikov Act repeal in the second term."

The senator brightened.

"And the president would do events with me in South Carolina?"

I didn't want to commit the president. Even if I did succeed in getting Oleg to play ball, it was possible Mr. Trump might decide to continue tormenting Squiggly, for the sake of tormenting him. Mr. Trump often does this. Not to be cruel, but as a management technique, a way of maintaining dominance. That was important to Mr. Trump. His philosophy, like that of Socrates, was: "It is not enough that I win; others must suffer."

I said, "Let's hope Oleg and I have a meeting of minds. In that event, then I think happy days will be here again."

The senator looked confused. I realized I had accidentally quoted the Democrats' anthem instead of Mr. Trump's, "We're Not Gonna Take It," by Twisted Sister.

I corrected myself. The senator seemed to relax.

"Y'all have a productive time over there," he said, walking me to the door. "I understand about Interpol, but the Vatican? Seems like a strange place to meet a Russian oligarch to talk him out of releasing adult-themed movies featuring a president of the United States. But it's a strange world. And getting stranger by the day."

25

This time the CIA disguise person outfitted me as a Roman Catholic monsignor. He explained that a monsignor is one rank up from a regular priest, a sort of clerical NCO, identifiable by the scarlet buttons and trim on the cassock. He said Catholics would be less likely to engage me in casual conversation than they would a regular priest.

"They see the scarlet and they get stage fright. Very hierarchical, Catholics."

I wasn't thrilled, but he seemed to know what he was talking about.

"I'll be on a flight to Rome," I pointed out. "What if there are other priests or monsignors on the plane and they want to talk theology or play bingo?"

He considered.

"Tell them you're making a pilgrimage to atone for sexually assaulting underage boys, and you need to concentrate on your penance."

Wonderful.

I was seated in coach as part of my cover. It had been a while since I sat in what Mr. Trump calls "Loser Class." But I appreciated that a monsignor sitting in first, sipping champagne and watching a movie with people having sex, might compromise my religious cover. Still.

Sitting in the back with the other losers got me thinking about Mr. Trump's wealthy evangelicals and their fleets of private jets. Our own Pastor Norma Damdiddle had recently upgraded from a Gulfstream 5 to a 7. She was very pleased with it because it cruised at a higher altitude, which she said made her feel "closer to heaven." I'll bet.

The lack of legroom and attendant risk of a thrombosis, along with the prison-quality food—a subject I can speak of with authority—and the considerate individual in front who insisted on reclining so my tray jammed up against my chest all made me feel that I actually was doing penance, if not for fondling underage members of my flock. Seldom have I been so happy to land.

The airport in Rome is named after Leonardo da Vinci. Very classy, naming the airport after a painter. I made a mental note to suggest to Mr. Trump that he rename Newark or West Palm after some painter. Perhaps after his favorite artist, Jon McNaughton. He did the amazing painting titled *Exposing the Truth*. It depicts Mr. Trump strangling Robert Mueller by his own necktie and holding a magnifying glass up to Mueller's eyeball. Stunning. Mr. Colonnity is a major collector of McNaughtons. He owns the one showing the Founding Fathers gathered around the park bench, imploring Obama to stop snorting cocaine.

My visit was unofficial. But Judd said that as a matter of protocol, our embassy in the Holy See (why do they call the Vatican that?) should be informed. Also, Miriam said she needed to let the CIA folks know, in case something happened.

Our ambassador to the Holy See was Clytemnestra Neuderscreech, wife of former Speaker of the House Salamander

"Sally" Neuderscreech. Sally had been a major deficit hawk until Mr. Trump came into office. His view now was that annual trillion-dollar deficits were "vital to uninterrupted prosperity."

Sally had briefly been on Mr. Trump's short list for VP. He endured the ritual humiliation of coming out to Wetminster and standing next to Mr. Trump on the front steps for picture taking; then learning via tweet on the drive back into Manhattan that Mr. Trump had scratched him from the list. Mr. Trump found him a bit of a talker ("never shuts up") and an untidy eater ("sprays food—disgusting").

But Sally sucked it up and campaigned for the Trump-Pants ticket. His considerably younger (and third) wife, Clytemnestra, was a devout Catholic, except for having had a long affair with Sally while he was still married to Mrs. Neuderscreech number two. She made Sally convert to Catholicism. That meant getting him an annulment, invalidating his prior marriages in the eyes of the church. (Don't ask—not my religion.) After being scratched from the VP short list, Sally lobbied fiercely for the secretary of state job. But Mr. Trump said, "I can't have him spraying food on heads of state." As a consolation prize, Clytemnestra got the ambassadorship to the Holy See. Catholics say the workings of grace are a mystery. I can see why they say this. We Jews say, "Go figure."

As I descended the elevator to baggage claim I was surprised to see a person holding up a sign: Signore Nooterman.

"Signore Nooterman?" He had a photo of me on his clipboard.

"I . . ."

"Ah," he said apologetically. "*Monsignore* Nooterman! Forgive! It seems there have been a miscommunication. All is well. All is well. Welcome to Rome. The flight was good? Ettore is my name. And here is our driver, Massimo. You have many baggages? The ambassador is waiting for you. This way, please."

Ettore led the way to what looked like an armor-plated vehicle. Beside it stood two machine-gun-toting carabinieri in berets and shiny boots and white patent leather chest straps—very stylish, the Italians. The meter maids look like runway models. I'd be happy to be ticketed by them.

I needed to phone Judd to ask him what the hell. But I didn't want to have the conversation in Ettore's hearing. More urgently: what would the devout Ambassador Neuderscreech make of a Jewish White House chief of staff showing up on her doorstep in the uniform of a Roman Catholic monsignor? She'd have views about that.

"Of course, you have been to Rome before," Ettore said, "since you are a *monsignore.* How good that President Trump has a member of the clergy for his chief of staff. I did not know. So, the drive will take us maybe some forty-five minutes. Your first event is . . . allow me to look"—he consulted his clipboard—"at eleven thirty, so you will have some few minutes to freshen up."

First *event?*

"May I?" I asked, reaching for his clipboard. I read:

> Schedule of the Honorable Herbert Nutterman
> White House Chief of Staff
> and
> Counselor to the President of the United States

11:30 A.M.: Greeting by Her Excellency Ambassador Clytemnestra Neuderscreech.
11:45 A.M.: Meet with embassy staff. Brief remarks by AN
  and HN.

I read the rest of the schedule with mounting panic: there was to be a luncheon with something called the Greater Mediterranean Security Conference. ("Remarks: twenty minutes, followed by Q and A.") A tour of a leather goods factory, presumably in hopes of being exempted from the president's new 50 percent tariff on luxury goods produced by NATO countries. Then back to the embassy for cocktails with the Knights of Malta. Dinner ("Black tie; decorations optional"). Attending: Ambassador and former Speaker Neuderscreech, Cardinal Maravilla, Cardinal M'Kwaampu, various other princes of the church, two members of the Italian Parliament, a former race car driver, an actress whose name I vaguely recognized and her husband, a tire magnate. ("Toast to the president of the United States, followed by brief remarks. Suggested theme: America First and Post-NATO Transatlanticism.)

Some "unofficial visit." Why didn't they throw in "Fanfare for the Common Man"? Somewhere, something had gone very, very wrong.

"I think there's been a misunderstanding," I said to Ettore.

"Yes?"

"It seems you were sent to meet Herbert Nutterman, the White House chief of staff."

"Yes?"

"That's not me. Sorry."

Ettore frowned, looked at the photo of me on his clipboard, then at me.

"But . . . ?"

"Yes, we do look a bit alike. And the spelling is similar. But as you see, I'm with the church." Should I add, for verisimilitude, that I was on a pilgrimage to atone for fondling altar boys? Might move things along.

A look of panic came over Ettore.

"You are . . . *not* chief of staff Erburt Nooterman?"

"Alas."

Ettore spoke in machine-gun Italian to Massimo, who executed a U-turn that still haunts my sleep even after all these years. Twenty minutes later we were back at Leonardo da Vinci, Ettore grim-faced and perspiring. Massimo extracted my bag from the trunk and dumped it unceremoniously on the sidewalk. Ettore dashed back into baggage claim to locate the echt Signore Nooterman.

I hoofed it to the taxi line. On the way in to Rome I called Judd and demanded to know why I'd been greeted with pomp and circumstance when I was here incognito. I had to be circumspect, as the purpose of my mission was known only to the president and myself. Even Miriam wasn't in the loop; all she knew was that I was on a "private assignment for the president."

"Man, that *is* a mess," Judd said. "The embassy must have gotten a bit overexcited about having the White House chief of staff in town. Take it as a compliment."

"Well, call them and tell them my visit got scrubbed. And that I won't be attending dinner with the Knights of Malta and Brunella Piccatta."

"Brunella Piccatta? The actress?"

"I think that's the name. It was on the list, along with the thirty *other* people attending."

"Sure you want to bail on dinner with Brunella Piccatta?"

"I'm not here to ogle movie stars, Judd. I'm on a highly sensitive mission."

"If you say so. But most people would kill to have dinner with Brunella Piccatta. Can you give me some idea why you're in Rome? Is it some international conference on molybdenum?"

"Just call the embassy," I said, and hung up.

As rendezvous spots go, you can't do better than the obelisk in St. Peter's Square. There's no ambiguity to "Meet me at the obelisk in the middle of St. Peter's Square." That said, it seems odd to me that a sixteenth-century pope put a 330-ton "representation of the erect phallus of the Egyptian god Osiris"—according to my guidebook—smack-dab in front of a church dedicated to Saint Peter. How do you say "Whatever" in Latin?*

Oleg was there with a half dozen of his ex-Spetsnaz bodyguards. He took in my clerical garb.

"Cardinal Nutterman! Eminence! I was going to come as Orthodox patriarch, but there was not enough time to grow the proper beard."

The strain of the flight and the morning was such that I needed to sit. But the Catholic Church, in its wisdom, does not provide amenities in St. Peter's Square proper. I proposed that we step a few feet outside of sovereign Vatican territory, to a sidewalk café.

Oleg assented. His myrmidons set up a perimeter. We ordered espressos and biscotti.

"The president is very disappointed in you, Oleg. We're doing everything we can to repeal the Glebnikov Act. And you release that video?"

"She's talented, Miss Sri Lanka. That thing where she rotate—"

"Oleg, I didn't come here to review the movie."

"Pity. Wait till you see Miss Okinawa. You will say, 'Banzai!'"

"I'm sure. Look here, Oleg," I said forcefully. "You seem not to realize that humiliating the president of the United States will only mean that he won't have another term. *Then* where will you be?"

"Where I am now. Not in America."

"Do you think a Democrat president is going to make Glebnikov Act repeal a priority of his first hundred days?"

"No. This is why we must do repeal now. Before election."

"But, Oleg . . ." Sisyphus on his worst day was not more frustrated than I.

* *Quisquis.*

159

Then suddenly: *pop-pop-pop-pop.* I thought it was fire-crackers or backfire farting from a passing Vespa. But there was another sound, of shattering glass. I looked and saw holes in the front of the café. These were gunshots.

Oleg's private army was on him like a rugby scrum. I was knocked aside, to the ground. Vehicles screeched up, one nearly running me over. Oleg and his protective carapace disappeared into them and off they roared.

I lay on the pavement as a crowd gathered around. Exclamations, gasping, people crossing themselves. I wanted to get up and make an exit but couldn't seem to get my limbs organized. Shock, probably, and no wonder. I don't generally expect a hail of bullets with my espresso and biscotti.

I felt a tug at my armpits. Someone was lifting me up. An American voice said, "Let's get you out of here, Padre."

Wailing police sirens now joined in the general hubbub. Another vehicle screeched up out of nowhere. My savior shoved me into the back seat and off we went.

He began to grope me.

"What are you *doing*? Stop that!"

"Relax. Checking to see if you got hit."

"Who are you?"

"Director Jones asked us to keep an eye on you."

"CIA?"

"Whatever."

"What the hell happened back there?" I said.

"Not sure. One possibility is someone tried to take you and your Russian pal out."

At this point I—I don't want to say "fainted"—succumbed to shock and passed out. When I came to, I was on a private jet, on my way back to Washington. The flight was a significant improvement on the one over.

26

"**M**iriam said you got into some kind of fuckup over there," the president said. "Next time, be more careful. So, did you talk sense into that Russian prick?"

Mr. Trump is not one to waste time comforting an employee who's just narrowly escaped assassination.

"I made a strong argument against releasing seventeen more videos," I said.

"And?"

"I think I was making progress until our conversation was complicated by gunfire."

"Miriam says they don't know who it was. But she *never* knows. Totally useless. I'm considering firing them all and starting my own CIA. Then if I asked questions? They would have answers, believe me."

I wasn't looking forward to the next part.

"Unfortunately, sir, the incident seems to have had a"—I didn't want to say "disastrous"—"deleterious impact on our relations with Oleg."

The president frowned, as only Donald Trump can frown. His face scrunches into itself and becomes a gargoyle. You expect water to spout from its mouth. Mr. Trump must have come out of the womb frowning and muttering, "*Disgusting.*"

"Oleg left a message on my cell phone. If you'd care to hear it . . ."

The president gestured for me to play it.

"*You fucking try to fucking kill me, you piece of shit? Fuck you. And fuck your motherfucker boss.*"

Mr. Trump frowned more deeply.

"He thinks *you* tried to kill him?"

"I took his meaning to be collective. As in the US government tried to kill him. He seems to think it was a trap, with myself as the bait."

"Why would we do that?"

"Motive-wise, I suppose to keep him from releasing further movies."

"What a crock. I didn't order a hit on Oleg. At this point, I would. But not with you sitting next to him."

"Thank you, sir. Greatly appreciated."

"You and I are the only ones who know about the thumb drive, right?"

"Correct, sir."

"Not even Miriam? Miss Know-Nothing?"

"She only knew I was going to Rome on a private mission. She wanted to have her people look out for me. And thank God she did, or right now I'd be explaining myself to some Italian prosecutor. You saw what they did to that poor American girl, Amanda Knox."

Mr. Trump snorted. "So now what? I star in seventeen more movies between now and the election?"

"I agree that the optics are not optimal, sir," I said.

"I'd say very far from optimal, Herb. This is completely disappointing."

I rather boldly proposed that there might an upside.

"As you yourself said, sir, you could shoot people on Fifth Avenue and people would still vote for you. No one's getting shot in these movies. For all we know, your base might . . ."

"What?"

". . . enjoy them. The male portion, at any rate."

The president considered.

"Make America Hard Again. Why not?" I could hear the turbines of his stable genius humming. "What about the women?"

"It might raise an eyebrow or two. But with a little spin by Mr. Colonnity and Mr. Fartmartin, the ladies might be persuaded that you were just being a thorough judge. You were doing in-depth interviews. The contestants couldn't resist your magnetism. And before you knew it, they were hurling themselves at you and taking appalling liberties."

The president nodded. "They do throw themselves at me. You can't blame them. Drives Melania nuts."

"I imagine it does, sir. But I'm sure that Mrs. Trump understands. After all, she herself found Donald Trump irresistible, did she not?"

"What about my evangelicals?"

There had been cracks in our evangelical support. But hairline cracks, nothing to shake the foundations. One holier-than-thou evangelical journalist had written a snarky editorial calling Mr. Trump "the Antichrist." He changed *his* tune after the Aryan Soldiers of the Almighty Evangelical Brotherhood tried to stone him to death.

"We'll want to get Pastor Norma's thoughts," I said. "But these folks think you walk on water, sir. Your support among white evangelicals is something—I say this with respect—that Jesus Christ himself would envy. Now, if some of them want to quibble about your ministry to the Miss Universe contestants, our message should be: 'People love Trump. And Trump loves people back. Is that a sin?' Okay, fine. Donald Trump cops to not being one hundred percent perfect. But what Trump is also *not* is a radical, left-wing, gun-confiscating, fossil-fuel-banning, transgender-promoting, war-starting, Mexican-hugging socialist who hates America." I added, "I'd love to get Katie's thoughts on this."

The president considered.

"Or we just say the videos are fake. Cleaner. And frankly, Herb, I'm getting tired of having to bend over backward for these assholes."

"The . . . ?"

"Evangelicals. I mean I love them, but they creep me out. They come in here to pray over me and touch me. I hate that."

"I think that's part of the whole evangelical thing, sir. Touching. The so-called laying on of hands."

"Yeah, well, I hate it. From now on, you tell them before they come in: 'It's great that you want to pray over him. But Trump doesn't like to be touched.'"

"I'll make a note to do that," I said.

"Meanwhile, you and Buttplug can quit with the Glenikov Act repeal."

"Are you sure, sir?"

"If Oleg's going to be an asshole, why should I spend political capital trying to convince everyone we're facing a mollinum . . ."

"Molybdenum."

"Whatever. Crisis. He can take his precious metal and shove it up his Russian ass."

"Sir," I said, "Oleg is already in a rage. Bad enough he thinks we're trying to kill him. But if he sees that we're giving up on repeal . . . who knows what he might do? Surely it's better to have a Russian oligarch inside the tent pissing out, than outside the—"

"Fuck Oleg. I'm done with him."

If you say so, sir, I thought. *But is Oleg done with* you?

27

O ver the following days I kept a nervous, vigilant eye on the media coverage. My CIA guardian angel had gotten me out of there before any of the gawping tourists and passersby managed to tape viral-quality iPhone videos of me. Oleg's handlers, too, had done efficient work, bundling him off before some sidewalk Zapruder immortalized his presence. In yet another miracle, the CCTV security camera near the café was out of order at the time. Nice as it would have been to have a picture of our assailant, I was content to leave well enough alone.

The Italian authorities were interviewing witnesses. A number of them said that one of the people involved was a monsignor. People who lurk about St. Peter's tend to be the type who recognize clerical garb. The hunt was on for "*Il Misterioso Monsignore*"—The Mystery Monsignor.

Miriam—bless her—performed two mitzvahs: she got her people to get Italian immigration to "lose" the photo taken of me on entering the country and to plant a story in *La Bestia Eterna*, a leading Vatican newspaper, quoting an anonymous colonel in the Swiss Guard that the shooting was "a quarrel about papal infallibility that got out of hand." That triggered a cyclone of competing conspiracy theories on social media, including a plot to blackmail the pope for siring a love child by my almost dinner partner Brunella Piccatta. Dan Brown's next blockbuster Vatican thriller. That might have been the end of it had it not been for the US embassy in the Holy See. Holy See, Holy do.

I was in my office watching Katie Borgia-O'Reilly on Fox. She was swatting away media questions about Oleg's latest video release, this one featuring the future president enacting Kama Sutra positions with Miss Myanmar. We were now up to episode four of what Democrats, the liberal media, and Never Trumpers were calling *The Apprentice Does Moscow*.

Again I was in awe of Katie's skills. There are spin doctors, and there are centrifuges. Iran should hire Katie to centrifuge their uranium. She'd spin those isotopes into enough uranium 235 to blow up Israel *and* the world.

Once, during a meeting where we were morosely anticipating the possibility of a second impeachment, Katie, without batting an eyelash, came up with: "How many presidents can claim the distinction of having been impeached *twice*?" It took my breath away. It almost made me wish we'd had a second impeachment. Thankfully, we were spared that when Attorney General Barr audaciously invoked his theory about the "Divine Unitary Executive Right."

Now here she was, Trump's La Pasionara, in full voice. Not only was Katie denying the authenticity of the videos, she was suggesting that the Democratic National Committee had made them. And that the Miss Universe contestants were actually "human trafficked sex slaves."

I was so absorbed in this bravura performance that I didn't hear Caramella buzz me. She had to come into my office to tell me that Blyster Forkmorgan, chief White House counsel, was on the phone.

"Herb. Sorry to bother you. Listen, I just got a call from the head of the FBI's DC field office. By any chance were you in Rome last Tuesday?"

Not good, I thought.

"Rome," I said. "Rome . . . Italy?"

"Yeah. That Rome."

"Hm," I said. "Let's see. Last . . . Tuesday, you say? Even with Alzheimer's you'd think I'd remember something like that."

Yes, yes, I know: cracking wise about progressive mental deterioration was in questionable taste, but I was a bit rattled.

Switching gears, I said, "Why do you ask, Blyster?"

I sensed that Blyster, easily the busiest member of the Trump administration, was losing patience.

"Well, Herb, it seems they're following up on a report out of our Holy See embassy. Did you happen to hear about that incident in St. Peter's? A shooting? Involving some mystery monsignor?"

"Good heavens. St. Peter's, you say? Is the pope all right?"

"Yes, Herb. The pope is fine. He wasn't involved. It was a shooting outside St. Peter's."

"Yes," I said. "Now that you mention it. Been a bit busy . . ."

"Well, someone at our embassy there told the cops he thinks he met the mystery monsignor. And—this'll sound crazy—but that it was you."

"I gave up the Catholic drag scene years ago."

Blyster didn't laugh. It occurred to me he might be Catholic.

"They'd like to talk to you."

"Who?"

"The FBI."

"What about?"

"*Rome*, Herb."

"Oh, honestly. Is that necessary?"

"Normally, I'd say no. But Italian immigration swiped what appears to be your passport on the day of the shooting. There's no photo attached, oddly. But it was your passport."

"Hm. That *is* strange."

"Look, Herb, you don't have to tell me anything. Actually, it might be better if you didn't. But it's the FBI. And they'd like to talk to you. What do you want me to do?"

I thought: *What would Katie say?* I channeled her.

"Well isn't that something," I said. "Another FBI coup attempt? The deep state never rests, does it."

Silence.

"I can't speak to that, Herb. What do you want to do?"

The answer was: jump out the window. But as my office was on the ground floor, that wouldn't accomplish much. Another end-of-life option was violently banging my head against the desk. Maybe Jeff, my Secret Service buddy, would lend me his Glock 9.

I heard a voice, the voice of my late mother: *Schmuck, get a lawyer!*

I groaned, as I often did when Mom dispensed advice. But she was usually right. And we wonder why so few young people these days are inspired to go into government service.

28

Their names were Winchell and Wheary. FBI agents come from the same mold: late thirties, athletic, polite, respectful, declining coffee but thanks. I was hoping to hear *This is strictly routine, Mr. Nutterman*, but instead got a boilerplate warning about the importance of not lying to the FBI.

"You've heard of Martha Stewart, sir?"

"Yes," I said. Who hasn't heard of Martha Stewart? (For God's sake.) I could have added that my wife, Hetta, was a huge Martha Stewart fan. Subscribes to all Martha's magazines, loves her recipes, all the nice touches. Putting bay leaves in your pillowcase.

"Then you'll remember that Martha Stewart went to jail not because of the stock transaction, but because she lied to the FBI?"

"Sure you don't want coffee? So you were saying?"

"Mr. Nutterman, were you in Rome last Tuesday?"

"Now that you mention it, I think I may have been. I'd have to check my calendar."

"So you *were* in Rome?"

"Is that a crime?"

"No one's accusing anyone of a crime, Mr. Nutterman."

"Sure you don't want a cookie?"

"Were you involved in a shooting incident just off St. Peter's Square?"

"Well, that would depend on your definition of *involved*."

Meaningful "bingo" glances between Special Agents Winchell and Wheary.

"Mr. Nutterman, are you the person being referred to as the mystery monsignor?"

"That could be within the realm of possibility."

"Is that a yes?"

"Depends on your definition of yes. It's not a no."

More rapid eye movement between the G-men.

"Sir, may we ask: What were you doing in Rome?"

Good ground, here: "I was on a sensitive mission on behalf of the president of the United States."

"Can you tell us what it was about?"

"Now, gents, as I said, it's sensitive."

"Was the purpose of this mission to meet with someone?"

"Well, I didn't go to Rome to feed the pigeons."

Frowns.

"Mr. Nutterman, were you involved in the shooting?"

"More like *present at*. And let me tell you, gents—Churchill was right. It is exhilarating, being shot at without effect. Damn near crapped my cassock."

"Would you be willing to talk to the Italian authorities about it?"

"Absolutely not. You saw what they did to that poor American girl, Amanda Knox. Look, guys—no one died. Besides, I was there on a diplomatic passport. On a confidential assignment, so I and the—ahem—president certainly hope we can rely on your discretion. And now"—I glanced at my watch—"if you'll excuse me, I'm afraid I'm a bit busy running the US government. Give my regards to Attorney General Barr. We're all huge fans, here. Thanks for coming in."

All in all, I felt I'd handled it rather well. And without a lawyer sitting there, breathing at a thousand dollars an hour. Surely it looks better when you don't have a lawyer there, saying, "My client doesn't have to answer that. Back off, Gestapo pig."

I called Blyster to report in but he said he didn't want to know.

I called Secretary of State Pompeo. One of the nicer aspects of being White House chief of staff is that cabinet members have to take your call.

"Mike," I said. I could hear him bristling. (Pompeo rhymes with pompous.) He prefers to be called "Mr. Secretary." Likes to throw his weight around, and does not lack for weight.

"*Her-b,*" he said, making it sound nerdy, like something you flavor soup with. "What can I do for you?"

"Just wanted to check with you. Is the mission of our embassy to the Holy whatever—the Vatican—to embarrass the president of the United States?"

That got Mr. Secretary's attention. I heard pores opening, sweat bubbling up, trickling. By the time I hung up, I was confident Ettore and Massimo and any other blabbermouths on the embassy payroll there, including Her Excellency Madame Neuderscreech, were about to be fitted with muzzles and a short leash.

That night, Hetta made a quiche for dinner. It was excellent. I complimented her, as I always do, and what do you know? The recipe? Martha Stewart.

29

Why the Republican National Committee chose to hold the convention in Charlotte, North Carolina—in *August?*—was beyond me. (I was not involved in the decision.) As a hospitality professional, I was appalled. Why not just hold it in a Turkish bath? Had no one considered the impact of that swampy southern heat and humidity on Mr. Trump's complex coif? Answer: obviously not. I get that siting a convention is a political decision. Still. This would not have happened on Herb Nutterman's watch. That said, you could feel the excitement building. It was palpable. Like the air in Charlotte in late August.

The damage from Oleg's biweekly episodes of *The Apprentice Does Moscow* had been far less than I'd feared. They were actually proving highly popular, at least among the male portion of the base. At the rallies, chants of "Lock her up" had given way to "Keep America hard!" We tried to tamp that down, but Mr. Trump slyly encouraged it.

Not everyone was cheering, mind. Word from the East Wing was that the first lady was "not thrilled." And who'd expect her to be? But pro that she is, she kept her game face as she stood by Mr. Trump's side—*not* holding hands, everyone noticed—looking straight ahead with that icy-cool, Slovenian sphinxy stare.

I wondered: *What's goes on inside that gorgeous head? Is she thinking: Am I the luckiest girl on earth?* Or: *Beam me up, Scotty.* Sometimes it looked like she was thinking, *I envy the dead.* Not an easy read, Mrs. T. It can't have been much fun for her when Oleg released the video of Mr. Trump "interacting"—the verb Katie and I had devised—with Miss Slovenia.

Katie sensitively reached out to Mrs. T to see if she wanted to spend some "girl time" with her and Ivunka at a spa where they immerse you in jellyfish—apparently very rejuvenating. Mrs. T declined, saying she needed to practice her convention speech announcing her new cause: training highly attractive young women from third world countries to spot fake jewelry. The anti-cyberbullying campaign never really got traction.

I worked on Mr. Trump's acceptance speech with our speech-writer, Stefan. Stefan is a highly skilled wordsmith, but I felt that the early drafts were—I don't want to say "harsh"—a bit overedgy.

Mr. Trump was certainly entitled to make the convention a victory lap. Still, I felt that lines like "I will unleash apocalypse on our enemies!"* and "John McCain rots in hell, where he will soon be joined by Mitt Romney, a devout *Moron!*" while appealing to the harder core element of our base, might scare the children and frighten the horses, as the saying goes.

Speechwriters, being writers, tend to be—I don't want to say "hothouse orchids"—protective of their prose. Stefan resisted

---

* I also worried that Mr. Trump might have difficulties pronouncing "apocalypse," which at first he thought was a Caribbean dance.

all my suggestions. As he saw it, I was painting mustaches on his *Mona Lisa*.

I suggested changing the McCain line from "rots in hell" to "John McCain and Mitt Romney and I may have had our differences, but John was an American hero whom I hugely admired, and Mitt is a fine man." That went down like a gallon of prussic acid.

For reasons perhaps best left to psychologists, Mr. Trump loathed John McCain. Despite heavy opposition from the navy, he finally got them to decommission the USS *John McCain* and sell it to Bolivia, for ten bolivianos on the dollar. It was far from clear what landlocked Bolivia intended to do with a destroyer, but I was done arguing with the president about it.

In the end I did manage to get Stefan to dial back some of his more incendiary rhetoric. We changed "Charlotte suffered horribly during the War of Northern Aggression. But look at her now!" to "Charlotte. Incredible city. *Hot enough for you?*"

Ten days before the convention, everything was going smoothly, when the *Washington Post*—and may *it* rot in hell— came out with a real humdinger:

> PANTS TRIED TO PERSUADE CABINET TO INVOKE
> 25TH AMENDMENT, REMOVE TRUMP, SOURCE SAYS

On the holy shit scale of one to ten, this was a twelve. Katie's reaction, right out of the gate, was, "Well, at least it's not another 'Mike Pants Worships at Satan's Altar' story." But not much comfort there. I was deluged with calls from frantic cabinet members denouncing the story, offering to chop off their pinkie fingers—anything—to demonstrate their loyalty to Mr. Trump.

The nut (I choose the word carefully) of the story was that the vice president and twenty-two cabinet members had con- vened at Camp David to "participate in a nuclear war game scenario. Whereupon, Pants announced that the president had 'gone completely off his nut,' and passed around a document for them to sign invoking the amendment and removing Mr. Trump from office. A majority is required. According to the *Post*'s source, "the motion failed by three votes."

Well.

Most vice presidents, confronted with a story like this, would start gibbering like a chimpanzee and hurling the feces. Not Mike. Good old stolid, evangelical, non-Satan-worshipping Indiana Mike merely shrugged and said in his tranquilized monotone, "That's not *my* recollection of the meeting."

Mr. Trump was livid. And who'd blame him? He wanted to fire "every other" cabinet secretary. Stefan told him that's how "you know who" would have handled it. (*Danke*, Stefan.) Fortunately, Jored, Ivunka, Katie, and I convinced him that a "night of the long knives" going into the convention would make for terrible optics.

"Fine," he snorted. "I'll do it after the election. Fuckers."

There was something smelly about the story. In the history of the vice presidency, there has never been a more—I don't want to say "supine"—team player than Iron Mike. But there was also something odiferous about all the denials. And the timing.

The Camp David meeting had taken place the day after the infamous press conference in Helsinki at which Mr. Trump drew gasps by saying he believed Mr. Putin that Russia didn't interfere in the 2016 election. Not a high point.

And I must say, I've always found it interesting that a few weeks before the story broke, former UN ambassador Cricket Singh spent one whole hour in the Oval with Mr. Trump. Just the two of them.

Mr. Trump gushed after the meeting.

"She's terrific. Smart. Hot. Brown. If we ever need a replacement for Mike, that little Indian is at the top of my list."

Hm. But I'll leave it at that.

30

Caramella buzzed to say that former speaker Salamander Neuderscreech was on the line. My bowels shriveled. There could be no good reason for this call.

"Sally, what a pleasant surprise," I lied. We'd met years ago when he and the current Mrs. Neuderscreech were guests at Farrago-sur-Mer. He was miffed at checkout to learn that his stay had not been comped. I mollified him by taking off the minibar charges, which were considerable, indicative of an insatiable appetite for macadamia nuts.

"How are *you*, Herb?" he said with a somewhat oily inflection.

"Busy, as you might imagine, what with the convention approaching." For a hopeful, fleeting moment I thought he might be calling about tickets or VVIP arrangements. Alas.

"We missed you in Rome. What happened? Cly had a great day lined up for you. We had Brunella Piccatta seated next to you at the dinner."

"My apologies to Her Excellency," I said. "Some wires must have gotten crossed. It was an in-and-out visit. We only let the embassy know out of courtesy. Let us know if you're coming to DC."

"Actually, I'm here."

What joy.

"I'd like to stop by. Out of courtesy."

"It would be great to see you. But it is a bit busy at the moment."

"Oh, I think you'll want to hear what I have to say, Herb."

Actually, the last thing I wanted to hear was whatever he had to say. But in he came.

I hadn't seen him since he and "Cly" had left for the Eternal City. Sally was always portly, but from his considerably more ample figure, it appeared he'd been snout-deep in the pasta and the macadamia nuts.

"How is Cly?" I asked. Out of courtesy.

"She's in heaven. She's got His Holiness eating out of her hand."

"Wonderful," I said. "Then we'll be able to count on his support in the next world war."

"What?"

"Nothing."

"We had a bit of excitement recently," he said.

"Oh?"

"A shooting. In St. Peter's."

"That is exciting. I heard something about it. St. Peter's. Is nothing sacred these days?"

"You *heard* something about it?" He chuckled unpleasantly. "Herb. You were there."

"I was?"

"It happened the day you were in Rome."

"Now that you mention it, that's right. I heard about it on the plane, flying back. Dreadful business."

"*Il Mysterioso Monsignore,*" he said. His three-hundred-pound body jiggled like an outsized Jell-O mold. And now, with the lunatic glee of a carnival barker, Sally unveiled his agenda.

"Our security people tell us Italian immigration has a photo of him at Leonardo."

"Really? Well, good."

He grinned. His pudgy face, beady little eyes, and bared teeth gave him the look of a malevolent Pillsbury Doughboy.

"I'll give it to you straight up," he said. "I think the president should drop Pants from the ticket and replace him with me."

This I hadn't expected.

"Gosh, Sally. That's rather a big ask."

"Pants is baggage. Between the satanism and invoking the Twenty-Fifth? Come on. Devil worship *and* mutiny? How do those two factors help the president?"

I didn't see much point in arguing it on the merits, there being no merits. So I gave him my standard "I'll definitely pass it along to the president."

"*Oh,*" he said with an evil pixie grin, "I think you can do better than that, *Monsignore.*"

"Should I take that as a compliment, Sally?"

"Any way you like," he said.

I considered.

"For a miracle like the one you have in mind, you'd need more than *monsignore* mojo. If the pope is, as you say, eating out of Cly's hand, wouldn't he be a better advocate with the big guy upstairs?"

"Oh, I have great faith in monsignors."

I was tempted to shut this pantomime down by telling him the truth: *Sally, the president doesn't like you because you talk too much and you spray food.* But there are times when truth is a luxury.

"Assuming," I said, "that the president prefers to stick with his devil-worshipping, mutinous VP, is there some other position in the federal government that would be of interest to you?"

He received this with a thoughtful look of *now we're talking*.

"The second term is going to present unique challenges in the field of foreign policy," he said.

I inwardly groaned as he embarked on a *tour d'horizon*.

"Secretary of state?" I interjected. "You'd be fabulous."

"I think so, too," he modestly agreed. "See, if you look at history in terms of alternating concentric cones—"

"Sally, you had me at *monsignore*. I'll do what I can. But for miracles, you're going to need the big guy."

"Why is a *miracle* required?" he said, suddenly peevish. "I'm by far the most qualified. And if I may say, the most . . ."

I perceived that there would be no stopping this bulldozer tour d'horizon on the theme of the wonderfulness of Sally Neuderscreech. I let him blow on. And blow on he did. Of the seven cardinal virtues, Sally had dispensed with humility. Maybe he was a "cafeteria Catholic," the type who picks and chooses off the doctrinal menu.

I informed the president, whereupon *he* launched into a tour d'horizon (my third of the day), enumerating the many reasons why he loathed Salamander Neuderscreech and how he could go rot in hell along with McCain. I said I couldn't agree more, but that detestation alone didn't solve the objective problem, namely that we were being blackmailed. Sally had made it pellucidly clear that if a plum did not fall off the Trump Tree into his lap, he was going to take a chain saw to it.

The president looked at me.

"I'm not being blackmailed. You're being blackmailed."

Presidents inevitably adopt the so-called royal we, as in "We have accomplished great things." When things go south, they invariably switch to the second person, as in "You have brought disgrace on my administration."

"Understood, sir, but I'm not sure that would be the end of it."

"Herb, how far back do we go?"

"A long and happy way, sir. Herb Nutterman is no Mickey Cohen. Herb Nutterman can keep a secret. Have no doubts on that score. I'm only saying that these things have a way of . . . What I'm trying to *say*, sir, and not saying well, for which I apologize, is that *in* the event I am summoned to account, I'm not confident the authorities—much less the enemies of the people—will be satisfied with just my head. I'm fond of my head, but it's no trophy to match yours."

The president frowned, indicating that he got what I was driving at.

Normally in a situation like this, the American president would call the Italian prime minister and that would be that. *Finito la commedia.* But Mr. Trump had recently tweeted that that the Italian government "couldn't run a pizza parlor, never mind a country. SAD!"

In his defense, the Italian Parliament was—again—in disarray. Yet another financial minister had committed suicide, and there had been shoving matches among the deputies. Still. The president's tweet certainly did not win Italian hearts and minds. It fell to Secretary of State Pompeo, himself of Italian ancestry, to aver mendaciously that the president's statement had been "taken out of context."

The president grumbled, "Why the fuck were you dressed up as a priest?"

"CIA's idea, sir. They thought it would make a good fig leaf."

"CIA," he snorted. "Imbeciles. Morons. If the photo gets out, you'll have to say you were going to a costume party."

I imagined myself explaining it to Agents Winchell and Wheary.

31

Whoever defined history as "one fucking thing after another" was onto something.

The day after my delightful visit from former Speaker Neuderscreech, Miriam phoned to say she needed to see me. "ASAP."

She arrived in my office with a bombshell that threatened to turn Mr. Trump's victory lap into a demolition derby. I could hear the fuse hissing.

"Herb, we have a problem."

I didn't much like that "we."

"It's not a hundred percent solid, but we're picking up indications the Russians may know about Placid Reflux."

On the holy shit scale of one to ten, this was a twenty.

"Miriam," I moaned. "We're about to go into the *convention*."

"I know. Suboptimal timing."

"Bathyspheric. What do we do?"

"I think it's time you told the president."

I didn't at all like that "you." I realize that there are few sights more—I don't want to say "pathetic"—deplorable than government officials playing Hot Potato. Still.

"Miriam," I said, "this being intelligence, surely the appropriate messenger is the director of national intelligence."

She nodded. "Okay. But you and Judd need to be there. He's going to want to know why you and he didn't tell him about Placid before."

"Maybe," I said, tossing the potato back. "But I imagine his first question will be why *you* didn't tell him."

"True," Miriam said, digging in her Manolo Blahniks, "and my answer to that will be: because, sir, your chief of staff and your NSC director determined it was best not to tell you."

She had me there.

"Very well," I said. "If your plan is go full Nuremberg, fine. But don't think that's going to spare you from execution along with the rest of us. Meanwhile, can we agree that the first head to roll should be Admiral Murphy's? He is the Dr. Frankenstein of this monstrosity."

"Let's take a step back, Herb. The time line, the who-knew-what-when, that shouldn't be our focus."

"The fact that we all hid it from the president?" I said. "Oh, I'm pretty sure that's going to be *his* focus."

"Herb. You're missing it. It was never about hiding it. It was about protecting the president. What does any president want, more than anything?"

"Reelection?"

"Plausible deniability. Coin of the realm."

"That's not going to be an easy sell."

"It's worth a shot. Meanwhile, we'll let Murphy—poor bastard—take ownership. But if it turns into a season finale of *The Apprentice*, with him going around the table saying, 'You're fired. You're fired. You—you're fired,' you might point out that sacking his national security brain trust on the brink of a shit storm isn't the smart play."

"Fix now, roll heads later?"

"Something like that."

I thought it best to have the meeting in the Oval rather than the Situation Room. It's a calmer environment. The Sit Room—with the DEFCON level indicator (showing how close the world is to blowing up) and the maps and monitors on the walls displaying real-time drone feeds and Tomahawk missiles launching—is inherently not calming. Personally I find it nerve-racking.

"Miriam," I said, "why don't *you* start us off?" My plan was to say as little as possible and blend into the furniture.

"Mr. President, our people in Moscow assess that Russian intelligence may*—I emphasize *may*—be on the verge of determining that their election was compromised by a US cyber-intervention."

The president stared. "*What?*"

I said, "Admiral Murphy, why don't *you* take it from there?"

Admiral Murphy didn't flinch. In his place I'd have been in full chimpanzee-gibber mode and hurling the feces. But Murphy manfully and lucidly explained about Placid Reflux, emphasizing its autonomous aspect. He reminded the president that he had in fact been briefed about its existence before taking office.

"No one ever told me about this," the president said.

"You had a lot on your plate, Lord knows. But it was in your briefing book." Admiral Murphy pulled a thick folder marked "Eyes Only" for the President from his attaché case. "This one, sir. 'US Cyber Capabilities: Opportunities and Liabilities.'"

---

* "Assess" is CIA-speak for "We believe" or "We think" or "Who the fuck knows?"

The president regarded it with distaste. The binder was thick as a bone-in round-eye steak.

"I don't have time to read that crap," he said.

Miriam said, "It is a lot to absorb, sir. Admiral Murphy didn't want to overwhelm you. Only to acquaint you with CyberCom's various modalities of—"

"Yeah, yeah. Okay," the president said impatiently. "So you're saying this, this thing . . ."

"Activated autonomously," Murphy said. "Correct, sir. AI has greatly enhanced the performance parameters. A program like Placid Reflux is called a 'hibernator.' They go into a state of deep sleep, making themselves virtually impossible for the enemy to detect. But they're still receiving. When their sensors detect predetermined indicators . . ." Murphy went on, folding in terms of such technical complexity that no one but himself understood what—the hell—he was talking about.

I telepathically prompted: *Get to the Obama part.*

I'd done some kibitzing prep with Murphy before the meeting, suggesting that he emphasize that Placid Reflux was authorized by the Obama administration.

Mr. Trump had devoted his entire presidential agenda to erasing the Obama legacy so thoroughly that future historians may not even realize there was an Obama administration. With a bit of spin, he could turn this calamity into a win by saying it was all a plot by Obama—*and* Vice President Biden—to sabotage his relations with Putin. And why stop there? He could suggest that Placid Reflux hadn't activated "autonomously." That Obama and his conniving former VP—in concert with the deep state, of course—had a remote control device with which to activate it and destroy his presidency at their pleasure. Katie could knock this right out of the park.

Admiral Murphy finished. Mr. Trump sat back, looking dazed and defeated. The only time I'd seen him this pensive was when the Palm Beach officials turned down our application for a helipad at Farrago-sur-Mer.

He glanced at me as if to say, *What the fuck, Herb?* I raised my eyebrows and shrugged, to convey that I, too, was appalled by the fiendish machinations of Obama and Biden. So much for the fabled "fraternity of former presidents."

He remained silent for ten, fifteen seconds, an eternity in Trump time. He said to Miriam, "Are you telling me that Putin *knows* about this?"

"We don't know that for a fact, sir, but CIA assesses that they might be vectoring in on it."

"Of *course* you don't know 'for a fact,'" he exploded. "The CIA never knows anything 'for a fact'! Why? Because it's got its head up its *ass!*"

The Oval trembled beneath us as Mount Trump erupted. Through the hot ash and toxic fumes I caught Miriam's eye and signaled: *Sit tight. Say nothing. This too shall pass.*

After considerable bellowing and slamming of fists on the Resolute desk—thank heavens for the sturdy timbers of HMS *Resolute**—Mr. Trump tired. A nervous calm descended on the Oval.

"So where the fuck does *that* leave us?" he said.

Miriam said, "Sir, if the Russians do figure it out, we'll know. I know that you disagree with the intelligence community's assessment that they interfered in 2016. But if they do trace this to us, you could legitimately say that it's nothing more than symmetrical proportionality."

Mr. Trump groaned. "What is that in *English?*"

"Tell Putin: 'Okay, we're even. You quit messing with our elections, we'll quit messing with yours.'"

---

* The desk, made from that noble warship, was given to President Rutherford Hayes by Queen Victoria in 1880.

The president scowled.

Miriam quickly added, "Now, it hasn't come to that yet. It may not come to that. The purpose of this meeting is simply to alert you to the possibility that it might."

"What if they already know?"

"Negative, sir," Admiral Murphy said in a naval way. "Not possible. We'd know."

"Yo, Dr. Frankenstein—I wasn't talking to you." Mr. Trump turned back to Miriam. "Suppose he does know. Am I supposed to sit on my ass and wait for Putin to retaliate—by electing the fucking Democrats?"

I saw my opening.

"Sir, if I may? You have been stalwart in publicly rejecting—sorry, Miriam—the intelligence community's assertion that the Russians interfered in 2016. You have valiantly defended Mr. Putin against that charge. I simply cannot believe that he'd do anything to hurt you in the coming election. If—*if*—the Russians ascertain that this golem was behind Zitkin's victory, I say let's put the blame where it belongs. On Obama and Biden. I hardly think Mr. Putin would deploy his army of trolls and bots or whatever they're called at the service of the Democrats." I added, "Not that Russia interfered in 2016."

The president considered. Miriam, Judd, and Admiral Murphy left the Oval with their heads intact. I remained with the president.

"Now it all makes sense," he said.

"How so, sir?"

"Herb. You're missing it again. It's not Oleg who's blackmailing us. It's Putin. Oleg wouldn't blow his nose without permission from Putin. Putin is punishing me for stealing his election. He thinks I was behind this fucking jack-in-the-box."

"Sir, are you certain?"

"Yeah I'm certain. This whole time we've been trying to make Oleg happy again, we should have been making Putin happy again."

Which Mr. Trump set out to do a few days later, in the middle of his acceptance speech; and in true Trump form, without telling anyone what he was about to do.

32

I was sitting with Stefan during the president's speech at the Spectrum Center in Charlotte. Stefan was purring like a Persian cat. Mr. Trump was knocking his lines out of the park, one by one. He'd stumbled by referring to "Charlotte, South Carolina." But no big deal. The place sounded like the Roman Colosseum on a day of major bread and circuses. At one point, Mr. Trump spread his arms wide and said, à la Russell Crowe in *Gladiator*, "Are you entertained, or what?" (The actual line is, "Are you not entertained?") The answer was: you bet we are! They were lapping it up. Never has so much "red meat" been tossed from a podium.

He was awash in applause, and so far—thank God—there had been no chanting of "Make America hard again!" (We'd put out the word among the delegates and spectators: ix-nay.) The only bump so far had been the Church of Satan's (unsought) endorsement of Mike Pants. It was going so well I almost felt sorry for the Democrats. Victory in November looked like low-hanging fruit. Then as I was scribbling notes I heard Mr. Trump say: "Russia."

Stefan nudged me. He pointed to the text on his lap. There was no "Russia" on the page.

Mr. Trump had gone off-text a few times, but he hadn't threatened anyone with nuclear holocaust or 100 percent tariffs. Nor had he mentioned John McCain roasting in hell. He did go on a bit about "Mitt Romney, the devout Moron."

"Russia . . . Let's talk about Russia, folks. Now, Loser One and Loser Too,* who hate America . . ."

Boos. The people loved "Loser One" and "Loser Too."

". . . along with all the other Democrats who hate America . . ."

I winced.

Stefan said, "Herb. They do."

Mr. Trump continued: "They also hate Russia. I asked myself—*Why?* The media . . . *Oh* yeah, folks, you remember them. The enemies of the people . . ."

Lusty boos.

". . . have been pushing the Russia collusion hoax from day one. Did you ever stop to think, folks—isn't it strange that the Democrats not only want to make America Socialist. Now they want Russia to be Communist again. What's up with that, folks?"

Roars. I couldn't recall the media approving of the Russian Communist Party. Mr. Trump must be making some larger point.

"I had to spend most of my first term dealing with the Russia hoax. Which was completely—excuse me, but there's no other word—*bullshit.*"

Roars.

"By the way, I've got some bad news for the media. Very bad. Wanna hear it?"

---

* As Mr. Trump exclusively referred to the Democratic presidential and vice presidential nominees.

Yesss! the crowd insisted.

"We're gonna win in November!"

Cheering. Roars. Stomping. Soda cans and chairs hurled at the media.

"I asked myself . . . by the way, folks, I gotta tell you, I *love* talking to myself. It's pretty great company, right? Me and myself? Oh yeah. So I asked myself: If the Democrats and the disgusting liberal mainstream media hate Russia, should *we* hate Russia?"

"Nooo!"

"Right! I mean, when you get right down to it, what's so bad about Russia? Why should we not like Russia? Am I right? I think I'm right. They're very religious, Russians. We like religion, don't we?"

Yesss!

"Russia's got the same problem with Muslims that we do. Right?"

Applause.

I winced. Mr. Trump had promised not to go after Muslims at this convention.

"I'm not talking about all Muslims. Only the nasty ones. If Muslims want to come live here? Okay. Maybe. We'll think about it. But they have to leave their suicide vests where they came from!"

Roars.

"That's reasonable. I think that's reasonable, right?"

Applause.

"What else do we like about Russians?"

I thought, *Please don't say, "They're white."*

"They're smart. And tough. Look how they kicked the crap out of Hitler. Did they kick the crap out of Hitler or what?"

The crowd applauded in agreement that the Russians had, indeed, kicked the crap out of Hitler.

"What else do I like about Russians? That they don't mess with our elections. But, folks—*shhh!* Don't tell that to the deep state! And to our so-called intelligence agencies! They've been peddling that crap before I was inaugurated. They don't want to hear that. Noo! It makes them very unhappy to hear that Russia doesn't interfere with our elections. And we don't want to make them unhappy, do we, folks? I mean—they might *impeach us!*"

The Spectrum Center shook so hard I thought the roof might collapse. The boss was cooking tonight.

"So you know what, folks? You know what I'm gonna do? And not just to upset Nervous Nancy Pelosi, who by the way should really do something about her teeth. Nancy—there's something called Poligrip. Please get some. And, folks, let's not upset Little Upchuckie Schumer and Shifty Schiff. Who are very disgusting people . . ."

Where was this going? Stefan was in a funk, shaking his head. The president wasn't just drawing mustaches on Stefan's *Mona Lisa.* He was painting Groucho Marx eyebrows, nose, and eyeglasses.

"So, folks, you know what I'm gonna do? I'm gonna invite Putin to the White House. How do you like *that*, folks?"

It took a few seconds for the "folks" to process "that." At first they didn't seem to know quite what to think. There were isolated shouts of "Yeah!" and "*Da!*" Then the cheering started and built, and built. I sat, frozen in my seat. Stefan's monocle fell from his eye. Any minute now the speakers were going to blast the Russian Men's Chorus singing the "Song of the Volga Boatmen."

Stefan looked at me miserably.

"Did you *know* about this?"

"No!"

Stefan was a full metal jacket Trumper, but he was not a fan of Russia. I don't want to misrepresent his views, but I think he'd have preferred for Hitler "to kick the crap" out of Stalin. I'll leave it at that. At any rate, Stefan was not happy. He sighed heavily and shook his head, muttering, "Not in the text. Not. In. The. Text."

My cell phone started vibrating. I couldn't move. I grabbed Stefan's speech text and flipped through it. There were maybe twenty minutes left, including some rather harsh words and a warning for Mexican president Labrador;* a pledge not to prosecute Pelosi and Schiff, provided they publicly apologize for the impeachment; and in a more upbeat vein, the announcement that Donald Jr. and Ivunka had "graciously consented" to run in 2024. "That's right, folks. Donald Jr. and Ivunka, on the same ticket. Not one but two Trumps! Is that amazing, or what? You know what D-I-N-A-S-T-Y spells? That's right, folks. Dynasty!"

A big finish. A real roof-bringer-downer. But at the moment, my sole thought was: *Katie. Find Katie.* This Putin invite required urgent, massive, full-on centrifuging.

I reached her on her cell. We had to scream, the cheering was so loud. Thousands of energized Republicans, stamping their feet in unison. (Actually, a bit scary.)

"HERB? WHAT THE *FUCK*?"

"I DIDN'T KNOW!"

"JESUS. OKAY, I'M ON IT!"

With my Secret Service guys leading the way, I made for the spin room. The message queue on my cell phone was an endless scroll of "WTF?"s.

A huge TV monitor displayed: TRUMP: MAKE *RUSSIA* GREAT AGAIN? MSNBC assholes. Another monitor showed Secretary Mike Pompeo, sitting next to Mrs. Pompeo, with a frozen smile. He looked like the progeny of Tony Soprano and Humpty-Dumpty.

---

* Andrés Manuel López Obrador, but Mr. Trump preferred this canine variation.

My phalanx of Secret Service guys opened a path through a maze of microphones and cameras and shouts of "Herb! Over here! Mr. Nutterman! What about the Putin invite?"

We pushed on, boats against the tide. Another giant monitor showed Mr. Colonnity and Mr. Fartmartin. They looked as though they'd eaten something that now wanted to come up. But they were doing their best. The caption said: NO, CORKY, BIGGER. WAY BIGGER THAN NIXON GOES TO CHINA. WAY . . .

I reached the spin room and spotted Katie. She was dressed to kill in a figure-clinging, slinky outfit of sparkling red, white, and blue sequins. A bit drag-queeny, but killer.

"Herb. Jesus fucking Christ."

"I know," I said. "But we have to run with it."

"Does *Putin* know? Please don't tell me they're pulling him out of bed. Why does he do this? I love him, but sometimes, Herb, I want to kill him."

Katie's magnetos were firing, the turbines starting to spin. A distant look came into her eyes. She looked like a droid, booting up. She went into rehearsal mode, speaking to herself.

"It's historic. Huge. More than huge. It's very, very, *very* . . . big. How many presidents would have the confidence . . . to . . . do . . . this? Answer? None . . . This makes Nixon in China look like going out to get milk at the 7-Eleven. What do I think? I'll tell you what I think. I think we're in the middle of a very major historical moment, is what I think. Everyone here tonight in this . . . spectacular Spectrum Center . . . in Charlotte . . . has to be thinking, *Wow, guess I'm part of history now*. History is taking place. Took place. Is still taking place. How often does that happen? Answer: not every day. Or even every other day. This is a major historical . . . thing. Donald Trump just won the election . . . The way I see it, this election is over. And out. If I were Loser One and Loser Too I'd seriously be considering killing myself right about now."

Brava. I wanted to stay and watch the actual performance, but more important was finding out what was happening at the Kremlin. Had Mr. Trump run this by Mr. Putin? What if Putin had learned about Placid Reflux and wasn't in any mood to be mollified by a state visit? (My understanding is that Slavs can be very sullen and pouty.) A terrible vision came to me, of Putin, stripped to the waist, his firm chest muscles glistening with sweat from chasing wild boar, rifle in one hand, the other hand raised, flipping Mr. Trump the bird. Not a good optic.

I got Pompeo on the phone. He growled at me and launched into a *This is no way to run foreign policy* lecture. I told him to shut the fuck up and find out what the deal was at the Kremlin and call me back. He hung up in a huff.

"Herb!"

I turned. Squiggly. Senator Biskitt.

He put his sweaty little face unpleasantly close to my ear. He smelled of hair tonic and bourbon. He moistly whispered, "You might have given me some warning about this. Holy kamoly. It's one thing to deny that he messed with our election. But . . . this? Lordy. My people really don't give a hoot, either way, really. But some of them are gonna be asking why we have to put him up at the damn White House. Heck, reason we *got* all these military bases in South Carolina here is because of Russia. By the way, someone oughta point out to him Charlotte is in *North* Carolina."

I wasn't in the mood for this.

"Well, Senator," I said, "maybe if you'd gotten the Glebnikov Act repealed, as you promised, the president wouldn't have had to resort to extreme measures to make Putin happy."

His little face fell.

"Now hold on. Just *hold on*. I worked my dang butt off, wrangling votes for that. Are you telling me the president blames me for not convincing the US Congress that the end of the world is at hand on account of we don't have enough of some metal no one's ever heard of?"

"You can make your"—I almost said "pathetic"—"excuses to him in person, Senator. Meanwhile, the train of history is leaving the station."

I don't know where that came from, but it had a stately ring.

I left Squiggly perspiring and probably in need of more bourbon as the microphones and TV cameras closed around him like a swarm of locusts. There was something biblical about it.

Huge roar. I looked up at the stage. President Trump and Vice President Pants were standing with their families. A Niagara of red, white, and blue balloons cascaded from the rafters. The speakers boomed out Beyoncé: "Proud to be an Ameri-*caaaaaan*, where at least I know I'm *freeeee . . .*"

Time seemed to stop. As Katie had said, history was happening. And I was in it. Whatever was going on at the Kremlin, I stopped caring. I stood there, taking it all in, proud—yes—to be an Ameri-*caaaaaan*.

My transcendent moment of schmaltz fizzled as I resumed thinking about what might be going on at the Kremlin. I felt light-headed.

My phone vibrated. Pompeo.

"It's a go," he said. "Next time, fucking warn me."

I exhaled. I felt my heartbeat resume normal sinus rhythm.

The Kremlin issued a statement the next morning: President Putin "graciously" accepted President Trump's invitation "in a spirit of mutual cordiality and respect."

Comrade Zitkin, meanwhile, denounced the invitation as an act of "heinous interference" in the upcoming Russian election.

It seems we'd come full circle: everyone was interfering in everyone else's election. A brave new era in democracy.

I'd told Judd under no circumstances to bring me further transcripts of phone intercepts. I felt dirtier and dirtier with each one I read. It was like going to a peep show. (Not that I have even been to a peep show.)

But by this point I did want to keep up with Anatoli. It's hard to explain, but somewhere along the line I'd conceived a feeling of—call it—friendship for him. I know it may sound preposterous. Still.

So when Judd alerted me to a transcript of a TV interview Zitkin had done—*that* I did want to read. Anatoli hadn't gotten much coverage in Russian media since he won that first election; the Kremlin had seen to that. This interview was on some Moscow cable channel show that aired at the non–prime time of 3 a.m. The Kremlin censors must have been asleep.

HOST LEV SCHMETNIKOV: Welcome to this week's episode of *Bez Raznitsy*. ["Whatever"] I am of course your host, Lev Schmetnikov, and tonight my guest is Anatoli Zitkin, chairman of the Communist Party. Welcome, Comrade Zitkin.

ANATOLI ZITKIN: Thank you, Comrade Schmetnikov. I compliment you for having the bravery to have me on your show. The Kremlin has effectively banned me from appearing on our news outlets. Since this is a live broadcast, I hope that you have barred the doors, in case the organs of state security wake up and come to break them down.

L. S.: That's funny. May I call you Comrade?

A. Z.: If you like. To be honest, I find it condescending to be called Comrade by non-Communists. But if you are feeling

Marxist-Leninist inclinations, then by all means call me by this fraternal appellation.

L. S.: Well, shall we get right to it?

A. Z.: All right. Unless you prefer to spend our hour together talking about the weather.

L. S.: Ha! That's good! Okay, so, how do you explain that you got more votes than Putin in the last round? All the polls had you sixty points or more behind.

A. Z.: Thank you for this question. There are two explanations possible. The first is that it was a miracle sent by God. I am an atheist, but should this turn out to be the case, I will take up religion, opiate of the masses or not.

The second possibility is that it was some nondivine form of intervention. A computer hacking. By who? No one seems to know. President Putin has exculpated his friend President Trump. Anyway, why would America want to make Russia Red again? Meanwhile, Putin seems eager to blame Ukraine. Perhaps for reasons that will become clear in the days ahead.

L. S.: How do you mean?"

A. Z.: Well, it's a nice pretext to invade the rest of Ukraine, isn't it? Did I say "invade"? Sorry. I meant "liberate."

L. S.: You're going to get us both in trouble.

A. Z.: Let's hope President Putin is asleep. Though we are always being told by his press secretary how hard he works. But if he is watching, then I wouldn't, if I were you, give any speeches from the *lobnoye mesto* in Red Square.

L. S.: You've run for president now, what, three times? Why do you keep running?

A. Z.: To annoy President Putin. And as you saw from my speech in Red Square, it seems to be working.

L. S.: And if you win the runoff election? What will be your first order of business?

A. Z.: To restore Russia's wealth to its proper owners. The proletariat.

L. S.: Ah, yes. We haven't seen much of them lately, have we? Where is their wealth currently?

A. Z.: In Swiss bank accounts. Cayman Islands bank accounts. Cypriot bank accounts. London real estate. The Trump Tower in New York.

L. S.: Well, good luck with that. And Putin? Will you arrest him and put him on trial?

A. Z.: What, "Lock him up"? No, that's America, not here. I will thank him for his service and wish him a good retirement. He'll be eligible for a pension of thirty thousand rubles a month. [five hundred US dollars]

L. S.: Let's hope the president *is* sleeping. [laughter] So what do you make of this invitation to Washington?

A. Z.: Well, one good turn deserves another. Putin got Trump elected. It's only right that Trump should return the favor. Russians seem to be very impressed that Vladimir Vladimirovich has been invited to Washington. He has "hit the big time." It's nice to watch this romance between them. If I didn't know that Putin is so butch, I might begin to wonder, you know.

[INTERVIEW ENDS HERE—BROADCAST INTERRUPTED]

33

Mr. Trump was riding high, delighting in the outrage the Putin invite had wrought among the coastal, wine-sipping, bed-wetting elites, now huffing and puffing that it just *proved* Putin "had something" on Mr. Trump.

What other possible explanation could there be, they whined and mewled on MSNBC and CNN, for inviting a journalist-and dissident-murdering dictator to the White House? Trump must be impeached *again*! Katie had a ready-to-go sound bite if it came to that. To this gnashing of teeth and rending of garments, Mr. Trump serenely tweeted: "YADDA YADDA YADDA! Socialist Dems and Enemies of the Peeple can't stand that I am creating a New World Order and making the WORLD GREAT AGAIN! Suck it up, Bitches! George Soros will soon be rotting in hell with John McCain!"

I know, but he just couldn't help himself.

In his defense, he really did believe he was making the world a better place. I'm no Henry Kissinger, but the world is one complicated enchilada. Meanwhile, I'll cop to some schaden-freude: it was satisfying to watch the mainstream liberal estab-lishment tie itself in knots.

Alas, our elation was short-lived. Leave it to Enemy of the People Number One—I refer of course to the *New York Times*—to declare "Aha!" when the videos of Mr. Trump and the Miss Universe contestants stopped popping up on Facebook.

Pleased as I was by the cessation of the pageant of carnality, the optics were far from ideal. Oleg was playing a clever game. By stopping the videos, he made it look like Putin, having been bought off with a White House invite, had stopped the peep show. Anyone with a pencil could connect *those* dots: Trump invites Putin to White House. Putin stops posting Trump porn. Again the air was rent with howls of "Quid pro quo!" To this day, I shudder when I hear that phrase.

"This looks *terrible*," the president said. "You've gotta get Oleg to keep posting the videos."

No one ever said working for Mr. Trump was a walk in the park.

"Sir," I said wearily, "may I point out that Oleg is convinced that we tried to assassinate him? And thinks I connived in the scheme. He's hardly inclined to do us a solid. Can't you take this up with Mr. Putin? If he's running the show, as you say he is, he must have the original of what's on the thumb drive."

But Mr. Trump was strangely reticent.

"No, no, no. Uh-uh. I don't want to bug him about something like this. It'd just give him something else to hold over me."

Else? Oy.

The president continued: "I not gonna have him gloating. Look, just tell Oleg we'll get the fucking Globnikoff Act repealed in the second term. Tell him if he doesn't start posting the movies—*now*—there's not gonna be a second term. Because everyone will say Putin blackmailed me into inviting him to the White House. Tell him I'll invite *him* to the fucking White House. Just get it done, Herb. This is very important."

Oleg was no longer taking my phone calls, so I had to visit Paul in jail again. I told him to tell Oleg a) we're not the ones trying to kill you. And b) you need to call me, unless you want to spend the rest of your life vacationing in non-Interpol countries like North Korea and Kiribati.

Paul reported that Oleg would "think about it." Great. It was like dealing with a sullen teenager. *Take all the time in the world, Oleg. It's not like there's any hurry. It's only a presidential election.*

Meanwhile the president was calling me every ten minutes, demanding, *"So?"*

I pointed out that Mr. Trump himself had a copy of the thumb drive with the eighteen videos. Why not just post them on Facebook ourselves?

Mr. Trump adamantly shook his head.

"No! Oleg needs to post them. It's gotta look authentic."

Authentic? What, for the sake of cinema verité? I sensed there was some "undistributed middle" here. Which is to say— something missing.

"Sir," I said, "not to be obtuse, but I'm not following you. Why does it matter who posts the videos?"

He said, "How's it gonna look if some four-hundred-pound fat kid in his bedroom figures out the movies are being posted from the fucking White House? You're not thinking at all clearly, Herb. This is very worrying to me."

He hunched his great shoulders together—Mr. Trump's way of squirming.

"Herb, what's on the thumb drive is very personal."

I certainly didn't know how to process that a) he wants the videos posted so a billion people can continue to watch him "interact" with the beauty contestants. But b) he doesn't want to hand over the thumb drive to our IT people. Because what's on it is "personal"?

"Very well, sir," I said. "But in that case, we're just going to have to hope Oleg stops sulking and plays ball. I don't see any other option."

"Lemme think about it."

Then it struck me: Was there something *else* on the thumb drive? I rebuked myself: *Schmuck, why didn't you view the goddamn thing?* But then I thought: *Um, nah.* There's a saying: "No man is a hero to his valet." Some things Herb Nutterman would rather not see. I don't consider myself a valet, but I preferred that Mr. Trump should remain my hero.

Meanwhile there was plenty going on to keep us all busy. Let the liberal mainstream media obsess about the videos. Most Americans weren't paying much attention. Sensible folks that they are, they were going about their lives, concentrating on more pressing matters, like wall-hopping Mexicans, affordable opioids, to vape or not to vape.

Mr. Trump was highly focused on the Putin visit. There were many meetings. One in particular sticks in the memory.

Present were myself, the president, Judd, Katie, former press secretary Beulah Puckle-Peters, now working with Pastor Norma in charge of evangelical outreach; and State Department chief of protocol, Lumpton Outersnatch IV.

Lumpton looked like his name: eastern shore, Ivy League, lean as a whippet, beautifully dressed, shoes you could see your reflection in, bow tie, horn-rimmed glasses, inbreeding going back to the Jamestown colony, incredibly polite—but then he *was* head of protocol. (You don't put rude people in charge of protocol.) Lumpton stood when secretaries came into the room with the coffee. He was very smart. He spoke Latin. I mean, he could carry on a conversation in Latin. I wondered: *With who?* How many people speak Latin? Aside from "quid pro quo"? Still—impressive.

When Mr. Trump was introduced to Lumpton, he scrunched his face and said, "Who the fuck named you that? I don't have time for that name. I'll call you"—he gave Lumpton a quick up and down—"Twiggy." I doubt Lumpton was thrilled to be named after an anorexic beauty icon of the 1960s, but being Mr. Protocol, he couldn't very well tell the president to go fuck himself.

As we filed in, Mr. Trump was finishing his midafternoon snack of two McDonald's Double Bacon Smokehouse burgers and a sixty-four-ounce Diet Coke. He crumpled the wrappers into a ball and tossed it at the wastebasket. It missed, but he said, "Swish!" Mr. Trump once told me it was important to lie about the small things as well as the big things. "You gotta stay in *tune*, Herb."

"Michael Jordan told me I could've been a pro basketball player."

"Guess you missed your true calling, sir," Katie said.

Beulah rolled her eyes. She wore heavy mascara. Her default expression was a scowl. Together, these gave her the look of a chief matron at a women's prison who's just learned that someone in Block Six is keeping a pet mouse, and Big Momma is *not* pleased.

She and Katie were not "girlfriends." They loathed each other, and competed for Mr. Trump's affection. Mr. Trump liked the tension between them and encouraged it.

They were from very different worlds. Katie was a size 2 cheetah in high heels from the New York suburbs. Beulah was a—I don't want to say "hippo"—full-figured, Bible-thumping, good old gal from Deliveranceville, Tennessee. I don't think she grew up with running water and indoor plumbing. But she had a good heart, and bore the indignities that came her way as a public face of the Trump White House with true Christian grace.

The day before the meeting, she'd been asked to leave yet another restaurant by its libtard owner, on the grounds that her presence was "making the other diners nauseous." First—how rude is that? Second, it's "nauseated," not "nauseous." Liberals. Spare me. They're always screeching about "diversity," then they tell the White House press secretary—and her family—to leave their restaurant? Would they do that to a black Beulah? I don't think so. As a hospitality professional, I found it disgraceful. Beyond the pale. Beulah wrote a memoir: *I Wasn't Hungry Anyway*. It's very good. I recommend it.

I don't think Beulah had met many Jews, but she couldn't have been nicer to me, personally. One time at Camp David, she offered me half of her BLT, then suddenly recoiled and blushed and started apologizing. Poor thing was mortified. To make her feel better, I ate it, even though I'm more of a tuna salad person. I think the incident speaks very well of her. I respected her faith, though I stopped shy of her view that Mr. Trump "was sent by God to save America."

The three TVs in the Oval were on, as usual, with the sound off. The one set to CNN showed a graph: POLL: MAJORITY OF AMERICANS "CONFUSED" BY PUTIN INVITE.

"Why are people confused?" Mr. Trump said. "What's confusing about it? Fucking idiots."

Beulah shifted in her chair. For someone who'd been raised in a home where "gosh" was considered profane, the Trump White House, where four-letter words were used as punctuation, must have taken adjusting to.

"How are my evangelicals doing with it?" the president asked.

"They're doing just fine, sir," Beulah said. "We're emphasizing that Mr. Putin is a man of deep religious faith."

"He is. Good. Keep doing that."

"We're also emphasizing that the Russian Orthodox Church is different from the Roman Catholic Church."

"It is? Okay. Does it matter? Is there a problem?"

"Some of our more fundamentalist evangelicals view the Roman church as—"

"The Whore of Babylon," Katie said, rolling her eyes. "Cretins."

Mr. Trump grinned. He enjoyed it when his girls started hissing at each other.

"Whore of Babylon?" he said, amused. "Really? Kinda harsh. I like it."

"Point is," Beulah said, soldiering on, "we're emphasizing that Mr. Putin is not Catholic. He's Russian Orthodox. They're different."

"How?" said the president. "Wait—let's ask Monsignor Nutterman."

I froze. Mr. Trump realized he'd stuck his foot in it and quickly changed the subject by rounding on Lumpton.

"Yo, Twiggy. How we doing? Everything good?"

"We are proceeding apace, sir," Lumpton said in his plummy voice.

"What the fuck does *that* mean? Twiggy. English."

"Sorry, sir. Everything is going very well. We are coordinating harmoniously with the Russian embassy."

"Good. Sergey is happy?" Mr. Trump said, referring to the Russian ambassador.

"He appears to be. Yes, sir."

"Well, let's keep him happy. Anything Sergey wants, he gets. Including blow jobs."

Katie thought this was very witty. Beulah and Twiggy reserved comment.

"We're gonna put him up here."

"Sir?"

"Putin. He's gonna stay here. At the White House."

Lumpton cleared his throat, WASP for *Are you out of your fucking mind, sir?*

"Sir, typically, heads of state stay at their own embassies. In certain cases we accommodate them across the street, at Blair House."

"No, no, no. We're not doing 'typical.' We're putting him here. It's a big honor, right? He'll be very impressed. You know, FDR had Churchill stay here during World War I."

Lumpton shot Judd a look: *Please* say *something.*

Judd stirred. "Sir, there are serious security issues."

"Like what? They're gonna plant *bugs*? Come on. He's staying here. Twiggy—do we know yet if he's bringing someone?"

Lumpton consulted his notes. "I have thirty-seven people in the immediate entourage, not counting—"

"No, no, no," the president interrupted. "You're being very slow today, Twiggy. Did you only have Grape-Nuts for breakfast? You need to eat more. Putin's divorced. I'm asking, is he bringing a friend? A squeeze. Someone told me he's dating some ice skater with tremendous *thighs*."

"Uh . . ." Lumpton shuffled through his papers. "I don't have anything on that, sir. Perhaps Mr. Wootten . . ."

The president turned to Judd.

"I'll have to get back to you on that, sir," Judd said. "The Kremlin tends to be guarded on those details. During the Soviet era, we didn't even know if Andropov had a wife. It's probably safe to assume that Mr. Putin doesn't lead a monkish existence."

"What's the name of that female rock group he threw in jail?"

"Pussy Riot."

Mr. Trump smiled. "Pussy Riot. Find out from the CIA who he's *shtupping*. Not that they know anything. Idiots. Twiggy."

"Sir?"

"Tell Sergey we would be very happy if he brings a friend."

"Yes, sir."

"Or two friends." The president grinned. "Then he could have a pussy riot in the Lincoln Bedroom. What would old Abe think of that, huh?"

"If I may, sir?" Beulah said. "Not to put the cart before the horse, but that could be a complication."

"How?"

As a hospitality professional, I knew right away what concerned Beulah. And I didn't envy the poor thing having to explain it.

The evangelicals had been stalwart in supporting Mr. Trump, a thrice-married man. They'd withheld comment during the "grab 'em by the pussy" unpleasantness, and the Stormy Daniels unpleasantness. And the other unpleasantnesses. There'd been no tut-tutting or *ahem*-ing or sanctimoniousness. They'd bitten their tongues bloody throughout *The Apprentice Does Moscow* videos. But a state dinner with a presidential mistress? Evangelicals had standards.

"Sir, not to be a Debbie Downer," she said, "but the leadership of the Evangelical Council might find it awkward."

Mr. Trump scowled. "What, you're telling me the president of Russia can't bring his squeeze because it might offend the fucking *evangelicals*?"

"I'm only raising it as a potential area of discomfort, sir."

"Jesus Christ," the president grumbled. Katie sighed heavily to show that she, too, found this unbelievably prudish.

"Excuse me," the president said rhetorically. "I thought it was the twenty-first century. I didn't realize we were still in the fucking Puritan era."

Katie and Beulah took off the earrings and went at each other. Katie declared she was tired of hearing about the "delicate sensibilities of these idiots." Who were they "to dictate morality to the president of the United States"? Beulah, now in full Big Momma mode, countered that white evangelicals constituted the president's single most loyal core. Their support had never wavered, despite "some challenging moments." (Delicately put, I thought.) What purpose was served, she said, by "making these folks sit down to dinner with some Russian strumpet with tremendous thighs?"

She immediately apologized to the president for her choice of words. No matter. Mr. Trump was loving it. He liked to watch the female wrestlers on the Fox show *Bitch-Mania Smackdown*. Fox had tried without success to pitch it as "family fare."

Lumpton came to the rescue with a proposal: Why not invite Russian Orthodox patriarch Kirill to the dinner? Seat him with the evangelicals. It would divert them from harrumphing about Mr. Putin's strumpet and her tremendous thighs. He'd regale them with stories about how Mr. Putin was making Russia Orthodox again.

Katie and Beulah wiped each other's blood from their fingernails. Beulah said she thought it was "Solomonic." Mr. Trump expressed his approval by not calling Lumpton Twiggy anymore.

Outside the Oval, Katie said to me, "What did he mean by that 'Monsignor Nutterman' crack?"

"Who knows?" I said.

34

Paul called from the pay phone at his luxury residence at the Metropolitan Correctional Center. Oleg had thought it over and was agreeable to a meeting.

I greeted the news with mixed emotions.

Where, this time? North Korea? Bhutan?"

"Russia."

"Russia?" I said.

"He says you tried to kill him last time. He only feels safe on home turf."

"It wasn't us who did the shooting," I said, weary of explaining. "I was there."

"Any progress on my pardon? This place is depressing, Herb. I'm going to end up like Jeffrey Epstein if you don't get me out of here."

I couldn't tell if Paul was threatening to hang himself, or if he was suggesting that someone might hang him and make it look like suicide. I didn't really want to get into it.

"The president said to tell you, 'Hang tight.'"

I realized this was an unfortunate choice of words. I sympathized with Paul's predicament. With the election approaching, the dozen odd members of the Trump White House Alumni Felon Association were sweating it out about pardons. But Mr. Trump could hardly free them in the middle of a general election. Talk about bad optics. I urged Paul to be patient. But patience is a tough sell to people who spend their days trying to avoid being shanked or sodomized.

Meanwhile—Russia? How was a White House chief of staff supposed to get to and from Russia in the middle of a presidential campaign without ending up on the front page of the *Washington Post*?

I explained the situation to Mr. Trump. He considered.

"Come on the Anchorage trip. You can duck out from there. The air force can fly you over and back. It's not far. Sarah Palin says you can see Russia from Alaska."

Mr. Trump's trip to Alaska was controversial. Our political people were having fits.

Senator Umtiq—a Republican—was the other Republican senator who'd voted to convict Mr. Trump. As a consequence of her vote, Umtiq was now facing a very tough primary challenge, and Mr. Trump was determined to campaign for her challenger.

I studied the atlas, looking for a place to have my tête-a-tête with Oleg. The only place that didn't look like an outpost of the Gulag archipelago was Petropavlovsk-Kamchatsky (pop. 180,000). Grim, to be sure, but less grim than anything within a thousand miles. On the plus side, there would be no need to go in Catholic drag. (I decided not to tell Miriam about this outing, in case the CIA wanted to dress me like an Orthodox patriarch.) I could be reasonably confident no one in Petropavlovsk-Kamchatsky would recognize me.

I searched the most expensive restaurants on Yelp. The choices were Da Vinci ("Very disappointing, Expensive"), Kalylan ("local folk restaurant with Dance"), and Pastrami Kamchatka ("Great wine and whole Kamchatka crab"). Pastrami? A no-brainer.

I slipped away from Mr. Trump's Anchorage rally while he was in the midst of a scorching denunciation, comparing Senator Umtiq to Benedict Arnold and predicting that she would soon take her rightful place in hell with John McCain.

The air force flew me across the Bering Sea in one of their small, unmarked planes. I was a bit nervous. Kamchatka air space is not historically known for hospitality. I didn't want to be a noodge, but I went forward to the cockpit several times to establish that Russian ground air defense knew we were friendly. We landed. I almost told the guys, "Keep the engines running."

Oleg was sitting at a corner table. (They prefer corner tables, Russian oligarchs.) Only half his normal private army was in attendance.

No sooner had I sat down than he started in with, "Why you try to kill me in Rome, Errbert?"

"Oleg," I said firmly. "Enough. Please. I didn't come this great distance to listen to you talk gibberish."

He rejoined that *he* had flown eight time zones. Hoping to end discussion on the topic, I pointed out that the bullets came just as close to hitting me as they did him.

"Russian oligarchs tend to have more mortal enemies than someone who's spent his entire career running hotels. So can we please move on?"

We ordered our whole Kamchatka crabs. I'd have preferred pastrami, but Kamchatka crab you can't get back home. To be companionable, I joined Oleg in shots of the local kelp-infused vodka—which I do not recommend—and we got down to business.

He listened to what I had to say.

"If Donald want videos to continue, why he don't post them? I gave you thumb drive."

I'd anticipated this question.

"Frankly, Oleg—and don't take this personally—there was concern that the thumb drive might contain malware or something else that might infect our computers. It's the White House. You can't just insert Russian thumb drives into our computers. I'm sure you understand."

He looked at me curiously.

"*You* don't look to see what is on thumb drive?"

"No. As I just told you. Out of concern for security."

He smiled.

"So, this explains. Now everything is making sense. Okey-dokey, arty-choky." He seemed greatly amused.

I asked, "Is there something on it other than your, may I say, highly indiscreet videos of Mr. Trump interacting with the beauty contestants?"

Our crabs arrived. I can report that Kamchatka crabs are identical to Alaska king crabs. Their six-foot leg spans make them look like the aliens in *War of the Worlds*. Oleg stuffed his napkin into his collar and dug in.

"What's word you use? For what Donald do with girls?"

"Interacting."

He laughed and snapped a meter-long crab leg in two with feral delectation.

"Interacting. Yes. *Much* interacting by Donald with girls. So . . . Donald tells eighteen girls: each of you will win, pussycat. But first you must make *interacting* with me.

"So. They make interacting. But—only one girl can win. Which is leaving seventeen girls unhappy. But Oleg, being good friend to Donald, says he will make okay. Oleg gives girls presents, money. Bling. Much bling. Bling, bling, bling."

"Yes, Oleg. I get it. Lots of bling. And?"

"It's expensive, making seventeen girls happy. But Oleg does. Because is good friend. But one girl—Katya is her name.

Miss Ukraine. Oh, she is *wery* unhappy not to win. She say, 'Fuck off with bling. This is not right. Donald promise me I win. I don't win. I will make *big* noise.'

"I say to her, 'Darling. No. Take bling. You are young. You are beautiful. You give men erection from distance of a thousand meters. Go be model, find nice rich husband.'

"But she says no. This is not right, not fair. Interacting with Donald was *wery* unpleasant. She will make fuss. Ukrainians. *Wery* difficult people. So."

Oleg tore off another primeval crab limb. I waited.

"Yes? I said.

"She died."

Oleg shrugged.

"She . . . *died?*"

"Um. Wery sad."

"Died . . . of what?"

"Who knows. Wirus, maybe."

"Wirus?"

"Um. From bacterias."

I was beginning to get a wery bad vibe.

"Oleg," I said, "are you telling me this woman died of . . . the same thing Glebnikov died of?"

"Maybe. Who knows?"

I tried to process.

"Oleg," I said, "is there something on the thumb drive *other* than the videos?"

"Yes, of course."

"What, exactly?"

"Some conwersations between me and Donald."

"About . . . ?"

"Me telling Donald that girls are making fuss. And he's saying, 'Can you take care of?' And I'm saying, 'Yes, okay.'"

I felt my chest constricting.

"He said . . . 'Can you take care of?' Yes."

"But that only means . . . Oleg. He didn't specifically ask you to . . . kill someone?"

"No. Of course. He mean give them bling, whatever. Whatever is needed to make them not make fuss."

I exhaled so hard I thought I might pass out from lack of oxygen. "Phew" does not begin to express my relief.

Oleg said: "Donald is wery naughty boy, yes. But he's not asking Oleg to extinkuish girl."

"Understood, yes. But you say this Katya creature died? What . . ."

"After contest, Katya is becoming girlfriend of Oleg. For a while, it's nice. She is wery, wery hot, this girl. But soon she is becoming big pain in ass. Making all kinds trouble for Oleg. So, she get sick from wirus. *Dasvidaniya.* Bye-bye, Katya."

I suppose smearing Oil of Oleg on a troublesome girlfriend is one way of saying, "I don't think this relationship is going anywhere." Still. Russian oligarchs. One despairs.

I said, "So, just to be clear, Oleg: there is absolutely no suggestion whatsoever on the tape that Mr. Trump asked you to . . ." I couldn't bring myself to finish the sentence.

"No, no. *But,*" he said, arriving at the nub of the matter. "Errbert. *Think* what media—enemies of people!—will say if they hear tape of Donald saying, 'Can you take care of?' And then knowing Katya dies. Would make big problem for Donald, I think."

As October surprises go, it would be, yes, a Category 5 lulu.

"Oleg," I said, "I must tell you that I find all this very disappointing. This is *not* how friends treat each other. Mr. Trump is hugely fond of you."

"Errbert. Listen to Oleg. Oleg *loves* Donald. Donald is my kind of guy. *Here* is how friends treat each other: I do you favor. You do me favor. All Oleg is asking is for Donald to make

Glebnikov Act go poof. He's president. He can do this. Look how Republicans wote to acquit him in Senate trial. All Donald have to do is tell them take away Glebnikov Act. Then Donald have four more years. So, let's have more crab. It's good, eh?"

I spent much of the flight back across the Bering Sea brushing my teeth and gargling with everything other than hydraulic fluid to rid my mouth of the foul aftertaste of kelp-infused vodka. I can't even think about it.

Mr. Trump listened to my report.

"I knew this was going to happen," he said casually, as if he'd predicted rain and here it was, raining.

He *knew* what was on the thumb drive? No wonder he didn't want to hand it over to White House IT folks to post it on Facebook.

"That asshole," he said. "He squirts nerve agent on his girlfriend and threatens to pin it on me? Fuck Oleg."

Mr. Trump's legendary refusal ever to back down is often attributed to his having been mentored by the infamous Roy Cohn. (Who may actually be rotting in hell.) I would only point out that it was Winston Churchill (former White House guest) who said, "Never, never, never, never give in!" Still. What a mess.

"In principle, sir, I agree. Fuck Oleg. But the optics—"

"Fuck the optics."

Next thing I knew, he picked up the phone and asked to be put through to some general at the Pentagon. I heard the word "drone."

I said to myself, *Nutterman, this is not a conversation you need to hear.* I made what the Brits might call an "Ovalexit," and a lot more quickly than they do their -exits.

If Katie had been privy to this, she'd have said, "How many presidents facing a horrible blackmail situation like this would have the courage to say, 'Fuck the optics'?"

35

With the Russian runoff election in early October, the Putin visit in mid-October, and our election in early November, it was shaping up to be a fall to remember.

Before leaving Pastrami Kamchatka with the ghastly tang of kelp-infused vodka in my mouth, I'd managed to persuade Oleg to give us until the end of October to get the Glebnikov Act repealed.

A stalling tactic at best, and probably futile. Getting 51 percent of the House and Senate aboard this legislative choo-choo was as likely as John McCain making snowballs in Hades. But desperate times call for desperate measures.

I implored Mr. Trump to get Mr. Putin to intercede with Oleg. But he waved that away.

Frankly, I was beginning to suspect that he *had* asked Mr. Putin and that Mr. Putin was being cagey, in order to maintain leverage. Maybe all along Putin had been using Oleg as a proxy blackmailer. Poor Mr. Trump. Bad enough to be blackmailed by one Russian. But two—and one of them president? Sub-suboptimal.

While reviewing the invitation list for the state dinner, I saw that Mr. Trump had crossed out Senator Biskitt's name. He was highly displeased at Squiggly's failure to wrangle a majority of senators to our cause.

Squiggly was now putting all his energy into getting the Joint Chiefs to sound the alarm over the Molybdenum Gap. But the JCs were having none of it. To help, I got Mr. Trump to okay Squiggly telling them that he was considering mothballing two carrier battle groups *and* converting all military-base golf courses into bombing ranges. That might bring them around.

I wondered if I should tell Squiggly he'd been dropped from the guest list. It was the hot ticket of the social season. Maybe it would light a fire under his little rear end.

The president certainly wasn't one to hide his ire under a basket, as the saying goes. He'd done two rallies for Squiggly in South Carolina without so much as mentioning his name. Instead, he'd gone into rhapsodies about the wonderfulness of former governor Cricket Singh. Poor Squiggly stood there on the stage, smiling bravely, like the only boy on Sadie Hawkins Day who doesn't get chased by the girls.

I decided not to tell him he'd been dropped from the Putin dinner. It would only demoralize him. Better he should "stay frosty" and keep working on the chiefs.

The Democrats—that is, "Loser One" and "Loser Too"— had set aside their touchy-feely campaign theme, "Come On, America—We Are *So* Much Better Than This!" to assail him over the Putin invite.

"If Donald Trump wants to sell his soul to the devil, that's his business," Loser One thundered, shaking a bandaged hand in the air. (He'd sprained it pounding the podium during a previous speech.) "But I don't like him putting America's soul up for sale! I won't have it! And the American *people* won't have it!"

Loser Too was doing her best to sound the tocsin of outrage, but she was struggling. She gave the impression she'd rather talk about Medicare extension, family leave, student debt relief, and how Wisconsin was coping with the influx of former Somali warlords who for unclear reasons wanted to live in Waukhegan.

She didn't like the idea of Vladimir Putin having a pussy riot in the Lincoln Bedroom, but her Midwest Mom "Hey, who's up for pie?" shtick hampered her from projecting red-hot indignation. Her tsk-tsking and tut-tutting was having some effect, though. Our pollster, Boyd Crampon, reported that her umbrage was "getting traction among midwestern women who belong to book clubs." Progress.

Former UN ambassador and Trump darling Cricket Singh was dispatched to the Midwest to sound the theme that "diplomacy doesn't mean you *like* the other person," and to assure voters that Mr. Trump "was definitely going to count the silverware before Putin leaves. You betcha!"

In the first debate with Loser One, Mr. Trump unveiled what he said was "the real reason" for the Putin invite, namely that he wasn't about to "sit on my ass and let Russia become Red again." I thought this brilliantly reframed the invitation as vital to national security, as opposed to caving to blackmail.

"We all know what happens when Russia goes Communist, folks," the president explained. "First, they kill everyone. Then whoever's left gets sent to Siberia. Then they put up the Berlin Wall. Not that I hate all walls. Some walls you need. But we're not gonna let Russia go Red. That's why I'm showing our support for Putin. We don't need another Nikita Stalin in the Kremlin. No way, folks. Not happening on my watch."

Chris Wallace, the moderator, asked, "But sir, isn't that tantamount to interfering in the Russian election?"

To which Mr. Trump neatly responded, "Yeah. So?"

That gave Loser One an opening to rehash the whole "Russia interfered in 2016" business. Yawn.

"You're not making America great again. You're making Russia great."

Mr. Trump was ready for that. He retorted: "Blow me."

The boss was firing on all pistons. I thought, *We've got this thing in the bag.*

But as the saying goes, "Whom the gods would destroy, first they make believe that the thing is in the bag."

I returned to DC to a message from my secretary, Caramella, that "Former Speaker Neuderscreech wants to speak to you. He said it's important."

Joy. And by the way, what kind of person goes around referring to himself as "former speaker"? Spare me.

"Yes, Sally?" I said, sounding very busy.

"I thought the president was simply magnificent last night."

"Yes. He was."

"It's looking like four more years."

"Let's hope. But I don't count my eggs until they're in the soufflé."

"There's been a development in the St. Peter's shooting."

"Oh? I haven't been paying much attention."

"Some tourist with an iPhone got a video of the person sitting with the Mystery Monsignor. They think it might be Oleg Pishinsky. Putin's pal. 'Oil of Oleg' Pishinsky."

"Really? Well, thanks for the call, Sally."

"What do you suppose *he* was doing at the Vatican? Going to confession?"

"Funny. Always good chatting with you."

"I'm predicting the president will end up with 289 electoral votes." Pause. "Barring an October surprise."

I inwardly groaned. "October surprise" is the generic term

for an eleventh-hour revelation that the leading candidate a) *was*, after all, born outside the US, b) was recruited by Chinese intelligence during a junior-year study-abroad program, c) keeps a statue of Robert E. Lee in his garden, with an eternal flame, or d) dispatched his chief of staff to Rome disguised as a Catholic priest to negotiate blackmail with a Russian oligarch wanted by Interpol.

"Good of you to call, Sally."

"Let's talk right after the election. I've discussed it with Cly and she's all aboard with the idea of me taking over at State."

"Very understanding of her. That's one fine lady you have there."

"Pompeo's in way over his head. But if the president insists on keeping him—though I can't imagine why he would—I could probably be talked into taking Treasury. But State is a much better fit for me."

"Well," I said, "now we really have an incentive to win."

I told the president about the phone call, rather hoping that he might pick up the phone and ask that general to order up another MQ-9 drone strike. But he just said, "What a prick," and went back to watching a tape of Mr. Colonnity comparing his debate performance to Cicero "opening a can of whoop-ass" on somebody named Catiline.

At this rate, I thought, I should install one of those take-a-number machines you see at the deli outside my office. Caramella could direct blackmailers to it, warning them that it might be a wait since there was a line. Honestly. Whatever happened to "Ask not what your country can do for you"?

36

Miriam called to say she needed to see me on a "somewhat sensitive" matter, and that she'd prefer to discuss it at her office, not the White House. That made me both curious and nervous.

On the way to her office in suburban Virginia, I told myself that 99 percent of what a director of national intelligence does surely qualifies as "somewhat sensitive." Still, I arrived at her office with a belly full of butterflies.

"Herb," she said, "I'm turning to you not because you're chief of staff, but because you and the president have history together. I know you care about him, personally. And I'm sure he . . . anyway, thank you for coming."

"What's up, Miriam?"

"The president has asked me to quote-unquote 'take care of' Oleg Pishinsky."

Take care of. That phrase, again.

"Oh?" I said blandly.

"Herb, in the hospitality world from which you come, that means one thing. In my world, it means something else. Entirely."

"Yes, I suppose. Oh dear."

"My reaction was more 'Oh shit.'"

I thought back to Mr. Trump picking up the phone to talk to that general.

"Did the word 'drone' come up, by chance?"

"Yes. Drone strikes are the one thing we do that he seems to approve. Intel? Not so much. The one time he said 'Good job' was when we took out Soleimani."

"Yes, he loved that."

Mr. Trump told the Pentagon he wanted a fleet of drones on permanent patrol above the Mexican border. He was displeased when they told him he could have them but that they couldn't fire on the migrants.

Miriam said, "I explained to him that taking out a terrorist leader with the blood of Americans on his hands was one thing. Training Hellfire missiles on a Russian citizen, on Russian soil, another."

"Valid point. Was he receptive?"

"He conceded the difference, yes."

"Good."

"He told me to do it by other means. He suggested giving Pishinsky a quote-unquote 'dose of his own medicine.' I took that as a reference to Novichok. A nerve agent we've taken to calling Oil of Oleg."

"I see. Well, I'm not saying I approve, but Oleg has been something of a royal pain."

Miriam stared.

"Herb. Help me out here."

"I'm trying, Miriam."

"What does Pishinsky have on the president? If it's some

Stormy Daniels–type thing, I don't want to know. But he's president, Herb. And Pishinsky is asshole-tight with the president of Russia. Which means that much as I'd rather not know, I need to know. So what the fuck's going on, Herb?"

I took a deep breath and told her. What else could I do? I sensed that Miriam did want to help.

"God," she said. "I so wish you'd brought this to me sooner."

We left it there—"for now," per our usual way. She thanked me for my "candor" and even gave me a hug. It's nice, ending a conversation about assassination with a hug. Takes out some of the sting.

On the eve of the Russian runoff election, President Trump tweeted: "Good luck, President Putin! Everyone in America except Loser One and Loser Too hopes you will crush Upchuckin' Anatoli Zipkin and his fellow Bolshevicks! Vote Putin! Keep Russia Great Again!"

It set off a predictable storm of howls. Mr. Trump does love to "set the tune." And people will dance. You'd think they'd know better by now. Really.

Loser One said that he was "goddamn well sick and tired of being called a Communist." It showed yet again Mr. Trump's talent—genius—for throwing the enemy off-balance.

Katie strapped on armor and mounted the ramparts. As always, she dazzled.

"Sadly, this just goes to show that Loser One and his Bolshevik running mate want Russia to fall under the hobnailed jackboot of Communist rule again. Gulag? KGB? Suppression of the church? Persecute the Jews? Bring it on! What's not to like about all *that*? Really, they should be ashamed of themselves. Meanwhile, patriotic Americans are standing shoulder to shoulder with the president."

I wondered if Katie would be spending another night at the Hay-Adams hotel across the street, rather than at home. The Borgia-O'Reilly marriage had been undergoing some pretty serious stress testing lately, between Katie's centrifuging and Romy serving as counsel to the Democrats during the Senate impeachment trial.

Then, with a bang like the secret police knocking on the door in the middle of the night, came the announcement that Anatoli Zitkin had won.

Really?

37

Really.

"What the *fuck*?" the president demanded in his now customary way of starting our morning meeting.

It was a reasonable question. Mr. Trump had ordered Admiral Murphy—aka "Dr. Frankenstein"—to shut down Placid Reflux. Now this?

Admiral Murphy launched into one of his convoluted cyber-yada-yada disquisitions on the "challenge" of shutting down "autonomous AI platforms." The president wanted to strangle him. He didn't want to hear this. I didn't much myself.

"I told you to use sledgehammers if you had to. Dynamite. Drown it in a fucking bathtub."

There were, of course, alternative explanations for Anatoli's stunning repeat victory. It was—theoretically—possible that a majority of Russians had decided that two decades of Putin rule were enough; or that Anatoli's pledge to "hang the oligarchs by their Hermès neckties" appealed to Russians who couldn't even afford ties made in Bulgaria; that Russia's youth found

Anatoli's podium-pounding, arms-akimbo, grumpy-old-uncle shtick more authentically Russian than Putin's cool, Cheshire cat affect. It was possible, too, as Patriarch Kirill was saying on Russian TV, that Zitkin's victory was the work of Satan, who was furious about the wonderful things "dear Vladimir Vladimirovich" (that is, Putin) was doing for the Orthodox Church.

Admiral Murphy assured the president that his "A-Team" had shut down Placid. But, he allowed, it was "theoretically possible she'd migrated to other servers." (Naval persons address ships and—apparently—machines by the feminine.)

The president's orange complexion glowed like a food-warming lamp.

"Migrated?"

I should have warned Murphy against using the M-word. Too close to "migrant."

"Without getting overly technical, sir, her algorithm is modeled on antibiotic-resistant bacteria. So when she detected we were trying to shut her down, she may have migrated to other servers and gone dormant, to evade detection. Then autoactivated and proceeded with her mission."

"The mission to start World War III? *That* mission?"

Admiral Murphy pointed out that Placid Reflux was designed with one objective only: to counteract and deter foreign interference in our elections.

"Judged according to that parameter, I'd say she's been a success," he said.

I wondered if inside Admiral Murphy's cybernoggin he was thinking, *If you'd punished Russia for screwing with our election in 2016, we wouldn't be in this situation. Sir.* But people probably don't get to be admirals by expressing what they really think.

"How am I gonna explain this to Putin?"

Admiral Murphy looked surprised.

"*Is* it your intention to explain it to Putin, sir?"

"He already *knows* about it!"

Admiral Murphy shook his head.

"Negative, sir. If they did, we'd know. We'd see their fingerprints. Of course it's your call, but as of now, there is no objective reason for you to explain anything to them."

The president looked baffled. He said to Miriam: "You *told* me they knew."

"Negative again, sir, with all due respect," Miriam said. "As you'll recall, I told you that we thought they *might* be on the verge of detecting. I must say, I'm reassured by what Admiral Murphy has just told us."

The president's brow furrowed.

He pointed at Miriam, then at Admiral Murphy.

"If this is some deep state bullshit, both of you are gonna spend the rest of your lives wearing orange. Meanwhile, you—Frankenstein—you're fired."

"If I may, Mr. President?" Miriam said. "What inference do you think the Russians will draw if you dismiss the head of US Cyber Command the day after Zitkin won an obviously rigged election?"

The president considered.

"All right. Frankenstein, you're unfired. For now. But stay tuned to Twitter."

The president's secretary buzzed to say that Secretary Pompeo was on the line. Mr. Trump picked up and listened.

"No, goddamnit, no!" he said. "Do *not* fucking call him to congratulate him! He stole the fucking election!" He slammed the phone down.

"He wanted to know if I'd called Zipkin. To congratulate him. Remind me—why is he running the State Department?"

Judd said, "We should issue a statement of some kind, sir."

The president reached for the remote control and unmuted Fox News. Mr. Colonnity's stentorian voice filled the Oval. As always, it was unclear if he was speaking to the viewer or to himself.

What does this mean? I'll tell you what it means. For start-ers, Brown Square is back to being Red Square. You want to know who's smiling? I'll tell you who's smiling inside that mausoleum there. Lenin. That's right. V. I. Lenin. His embalmed corpse is in there. Personally I find the idea of displaying the embalmed corpse of someone who died in 1924 disgusting. Would you take your kids to see that? *Come on, kids, let's go see Lenin's rotting corpse!* Imagine if George Washington's embalmed corpse was in a glass coffin in front of the White House. What would that say about us as a nation? I'll tell you what. *Nothing good.* What does it say about Russia that this revolting artifact is there in their front yard, like some grotesque Sleeping Beauty? My point? I'll *tell* you my point. I'm getting to it. Today that corpse is smiling. Because Russia is Red again. And that's exactly what President Trump warned of in his eloquent, beautiful tweet last night. Who *else* is smiling? Loser One. Oh yeah, *big* grin on that red mug. And his running mate, Krupskaya. Oh yeah. She's grinning, ear to ear. I can hear the clinking of vodka glasses at their campaign headquarters. They're probably all singing "The Internationale."

I whispered to Judd, "Who's Krupskaya ?"

"Mrs. Lenin."

"Yoko?"

"*Lenin.* The corpse's wife."

The TV screen split in two, showing a Fox correspondent standing outside the West Wing.

Mr. Colonnity said, "Amber Purr is at the White House. Amber, what's the reaction from the White House?"

"Nothing official so far, Seamus. We're waiting for reaction from the president. What we do know is that he is aware of the situation."

"Of course I'm fucking *aware* of the situation," Mr. Trump growled at the screen. He reached for his iPhone, buttock muscles collectively clenched.

Judd said, "Sir, perhaps it might be better to hold off until . . ."

The president ignored him, thumbs tapping away, like woodpeckers on Adderall.

The screen split into three, adding a corpulent, goateed man smoking a cigarette. He was identified as KGB defector Trofim Ulyakim.

"Mr. Ulyakim, thank you for being with us."

"Yes, Seamus. Always goot to be with you."

"Tell us—what's going on at the Kremlin right now?"

"I woot say probably carpenters are building gallows, for the hangings."

"Really?"

"No, Seamus. Am spikking in metaphor. But yes, there will be repercussings for this, sure. Putin is not happy. No. But for now, he's having mittings with top people to discuss what is next step. Will he accept result of election?" Ulyakim seemed amused. He took a puff of his cigarette. "I woot say, no."

"So you . . . hold on . . . don't go away, Trofim, I want to talk more, but we're getting a tweet from the president . . ."

The screen filled with a piping-hot presidential tweet.

Democracy is grate but something is FISHY about these election returns! Putin has made Russia great again. Why would Russians want to set the clock back to 1719? Mystery! Meanwhile Loser One and Loser Too are rejoicing! But the fat lady has not sung yet!!!!

Judd whispered to me, "Nineteen seventeen."

"What?" I said.

"The Russian Revolution."

"Did he just call Loser Too fat?"

"No. Opera reference."

Mr. Colonnity said, "There you have it, folks. Straight from the top. I say thank God Donald Trump is at the helm of the ship of state. At a time like this, we need his firm hand on the tiller of state. As he has just told us, something is stinky in Moscow."

Mr. Trump reached for the phone.

"Put me through to Putin."

Judd looked horrified. For a moment I thought he might wrestle the phone away from the president.

I signaled Miriam to say something. She was the senior government officer present. She shrugged.

Mr. Trump watched Fox as he waited to be connected.

The screen showed ancient footage of Lenin speechifying from what looked like *lobnoye mesto* in Brown/Red Square; people being denounced at the purge trials; starving Ukrainian kulaks; labor camps; Stalin smirking as nuclear missiles on trucks rolled past; the Berlin Wall going up; Khrushchev, banging his shoe at the US and hugging Fidel Castro; Brezhnev smirking beneath bushy eyebrows as even bigger nuclear missiles rolled by; CIA traitor Aldrich Ames, wearing orange, shuffling to court in leg manacles; Reagan in Berlin shouting, "Mr. Gorbachev—tear down this wall!"

The secretary came in.

"They have President Putin for you, sir."

"Vlad? Jesus fucking Christ, what the fuck is going on over there? This can't be right. No way those assholes could have won. Uh-huh. Uh-huh. Yeah? Good. That's what I'd do. Throw their Red asses in jail. Uh-huh. Uh-huh. Right. Say, Vlad, could Ukraine be involved? Maybe they used the same servers they did to help Hillary. Motherfuckers. What do you bet Biden's kid is mixed up in this? Collecting fifty big ones a month from some company that steals elections. Absolutely, I think you should consider that. In fact, it would be great if you would say so publicly. So you'll say you're looking into that? You're the best. Uh-huh. Yeah? No kidding . . ."

Miriam was shaking her head. I was pretty sure she was thinking, *Oh God, not again . . .*

The call ended. Mr. Putin wasn't in the mood for an extended chat. But then he had a lot on his plate today.

Judd asked, "What did he say, sir?"

"Number one, he's not going anywhere. Number two, they're gonna arrest whatshisname and the other Commies. Three," he added in tone of satisfaction, "he agreed with me that Ukraine's gotta be involved. I saved your sorry ass, Frankenstein."

None of us spoke.

"What? I knock it out of the park, and you all sit there like it's a funeral parlor?"

Judd said, "Well handled, sir." Someone had to say something.

Much as I wanted to praise Mr. Trump, I was—I don't want to say "aghast"—concerned that he'd blamed it on Ukraine. Though it had probably already occurred to Mr. Putin to do just that. Rather convenient, casus belli–wise.

Disgusted at our failure to fete him with confetti and huzzahs, Mr. Trump turned to his most dependable aide—his cell phone. His thumbs tapped away. A moment later, up on Fox came his tweet:

Just had perfect talk with present and future President Putin. Fake election! Zipkin and his fellow Reds will soon shiver in

Siberia! Ukraine likely in cahoots with the commies. Used same computer servers that helped Hillary in 2016! Lock them all up!

I called Miriam.

"I know Zitkin's a Communist," I said, "but he didn't steal the election. We did. It doesn't seem right he should spend the rest of his life wearing orange."

"Orange is the new red?"

"Miriam."

"Sorry. Bad taste. Oh, Herb, what can I tell you? The intelligence biz all too often boils down to a choice between shitty and shittier."

"Shouldn't Murphy's computer have anticipated this? That Putin would simply ignore the election results and throw his opponent in jail?"

"Yes. Unless Placid Reflux is playing a longer game. Putin can void the election and throw Zitkin in jail. But there may be consequences for doing that. It could weaken him. Make him look like what he is—a dictator."

"Not much comfort for Anatoli. What about your quote-unquote asset, Huggybear? He must be shitting himself about now."

"He is. As we speak, a very intense discussion is taking place at Langley."

"Are they going to exfilate him or whatever you call it? Get him out of there?"

"Well, there are those who want to do that. And those who want to leave him in place."

"Where do you stand?"

"Above the fray."

"Miriam."

"Herb. The DNI's role is not to micromanage. Langley will

make the right call. Which is to say, choose between the shitty choices."

Miriam detected the note of dejection in my voice. She asked me to come to her office. She had something to show me.

"I obviously don't need to point out how sensitive this is," she said, placing the transcript in front of me.

She pointed to the letters "XMHUG/B" on the top page.

"That's our guy Huggybear," she said. " 'Z' is Zitkin. This was recorded just after the results came in, around 2 a.m. Moscow time."

"And these blacked-out bits?"

"Redactions where Zitkin said Huggybear's name."

I read:

z: Well, [REDACTED] we're fucked for sure now.

XMHUG/B: How did this happen? Who did this?

z: I don't know. No one seems to. It appears we have a guard-
     ian angel.

XMHUG/B: Guardian devil, you mean. They're going to arrest
     us all.

z: Yes, I expect.

XMIIUG/B: Why are you so fucking calm?

z: I don't know, [REDACTED]. You know the saying, "Where
     there are no alternatives, there are no problems"?

XMHUG/B: No, I don't. And it seems to me that there are
     alternatives. We could renounce the results ourselves.

z: Not a very glorious ending.

XMHUG/B: Fuck glory!

z: Shall I tell you a secret, [REDACTED]? Part of me—not a
     big part, mind you—has always felt that you haven't really
     paid your dues as a Communist until you've—

XMHUG/B: Shat yourself in the middle of a speech in Red
     Square?

z: [Laughs] Well, yes, I paid those dues. But Lenin was in jail for one year, plus three years of exile. Stalin got—what?—eight months, and two years exile. Trotsky, four years in Siberia. Then the ice ax in his skull. Solzhenitsyn was eight years in the Gulag. He parlayed that into a Nobel Prize.

XMHUG/B: [Exasperated] What are you saying, Anatoli Ivanovich?

z: Only that if we do get sent away, it's not the end, necessarily. We'd be heroes. We'd have respect. Come back sanctified.

XMHUG/B: I've got a better idea. Leave Russia—quickly. And continue the struggle from there. Paris is—

z: [Laughs] I don't see them writing ballads about us if we do that, [REDACTED]. Come, old boy. Courage! We'll have time to write our memoirs. We'll be best-selling authors when we get out. Maybe we'll get a Nobel. I call dibs on the title *One Day in the Life of Anatoli Zitkin*.

Miriam said: "He's rather likable, isn't he?"

38

In due course, the Kremlin announced that the election results were "nullified in consequence of malevolent and criminal interference with the organs of electoral democracy." It was further announced that given the "grave nature of the situation," President Putin had "graciously consented to continue in office until such a time as another election can be arranged."

Poor old Anatoli and other top Communist Party officials were taken into "protective custody." The Ministry of Justice issued a statement that they were "cooperating with the investigation." Ominously for Ukraine, a further bulletin announced the discovery of "involvement by anti-Russian elements tied to the Kiev regime." Buttocks were clenching in Kiev.

Mr. Trump approved of these developments in a fusillade of tweets. He was looking forward "more than ever" to the upcoming Putin visit.

The liberal mainstream media was, needless to say, outraged. Putin had just nullified a national election without presenting so much as a shred of evidence that it had been rigged. And *still* Trump was rolling out the red carpet? Katie might yet get to unveil her brilliant "How many presidents can claim to have been impeached *twice*?"

Loser One and Loser Too found themselves between the proverbial rock and hard place. On the one hand, they didn't want to look pro-Commie by defending Comrade Zitkin's victory. On the other hand, the international community was loudly *ahem*-ing and tut-tutting about the "interminability of the Putin regime." Not a lot of gratitude for Mr. Putin for his gracious consent to stay on.

Further complicating things: the Dems were desperately trying to attract the disappointed postconvention Socialist millennials. The kids regarded Comrade Zitkin as a Russian version of their own beloved grumpy Uncle Pinko. They were denouncing the nullified election on Facebook and Instagram with taunts of "OK Putin." And wearing "Free Zitkin" T-shirts and hats. In France, people went about with "Je Suis Anatoli" buttons. (Arguably the least compelling political slogan in history.) At home there was talk of a concert in Madison Square Garden. Bruce Springsteen was rumored to be involved. (It turned out he was not.)

The Zitkin groundswell, such as it was, was creating pressure to denounce his jailing. But that risked alienating moderate elements of the Loser Coalition, short on sympathy for Commies caught with their pinkies in the cookie jar.

It was also complicating things for Mr. Trump. Was it appropriate, under the circumstances, to honor Mr. Putin with a state visit, red carpet, twenty-one-gun salute, and all the trimmings? The optics were not ideal.

Loser One was on surer ground, here. His campaign was messaging: "Rescind the invite!" Slogan-wise, a bit thin for the

Socialist millennials, who preferred more caffeinated slogans like "Capitalism sucks!" and "Down with heteronormativity!"

The Trump campaign capitalized on "Rescind!" by framing it as "Communist sympathizing."

Lots of moving parts.

The president always kept Miriam waiting. Rather than humiliatingly twiddle her thumbs in the West Wing reception area, she would come to my office to "hang."

I'd grown fond of Miriam, and she, perhaps, of me. I knew she disapproved of Mr. Trump, and as I always took his side, she surely must have disapproved of me; but she was always sweet to me.

My office TV was as usual on, sound muted, to Fox. Not because I didn't want to miss a word of Mr. Colonnity's Ciceronian monologues, or Mr. Fartmartin's baby-faced harrumphings about deep state coups—poor lamb; if only he knew—but because I needed to know what they were Trump-whispering, in case I had to manage it.

Fox showed Anatoli and his fellow Bolshies shuffling into the glass defendant's box in the Russian courtroom. He wasn't smiling.

I said to Miriam, who was knitting as she watched with one eye, "Is one of those Huggybear?" It was an indiscreet question, I realized.

"Funny you should ask," Miriam said, continuing to knit and purl. "Not that it's in the least funny. But that's what I've come to discuss with the president. We may have a problem."

By now a half dozen very glum-looking Communists were crowded behind glass in the courtroom, listening to a glum-looking prosecutor read out the charges.

Miriam did a head count.

"Looks like the full politburo," she said. "Minus Huggybear. That's the problem."

"How do you mean?"

"They've got him in the deep freeze."

"Barbaric."

"In isolation, Herb. Not an actual freezer."

"Ah."

"That means they're interested in him. And that's not good."

"Oh dear."

"Oh shit."

"Are they onto him?"

"Possibly. Huggybear is . . . well, there's no reason I can't tell you, for heaven's sake. He's just a tired old Marxist professor. Not the type to hold out when they attach the electrodes. If it comes to that, he'll start warbling before they even get him strapped in."

"Do you think he's told them?"

"Sure hope not. Maybe he'll distract them by reciting his favorite bits from *Das Kapital*."

I groaned. Outwardly. I no longer groaned inwardly.

"The president won't like that at all, Miriam," I said.

"No."

"Shouldn't we have given him a cyanide pill?"

"He's not high-level enough. Like I said, just a tired old Commie. It's not like he has access to nuclear launch codes or is up to speed on their biowarfare programs. We only turned him so he could identify promising students for recruitment."

"Then he wouldn't have much to give them, would he?"

Miriam seemed to hesitate. "No. But as the CP just won a rigged election, *and* as he's on the CIA's payroll . . . there'll be some dot connecting."

A secretary came to say the president would see her now.

"Good luck," I said.

"Thanks. Tell my husband and the children my last thoughts were of them."

Caramella buzzed to say that Senator Biskitt was on the line. I hoped he was calling with good news on the Joint Chiefs/ Molybdenum Gap front. But probably not. Why? Because that would be good news. And no one ever called me with good news.

"Say, Herb, a bunch of us senators were talking. They all got their invitations to the Putin dinner. Then Cricket Singh called me about something, all chirpy, but she's *always* chirpy, and she mentioned as how she'd gotten *her* invite. I checked with my office. Mine seems not to have arrived."

I groaned, outwardly.

"I was going to call you about it," I prevaricated. "But while I've got you—any progress with the chiefs?"

"I'm shakin' it, boss, I'm shakin' it. I even dropped a hint on them that the Armed Services Committee is considering turning all their golf courses into bombing ranges. Meanwhile, Admiral Fletcher—the CNO—he's all bent out of shape on account of the *McCain* decommissioning. I could threaten him with mothballing a couple of carrier battle groups. But he's likely to call that bluff."

"Well, keep at it. The president is counting on you."

"Right. So my invitation is on the way? Herb? You there?"

"Sorry. They're arraigning Zitkin and the other Reds . . . Wow . . . They just charged him with treason."

"Reckon that'll teach him to keep his little red mitts out of the ballot box. So, the invite . . ."

"They're *all* being charged with treason. Oy."

"Herb?"

"Senator?"

"Where's my damn invite?"

Deep breath.

"I'm afraid I don't have much good news for you on that, Senator. The president has decided to make the dinner more, uh, intimate. They've been paring the list pretty heavily. Culling, really."

Silence.

"Don't give me that, Herb. Don't give me that. Half the damn Senate is attending that dinner. Cricket *Singh* is attending. She's been out of government for two years."

"Has it been that long?"

"What's going on, Herb? This is no way to treat your friends."

I was tempted to quote "Ask not."

"You've been a rock of Gibraltar," I said. "And to think that only three years ago you were calling the president a 'kook' and a 'retard' and a 'disgrace to the human race' and all those other names."

"Then how come I'm being dropped like a sack of *cee*-ment?"

Awkward. Like the time I had to tell Governor Christie of New Jersey he couldn't sit in the president's limo because the president was afraid the tires would blow.

"I don't know what to tell you, Senator, so I'll just give it to you neat. Rightly or wrongly, the president feels that you've let him—and the country—down by failing to deliver on the repeal. The way I see it, I think you're a victim of the high standard you set for yourself."

Silence.

"Okay. But there is one thing you *can* do for me, Herb."

"Name it."

"Go fuck yourself."

So that went well.

39

A nd here's the irony: if Squiggly had called twenty-four hours later, there'd have been no reason for him to call.

The dinner was off. The Putin visit was off. Off, as in "not happening."

I was aboard Air Force One with the president and Katie and the rest of the retinue, en route to a big preelection rally in Philadelphia.

The president liked to watch "enemy TV"—CNN and MSNBC, that is—prior to rallies. He said it got his blood going, and also gave him fresh material with which to denigrate Chip Holleran and Jake Tapper and the other Trump bashers.

The president was glowering at Jake Tapper when Tapper suddenly paused in mid–Trump disparagement. He put a finger to his earpiece and furrowed his brow.

"Hold on . . . we're getting word out of Moscow . . . the Putin visit has been postponed. Or canceled. We'll get that clarified as soon as we can. Meanwhile, from the Kremlin comes the announcement that the upcoming visit to Washington by President Vladimir Putin of Russia is no longer upcoming. It is in fact not-coming . . ."

I was in the presidential cabin, handing Mr. Trump various documents to sign: deportation orders, notifications of intent to withdraw from various trade pacts, pardons for military personnel charged with crimes against humanity and such.

"*What* the fuck did he just say?" the president said. He muted CNN and unmuted Fox News, where Dana Perino and Juan Williams were discussing a report from London that Rudy Giuliani had fallen asleep with a lit cigar and caused a fire in the Ecuadorean embassy.

One of the military aides came in with a secure fax from our US embassy in Moscow.

It wasn't lengthy, but Mr. Trump doesn't like to read, so I read it to him. It confirmed what Tapper had just announced. Dmitri Peskov, the Kremlin spokesman who'd recently embarrassed Mr. Putin by wearing a $620,000 wristwatch, had issued a release: Putin would not be coming to the US, "owing to pressing matters of high importance."

"That's *all* it says?" Mr. Trump asked.

I nodded.

"Nothing about regrets or apologies?"

"No, sir."

"Why didn't he call me?" His expression changed from bewilderment to realization. "Motherfuckers!"

It took me a moment to decode this. I knew that yesterday Miriam had informed him that the CIA's asset—*what* an ironic term—was probably singing for his interrogators like the proverbial canary. Now Putin had just abruptly canceled a much-heralded visit to Washington, without so much as a courtesy call. Not hard to connect those dots.

I decided not to mention my talk with Miriam. Neither courageous nor forthcoming, I know, but this was not a caca of my making. And I've always felt that one should scoop one's own poop.

"Sir?" I said with faux innocence. "When you say 'Mother-fuckers,' to whom are you specifically referring?"

"The motherfucking deep state, Herb," he snarled.

"Sorry, sir? Still not following you, there."

The president was too livid to tell me (what I in fact already knew). He plunged into a silent, mineshaft-deep funk. I asked if he wanted me to tell the cockpit to turn back to DC, but he waved me away.

I went back to huddle with Greta and Katie. I couldn't tell them about Huggybear, but we had to have some response ready for the slavering beasts awaiting us on the tarmac in Philadelphia. (The press corps.)

I glanced at the TV monitor. It was set to MSNBC. The closed captioning said:

TRUMP-PUTIN BROMANCE! COITUS INTERRUPTUS? YOU'RE WATCHING EIGHTBALL . . .

"Herb," Katie asked, "is there something you're not telling us?" A sharp one, that Katie Borgia-O'Reilly.

I sighed.

"Katie, dear. This is an artichoke with many leaves. But for now let's take it one leaf at a time. What do we say in Philadelphia?"

"That on the whole, we'd rather *not* be in Philadelphia," she said, wittily inverting the W. C. Fields line.

The enemies of the people were waiting behind the Secret Service rope line like cattle, mooing and baying. Katie gamely approached on high heels as the rest of us scurried like beetles into the motorcade.

I got into "The Beast," the presidential limo, with Mr. Trump. The TV was preset to Fox. As we sped off, we watched Katie take up her position in the hot glare of the TV cameras and flashes—a thousand points of spite.

"Hi," she said girlishly. "Great to be back in Philadelphia. Great city. Love Philadelphia."

"What the fuck is she doing?" the president said.

"Her *best*, sir," I said a bit sharply. He scowled at me and returned his gaze to the TV.

Katie was beset by a tsunami of shouted questions. She gave them her raised-eyebrow *do-you-want-me-to-answer-or not?* What a cool customer, that girl.

The tsunami broke over her; the waters receded, swirling about her attractive ankles. She said in her—I don't want to say "zombielike"—robotic way, as if she were channeling from a spaceship hovering above Earth:

"The president completely understands why President Putin is postponing his visit. Look at all he has to deal with right now. An attempted coup by Communists. In a way, you might say that President Trump is dealing with almost the same thing, here. Sadly. What with this pink pair of Socialists running against him. Let's just hope they don't try to steal the election."

"He didn't postpone it," Mr. Trump growled at the TV. "He canceled it! Now the Kremlin's going to say, 'We didn't postpone it. We canceled it! Because Trump and Zipkin were in cahoots. And we've got proof.'"

The president had let the cat out of the bag. So I more or less had to ask, "Cahoots, sir? Proof?"

"Shut up, Herb. I'll explain later. I gotta concentrate on what I'm gonna say."

• • •

All in all, I thought the president did a commendable job at the rally, considering what must have been going on inside his head as he stood in front of twenty thousand people.

They'd had trouble filling the arena. At the last minute, thousands of unemployed coal miners and their families had to be bussed in. It must have been a thrill for them to be there, breathing the same air as their champion, the president. True, they were still waiting for him to make good on that 2016 campaign pledge to "bring back coal."

At first, their cheering wasn't what I would call "robust." But Mr. Trump soon warmed them up, telling them how the Democrats were going to confiscate their guns and give what few coal-related jobs remained to transgendered Guatemalan and Sudanese immigrants.

They liked his riff on Nancy Pelosi's "horrible teeth," though it appeared most of them didn't seem to know who Nancy Pelosi was. It didn't matter. What mattered was that Mr. Trump hated her. That was good enough for them.

Entertaining as it all was, I braced, waiting to see how he'd deal with the dead eight-hundred-pound Russian bear on the living room floor.

Katie joined me, a bit out of breath.

"Did he watch?" she asked.

"He thought you were magnificent," I said.

"Herb, what the fuck is going *on*?"

"Let's listen," I said.

"So tonight, on my way here, to *beautiful* Philadelphia. *Such* a great city. Philadelphia. Great people. Philly cheesesteak? Come on! Who doesn't love Philly cheesesteak? Am I right? You know I'm right, folks."

The coal miners didn't join in the paean to Philadelphia

cheesesteaks, but then they were from western Pennsylvania, where they probably have their own regional heart-attack-inducing cuisine.

I telepathically prompted: *Russia. You were talking about Russia.*

"So on the way here tonight, we got word from Russia"— telepathic message received—"that President Putin can't make it, after all. Is that sad, folks?"

The audience appeared to have no strong opinion.

"It makes *me* very sad. Why? Because I was looking forward to showing him what a great country this is. Washington? Not so great."

That brought them to their feet. You'd have thought he just announced free cheesesteaks or whatever suicide hoagies they have in western Pennsylvania.

He quieted the crowd.

"We were gonna have *such* a great visit. Very sad. But no wonder President Putin couldn't get away. Look what happened to him. Look what the Commies tried to do to him. They tried to steal the election!"

This didn't seem to bother the folks much.

"Let me tell you something, folks. You don't *do* that to Vladimir Putin."

No roars of approval, but enough murmuring to suggest general agreement that no, this was probably not a smart thing to do to someone named Vladimir.

"The reason I invited him in the first place? To show our support for him. After the disgusting Commies tried to steal the election the first time. What is with it Commies, anyway?"

For a moment I thought we were segueing into Henny Youngman "Take my wife—please!" territory. But then like a large orange matador, Mr. Trump deftly pivoted into an inspired descant about how after Mr. Trump crushed Loser One and

Loser Too, they were going to move "back" to Russia and run against Mr. Putin in the next election, on the Communist Party ticket.

"*Oooh*," Mr. Trump said, trembling and shaking his arms the way he does when he mocks people with degenerative muscle disease. "I bet President Putin is *sooo* scared!"

40

The next day the Kremlin clarified: the Putin visit was not "postponed." It was "canceled." Emphatic, terse, with just a hint of "And fuck you."

"I gotta call him," Mr. Trump said.

"Sir, are you sure that's a good idea?" I said. "What if he . . . what if he asks you directly if we were involved in the hack? What will you say?"

"I'll think of something."

"Oh, sir."

Much as I admired Mr. Trump's quick thinking and ability to charm—he had Kim Jong-un eating out of his hand within five minutes, though to judge from Dear Leader's physique, he'd probably eat out of anything—I strongly felt that improv was not advisable in these circumstances.

He picked up the phone and asked to be connected with Mr. Putin. I waited with him. We watched Fox. He became fidgety. He kept getting up to throw cans of Diet Coke at squirrels in the Rose Garden.

"Fucking tree rats. We need a wall around *that*," he groused.

Two hours passed, which is a lot of Fox and an eternity to a man accustomed to getting people on the blower, pronto.

His phone rang. He picked up, listened, frowned, and hung up.

"President Putin is unavailable," he said. "Unavailable? Herb. The president of Russia is not taking my calls? Well, that's just fucking great." He sounded so like my mother. (Though she didn't use four-letter words.)

"Shall we get Miriam's input?" I suggested.

He looked at me.

"Herb, do you not see that Miriam and Admiral Frankenstein are the reason Putin is not taking my phone calls? Fuck their input. I'll tell you who's going to get *output*. Miriam fucking Jones and Admiral Frankenstein. Deep state motherfuckers. I'm gonna fire both their asses." He paused. I could see the cogs moving as he thought it through. "*That* might make Putin happy again."

I told Mr. Trump that it was a bold move, to be sure. But that crippling America's intelligence infrastructure in order to appease America's principal—I didn't want to say "enemy"— adversary could have political costs.

The election was ten days off. I don't claim to be a political savant, but inflicting an October surprise on yourself struck me as unorthodox. Surely it's preferable to inflict it on your opponent.

"How many intelligence agencies are there?" he asked.

"Seventeen, I think."

"How much do we spend on these bozos?"

"Fifty billion? I'd have to—"

"Here's what I'm gonna do. I'm gonna fire the whole fucking bunch. That's *got* to make Putin happy. Look at the money we'd save. It's not like we're getting value for it. Right? Aside from the drones. The drones, we'll keep. We'll let the Pentagon run them. They'll love that. And the savings—we'll spend that on the wall. *Herb*," he said, suddenly excited.

"Sir?"

"We build the wall with whatsit called? Oleg's metal . . ."

"Molybdenum?"

"Yeah. That. Oleg'll make so much fucking money he'll be able buy the entire US Congress and Senate and get the anti-Oleg law repealed. Herb, do you see how brilliant this is? Everyone is happy. Putin. Oleg. The intelligence people? Not so much. But fuck 'em. They've had it in for me from day one, when they told those horrible lies about the size of my inauguration crowd. It's brilliant, Herb. You see how brilliant it is, right?"

I was without words.

So there it was, the Placate Putin Package—"3P" as he code-named it. He instructed me not to tell anyone. "The timing's gotta be just right."

I didn't like the sound of that. At all. The final debate with Loser One was in two days. Was he planning to unveil this three-headed monster then?

I returned to my office and pondered heavily. I was so gloomy I wouldn't have been surprised if a raven appeared and started tapping on the window.

I understood the president's urgent need to placate Mr. Putin. If Putin, or Oleg, released the tape of Mr. Trump asking Oleg to "take care of" the beauty contestants—with its odious (and I emphasize, false) insinuation that he wanted Oleg to give them all a rubdown with Oil of Oleg—that *would* be the October surprise from hell. Even the Ever Trumpers who'd offered to be gunned down by the president on Fifth Avenue might say, "Really?" On the other hand, maybe they'd just shrug and say, "Bitches had it coming."

I called Miriam on a secure line. Whom else could I turn to?

Miriam listened in her usual calm way. Unflappability in an

intelligence person is a good thing. I expected her to say "Oh shit" or "Suboptimal." But she just said, "Hm," which struck me as mild, considering.

"What do we do?" I asked.

"Well, Herb, I don't know that there's much we *can* do at this point."

"Miriam," I said, "I'm not asking for the 'Once more into the breach' speech, but there must be something."

She considered.

"Who does he listen to? Take advice from?"

"No one. He's always insisted that he's the smartest person in the room."

"He listens to those two baboons on Fox, doesn't he?"

I stiffened. "By 'baboons' do you mean Mr. Colonnity and Mr. Fartmartin?"

"Yes, Herb. Those baboons."

"I don't agree in the least with your characterization. But yes, he does listen to them. As you'll recall, Mr. Fartmartin talked him out of starting that war with Iran. Nice work. For a baboon."

"Okay. So, tell them everything you've just told me. If they're not baboons, they'll recognize 3P for what it is and Trump-whisper some sense into him, on live TV."

"Miriam. That's hardly a practical solution."

"Alternatively, you could inform Vice President Pants that the president is off his meds. And if he can tear himself away from carving satanic crop circles, he might do his duty and get the cabinet to invoke the Twenty-Fifth Amendment. And actually make America great again. By ridding us of this ghastly, toxic man."

"Miriam!"

Silence.

"Sorry. But God, that felt good. Okay, let me see if I can come up with something. I'll get back to you. Meanwhile try to stall him, eager as he is to dazzle the world yet again with his stable genius."

I hung up, reeling, and mulled. Her idea of using Mr. Colonnity and Mr. Fartmartin as Trump-whisperers might not be entirely far-fetched. I unmuted Fox.

Katie was standing outside the West Wing, a dozen boom mics aimed at her like jousting lances.

"I think it's very *obvious* why Mr. Putin canceled his trip. The left-wing, Communist-sympathizing Democrats have created an atmosphere of such hostility that Mr. Putin was probably concerned for his physical safety. And why shouldn't he be, with all the terrible things the Democrats and their vile henchpeople are saying about him? If World War III starts because the US and Russia aren't communicating? Blame *them*. They should be ashamed. They should apologize."

Katie always made me feel better. But this was no time for complacency. On to Armageddon.

41

Getting Mr. Trump to delay the rollout of 3P was tricky. There was a risk of backfire. He was always conceiving a brilliant idea no one else would have come up with, then forgetting it. A natural consequence of his superior intellect.

So I didn't mention it the next day, and I swamped him with stuff I normally wouldn't bother him with, to distract him. It seemed to work. As of late afternoon, no mention of 3P.

But few are the days in the life of a White House chief of staff that are jolt-free. Sure enough, Caramella buzzed to say a Mr. Pishinsky was on the line.

That he'd called me on a nonsecure landline—at the White House, for God's sake—did not portend well.

"Oleg," I said, "good of you to call. Why don't I ring you back on a more private line?"

"No, Errbert. What I have to say is for everyone to know."

That didn't sound good.

"*So,* my friend," he said in a hearty, oligarchy way, "how is coming repeal?"

"There's been progress," I said.

"Ah? Tell."

"The person with whom I am efforting that . . ." I didn't want to say Senator Biskitt's name on this open line.

"Biskitt," he said. "Squiggy."

So much for discretion.

". . . tells me he's making headway with his, er, military contacts. He's got them focused on molybdenum in a way I don't think they've ever been before. I think we can expect some good news on that front."

"Errbert. Enough with bullshit."

In desperation, it crossed my mind to poach a third of 3P and dangle the prospect of fifty billion bucks of molybdenum sales. What we monsignors call a Hail Mary pass. Still.

"Oleg," I said, "you've got to believe me when I say I'm doing my best."

"*Yes*, Errbert. Sure. But still no repeal. Still Oleg's money is freezing in American banks. Still Oleg can only wisit countries he don't want to wisit. So now Oleg is thinking, 'Fuck this bullshit.'"

That definitely didn't sound good.

"Election is when, Nowember 3? Okay. So, October surprise rewelation must be in October. So . . . Am looking at calendar. You have calendar, Errbert? October 31. What is Halloween?"

"A holiday."

"Okay. On Halloween, October 31, everyone get to hear on Facebook Donald asking Oleg to take care of naughty girls."

"Oleg—"

"Good-bye, Errbert. Tell Squiggy also fuck himself."

I called Miriam.

She listened to my latest report from the Valley of the Shadow of Oleg.

"Regular rodeo you're running there, Herb. Putin on line

one, Oleg on line two. Though Putin isn't actually on line one because he's not taking the president's calls."

I found Miriam's unflappability flippant under the circumstances, and told her so.

"Okay," she said wearily, as if I'd asked her to go back to the supermarket and get the right kind of milk. "I'll add it to my to-do list. After 'kill self.'"

I was furious. Here I'd just informed the director of national intelligence that the president of the United States had been threatened, and she'd more or less yawned. I was beginning to think maybe the president was right. For this we pay $54 billion a year?

I took a deep breath and marched down the hall to the Oval. I did not tell Mr. Trump about my phone call with Miriam, in part because I was still fond of Miriam, despite her pouty teenage girl attitude; in part because she might yet get off her DNI behind and do something.

I did tell him about Oleg's October surprise.

"Fuck Oleg," he said. "We'll say it's a fake recording."

I did not find this greatly comforting, but there it was.

The future passed in front of me. I saw President- and Vice President–elect Losers One and Too standing onstage, confetti and balloons raining down on them. The band playing "Happy Days Are Here Again." Loser One pledging to restore decency to the White House. Yay, decency. Loser Too prattling on about shattering the glass ceiling. Yay, shattering. What I did *not* see was Mr. Trump on a stage, conceding. No. I saw tanks clanking up to the White House. Heard a military voice on a megaphone: "President Trump! Sir, you have been defeated in a legitimate election. You must vacate the White House, or I will have no choice but to . . ."

Oh dear.

42

It was the morning of the day of the final presidential debate. The president was shortly due to leave the White House for Phoenix. I'd asked Stefan several times to show me Mr. Trump's opening and closing statements. He had not. That was a bit unusual. Stefan's Teutonic temperament had its downside; the upside was that he followed orders. (Like certain other people did back in the thirties and forties.)

This time, instead of asking, I put a bit of steel into in my voice and insisted that he bring them to me. I heard a click of heels on the other end. Presently Stefan arrived in my office.

I read and winced.

I'd been living in a fool's paradise, convinced that the president had forgotten about 3P. Here it was, under the heading "Second-Term Agenda."

Mr. Trump, a natural speaker, did not read fully drafted texts in debates. He preferred notes. Broad brushstrokes.

—MASSIVE OVERHAUL OF SO-CALLED INTELLIGENCE
COMMUNITY!
—HUGE SAVINGS—OVER $50 BILLION!
—USE THAT WHERE IT'S NEEDED! WALL!

The next bit, Stefan had wisely rendered phonetically:

—MO-LIB-DEN-UM BEST FOR WALL BUILDING! 100%
MEXICAN-RESISTANT! WILL NEED MASSIVE AMOUNTS!
PURCHASE WITH SAVINGS FROM SCRAPPING USELESS
INTELLIGENCE AGENCIES!

It appeared Mr. Trump had modified his "Fuck Oleg" attitude.

Stefan hovered nervously, as speechwriters do, fearful that
the tone-deaf philistine reviewing their pristine prose will start
fiddling with it.

"What do you think?" Stefan asked. Speechwriters pretend
to care what we philistines think, in order to soften us up. I did
not rise to the bait.

"The president loves it," he said before I could comment.
"It's bold. It's so *him*." This was Stefan code for: *It really doesn't
matter* what *you think, Herr Obergruppenführer.*

"Our intelligence services will certainly find it bold," I said.
The notes for the closing statement consisted of:

—"CLIMATE CHANGE"—TOTAL CRAP! AMERICAN JOBS
MORE IMPORTANT THAN AUSTRALIAN KOALA BEARS!
—NO PRESIDENT IN HISTORY HAS ACCOMPLISHED AS
MUCH AS I HAVE!
—LOSER ONE WAY TOO OLD TO LEAD AMERICA.
[[OPTIONAL: CLEARLY SUFFERING FROM DEMENTIA.
SAD!]]

—LOSER TOO ALSO MAKES NO SENSE. SHE SHOULD STOP
  BANGING HER HEAD AGAINST THE GLASS CEILING
  AND PREVENT FURTHER BRAIN DAMAGE!
—SECOND TERM WILL MAKE AMERICA SO GREAT IT
  WILL HURT!
—ONLY I CAN DO IT!
—THEN IT WILL BE DON JR. AND IVUNKA'S TURN!
—HOW GREAT IS THAT, FOLKS? [[ANSWER: *SO* GREAT!]]

"Sorry I won't be there to hear it," I said, handing it back.

"Not coming?" he said, feigning disappointment. Speech-writers prefer chiefs of staff not to be present so they can't make last-minute text changes.

"Alas," I said. "Someone has to hold down the old fort."

Stefan departed, happy. I buzzed Caramella.

"Get me Oleg Pishinsky," I said.

Today was October 30, the day before his threatened Halloween surprise. I was confident that the prospect of $50-odd billion in molybdenum sales would mollify him. It wasn't repeal, but with that kind of dough the president was right. Oleg could buy every member of Congress and have enough left over to build himself a megayacht the size of an aircraft carrier. For that matter, he could build an aircraft carrier.

Caramella buzzed me back. "His office said he's cruising on his boat on the Black Sea."

"They have phones on yachts, for heaven's sake."

"His secretary said they've been having a hard time reaching it. Might be a satellite connection problem. They'll keep trying."

"Well, keep at it. It's important."

Miriam called.

"There's been a development," she said. "Meet me in the Sit Room in half an hour. Bring the president."

"He's leaving for Phoenix."

"Herb, he'll want to see this. Trust me."

Half an hour later I arrived in the Situation Room with a grumpy President Trump in tow. He did not like to be told to do things. He scowled at Miriam.

"This better be good," he said.

Miriam had brought an aide. She nodded to him. An image came up on one of the screens. It looked like a satellite feed. She told the aide to zoom in on what appeared to be a boat. She circled it with a red laser pointer.

"This was taken two hours ago. The body of water is the Black Sea, about thirty miles south of the Crimean coast. This city here"—she circled with the pointer—"that's Sochi. The yacht," she circled, "is the *Maria Ivanovna*. Oleg Pishinsky's yacht."

The president perked. He murmured to me, "I've got a little present for Oleg tonight."

I didn't let on. Meanwhile, what was all this?

Miriam said something technical to the aide. The screen changed color slightly, revealing a blurry image of what looked like another boat, at a distance from Oleg's. Miriam circled it with the pointer.

"That's a Russian navy submarine. Akula class. Akula is the Russian word for shark."

"*Jaws*," the president remarked. "Great movie."

Two small, fainter shapes appeared in front of the submarine, moving toward Oleg's yacht.

"What are those?" the president said.

"Torpedoes."

"*What?*" Mr. Trump said.

"Type?" Miriam said to the aide.

"Sixty-five," he said. "Each warhead contains 420 kilos of high explosive."

I was experiencing a range of emotions, all of which could be boiled down to *holy shit*.

The torpedoes altered course.

"Target acquired," the aide said.

"Speed?" Miriam asked.

"Up to fifty knots, depending on water temp."

The image of Oleg's yacht suddenly blurred.

"Target destroyed."

"Jesus *Christ*," the president said.

"What's the depth there?" Miriam asked.

"Seventeen hundred meters."

"Can we have the room?" Miriam said. The aide left.

"What the fuck was that?" the president asked.

"Pending confirmation, it would appear that President Putin ordered his navy to sink Mr. Pishinsky's yacht."

"With him on it?"

I almost said, "Yes. I just tried to reach him and they . . ."

"I can't come up with a plausible scenario in which he'd sink the boat *without* Oleg aboard," Miriam said. She added, "It is theoretically possible he'd do that, as some kind of object lesson. But that probability I'd assess on a very low order."

"I wanna watch it again," the president said. I've never seen Mr. Trump look so pleased.

We were halfway through the third showing when an aide arrived to say that Marine One was on the south lawn to take him to Joint Base Andrews.

"I want a tape of that," Mr. Trump said to Miriam.

She and I were left alone in the Sit Room.

"What just happened?" I asked.

"I'd say Putin decided to keep Russia great by keeping the president in office. Four more years."

I may have technically been in some kind of state of shock. I was having a hard time organizing my thoughts into coherent speech. Miriam spoke in a Q and A format.

"Did Putin know that Oleg called you to say he was going to release the tape on Halloween? Yes. How did he know this? Because Oleg's phones are tapped.

"Why would Putin do this to an old pal? To prevent Oleg from releasing a tape that could cause the president to lose the election.

"Why would Putin protect the president? Especially if he thought Trump had messed with *his* election?

"Two possible explanations. One, he concluded that the hack on his election was a rogue op by US intelligence agencies—the vaunted 'deep state'—who were fed up with being denigrated and insulted. In that scenario, the deep state decided to retaliate on its own, without presidential authorization. And to leave a calling card. So as to piss off Putin enough to go public with whatever he has on the president.

"Explanation number two. Despite knowing that the US had fucked with him, Putin took a deep breath, sucked it up, and decided to forgo the pleasure of publicly humiliating Trump. Why? Because it's in Russia's interest to keep him in office. Four more years of making America great again."

She let that sink in.

I said in a Stepford Wife tone, "The second term is going to make America so great it will hurt."

Miriam stared.

"You should use that. See you round, Herb."

She left me alone in the Sit Room. As I said, I don't find it a pleasant place. Really, it gives me the willies.

Hetta and I watched the debate that night. It would be more accurate to say that I watched the debate. Hetta didn't even last through the moderator's opening spiel about the rules.

She went off to the kitchen and made clattering noises for the next ninety minutes.

Mr. Trump's opening statement had been whittled down. 2P was the new 3P. The money saved by overhauling the intelligence community would go to the wall, but molybdenum was no longer required. Apparently, titanium was sufficiently Mexican-resistant.

The headline in the *Washington Post* the next day:

PUTIN ASSOCIATE DEAD IN YACHT EXPLOSION:
OLEG PISHINSKY, SANCTIONED BY US CONGRESS,
HAD BEEN IMPLICATED IN DEATH OF JOURNALIST

My "shout-out"—and Senator Biskitt's—came four paragraphs into the story.

> White House Chief of Staff Herbert Nutterman and South Carolina US Sen. Squigg Lee Biskitt have been actively working to repeal the Glebnikov Act on grounds of national security. But a Pentagon source asked skeptically, "Who knew there was a Molybdenum Gap?"

Caramella buzzed, with words that have caused many a White House staffer's bowels to shrivel.

"It's Bob Woodward, from the *Post*."

43

Miriam resigned as director of national intelligence before Mr. Trump initiated his postelection overhaul of—as he continued to put it—"the so-called intelligence community."

I was sorry to see her go. Paradoxical as it may sound, I felt the country was less safe than it had been in her hands. Admiral Murphy also wisely abandoned ship, before Mr. Trump could sink it from under him. The chilling image of those torpedoes whirring toward Oleg still makes me shudder.

Miriam and Murphy teamed up, as many former intelligence persons do, to start a consulting firm. I gather it's been very successful. Their client list is impressive. I sometimes speculate—to amuse myself during napkin-folding classes here at FCI Wingdale—how many of their clients got to be president or prime minister or grand mufti or whatever thanks to Deep State Strategic Solutions, LLC.

Intelligence folks weren't the only ones to "get the chop" during the "night of the long knives." Mr. Trump doesn't like to fire people face-to-face—odd, considering he rose to fame shouting, "You're fired!" That pleasant task fell to Chief of Staff Herb Nutterman. For a time, anyway.

My workload was somewhat alleviated by virtue of Mr. Trump's predilection for firing by tweet; and by having Mr. Colonnity announce some sackings. Judd got his chop soon after the election. I remember him telling me once that working in the Trump White House was "like the Kremlin under Stalin—you're always waiting for that knock on your door in the middle of the night." Putting it a bit strongly. Still.

Mr. Trump liked to fire people when they were distant from Washington, as he did with FBI director Comey, who found himself on the West Coast, suddenly without a car or plane.

Mike Pompeo learned of his abrupt "emeritus" status in Tajikistan. That must have been a jolt. He had to wait three days before a seat opened up on Air Tajik. I wonder if he whiled away the time watching his successor, Cricket Singh, on CNN, outlining her vision of US foreign policy. I've not personally read Mike's memoir, *Why the World Hates America, and Why I Hate Donald Trump*. The reviews made it sound a bit bitter.

Someone else was not happy about State Department developments, or in his case, nondevelopments: Sally Neuderscreech.

Sally was on the phone to me within, oh, it can't have been more than thirty minutes after the news broke about Cricket's appointment. Boy, was he hot. I thought his language somewhat inappropriate for a spouse of the US ambassador to the Holy See. And him a Catholic convert. I'm no theologian—or even Christian—but my sense is that Jesus Christ, who by all accounts was a very decent guy, would not approve of calling someone a "Jew bastard cocksucker" just because he didn't get to be secretary of state. Shame on you, Salamander Neuderscreech. Excuse me: *former Speaker* Salamander Neuderscreech.

But wait—there's more. He then had the nerve to call me back the next day, to tell me he "felt bad" about calling me a

"Jew bastard cocksucker." *As well you should*, I thought. He then said that he could "see [his] way through to accepting the Treasury job." Talk about gracious.

I replied that I'd be happy to take that up with the president. As soon as the next ten-thousand-year-long ice age had thawed.

He didn't like that. That bought me another anti-Semitic-themed tirade.

And what do you know: a few days later, *L'Osservatore Romano*, the Rome paper that covers the Vatican, ran a photo of "*Il Mysterioso Monsignore*," namely me, next to the iPhone photo someone had snapped of Oleg. Oleg's mug was now very recognizable, owing to the massive news coverage his death had generated.

Miriam had gotten Italian Immigration to "misplace" the photo they'd taken of me when I arrived for my meeting with Oleg. Now—*miracolo!*—it had resurfaced. And wasn't my new friend Bob Woodward fascinated by that development.

Meanwhile, the *Post*'s rival paper, the *Washington Examinator*, whose Moscow bureau chief, Peter Glebnikov, had written the series that got him smeared with Oil of Oleg, was intensively covering Squiggly's and my efforts to get the Glebnikov Act repealed.

I won't rehash the whole sorry saga. It came as no great surprise when my old friends FBI special agents Winchell and Wheary paid me another visit. I thought it was a bit dramatic, taking me away in handcuffs. Caramella cried. Hetta saw it on TV and collapsed and had to be taken to the ER. Nice going, fellas. But you can't be too careful. I might have tried to shoot it out.

There was a TV in the DC detention center. It wasn't set to Fox, so I wasn't able to see Mr. Colonnity denounce me. (I watched the tapes of it later.) How gracious of him to say that I was "in way over [my] head," and that Mr. Trump "should have kept me handing out towels at Farrago-sur-Mer. Yet another case," he told viewers, "of no good deed goes unpunished. Once again, Donald Trump tried to help someone. And how did Herb Nutterman repay him? With perfidy."

Thank you, Mr. Colonnity. It would be nice to think that he didn't get those talking points from Mr. Trump himself. I prefer not to dwell on that.

The next day, while I was persuading a large man with swastikas and other Third Reich–themed tattoos on two-thirds of his body that I really did not want to have sex with him, I looked up at the TV—while groping for some blunt instrument—and there was Squiggly. He was scampering down a corridor in the Capitol, pursued by a mob of reporters with boom mics and TV cameras. And he *did* look like a penguin on an ice floe trying to escape a sea lion.

I read his—I don't want to say "outrageous lies"—quotes in the newspaper about how he'd been taking his orders from me, that he didn't realize I'd "gone rogue" and was acting entirely on my own, and that the president had no idea at all what I was up to. Mendacity, thy name is Squigg Lee Biskitt. At the risk of sounding bitter, I hope when Secretary of State Singh retires from diplomacy she'll challenge him for his Senate seat and trounce his little gerbil behind.

That sounds bitter. So as we say in Washington: I would like to revise my prior statement. Allow me to wish Senator Biskitt all the best. What a shame it would be for South Carolina if he were, say, run over by the trolley in the US Capitol. Or eaten by a sea lion.

Allow me also to say what an honor and a privilege it was to serve in the Trump White House. I may have left in handcuffs—suboptimal optics indeed—but with head held high. At least until Agent Winchell shoved it down as he put me in the car.

Epilogue

Tempus does not *fugit* in federal detention. I cannot say that these past four years have sped by.

But then along comes Friday, which is Pancake Day, and somehow another week has passed. We on the inside also get that TGIF thrill. Then it passes, and we confront the reality that although it's the weekend, we do not "have plans."

My principal lawyer—I accumulated a total of seven, at an average of $950 an hour—has spoken to Blyster Forkmorgan, chief White House counsel, a number of times about the pardon that Mr. Trump promised me. The reasons for why "this isn't a good time" vary. Once or twice, they sounded plausible.

But there's one thing Herb Nutterman values, even above his freedom, and that is his integrity. I would never—we've stressed this to Mr. Forkmorgan again and again—rat on Mr. Trump. Herb Nutterman will take his Trump secrets to the grave. And there are quite a few of those.

I don't know it for a fact, but my sense is that Donald Jr.— here's a harmless secret for you: his Secret Service code name was "Doofus"—along with Jored and Ivunka may have had a hand (technically, three hands) in keeping Mr. Trump's hand (for a total of four) from reaching for the pardon pen. Why? Because I told them they couldn't use Marine One to fly to the Hamptons. Smart move, Herb. Would it help to say I was only following orders? Not really.

Now that the end of Mr. Trump's second term is approaching, I remain hopeful that he will fulfill his promise to his favorite Jew. But if it doesn't happen, I'm at peace with that. Since I haven't shanked or sexually assaulted anyone, and because my napkin-folding classes have been a vocational success helping our "graduates" get jobs, I'm eligible for early release in eighteen months. How excited am I? Answer: very.

Miriam came to visit me, and how lovely of her was that? She looked tired. She'd lost weight, and she was never heavy. She said she's been working her tail off, flying back and forth between DC and some city in China whose name I didn't catch. (Wonder how their last election turned out.)

It wasn't a social call. She'd heard that I'd decided after all to write a book—this book.

I was impressed. How did she know that? She smiled and said once a spook, always a spook.

She said she was sorry about how things had turned out for me. She didn't think it was fair, or right. I shrugged and said, "*Feh*,"* though my actual feelings were more complicated than I let on.

She said she was glad I was writing a book. In fact, that was why she'd come. She wanted to help. To provide context. Might help with sales, she said.

Okay, I said, I'm all ears.

(I'm not putting all this in quotes because I wasn't taking notes. But this is what she told me that day in the visitors' room.)

---

* Yiddish expression for "Whaddya gonna do?"

The shooting in St. Peter's, she said, you remember that?

Do I ever, I said.

That was me, she said. I arranged that.

What?

Out it all spilled. By that point, she'd had it with Trump. The lying, the deceit—all this is *her* words, I emphasize—denigrating his own intelligence services, who *knew* that Putin had something on Trump. His refusal to accept their word that Putin had interfered in 2016. Everything. The whole horrible enchilada (again, her words). She'd decided: enough.

I'm not saying what I did was right, she said. But at the time, it sure felt right.

That's why you tried to have me killed in Rome? I said.

No, no, no. She smiled.

When she learned I was going to meet Oleg, she arranged for my monsignor disguise. (*Not* my best-ever idea, she said; I agreed.) She also arranged for her people in Rome to stage a nonlethal—she emphasized nonlethal—shooting.

Why? To make Oleg think that the meeting was a setup. That we *were* trying to kill him, to prevent him from releasing his Trump tape. That would piss him off enough to release it. And that would doom Trump. Right?

Wrong!

As it turned out, the base *loved* watching Trump hump beauty queens. How stupid was *I*? she said. She should have known. If a critical mass of people weren't offended by the "grab 'em by the pussy" tape, why would adult movies of him doing a lot more than grabbing them by the pussy move public opinion?

She said that US intelligence actually was starting to pick up indications that the Russians might trace the hack to Placid Reflux.

That's why I called you, she said, to tell you we had to tell Trump about Placid. Not to protect him. But if the shit hit the fan, Trump would shut down CyberCom and God knows what other US intelligence operations. Not good for the country.

But that turned out to be my second big mistake, she said. Because all it did was put Trump into a state of high freak-out. And what does he do? He proactively placates Putin by inviting him for a sleepover at the White House. So if Putin does figure out about Placid, maybe he'll shrug and say, fuck it, let's move on. He's getting feted at the White House. He's won, big-time.

Putin accepts the invite. But then Oleg stops posting the dirty movies. To fake—that word!—the appearance of a quid pro quo. So it would look like it was Putin who was posting them, and he stopped because he got his White House visit.

Why would Oleg do that? Because he was pissed that Trump had failed to deliver on the Glebnikov Act repeal. So he agrees to meet with you.

You order up an air force jet to fly you from Anchorage to Petropavlovsk-Kamchatsky. And google the fine-dining spots there for your rendezvous.

Yes, Herb, Miriam said, I *was* monitoring you. From the air force plane reservation, I knew where you were going. From monitoring your computer, I knew that you'd narrowed your choice of restaurants down to three. Just in case, we wired up all three. Thank God you didn't meet him in Paris.

So I was able to listen to your entire conversation with Oleg. By the way—*kelp*-infused vodka? Yuck. And now I knew about the other shoe Oleg was threatening to drop. The "take care of" Katya part. I like to think that would have been lethal for Trump. On the other hand, *who the fuck knows?* The Trump era has proved that Americans are capable of the most extraordinary moral elasticity.

When you got back to DC, your breath *still* smelling of kelp—poor Hetta!—I asked you to come to my office. And asked you what the fuck was going on.

That was a test. I already knew. But I needed to know if you were going to be honest with me. You passed the test.

Then Murphy's jack-in-box reactivates and elects Zitkin. Placid Reflux is a Terminator. If someone won't retaliate against Russia, it will.

So it's a Red dawn over Moscow. The Commies are back. Now the fan is so covered with shit the blades can't move.

But Putin's not going anywhere. Are you kidding? He's not going to accept this bogus result. He tosses Comrade Zitkin with his fellow Bolshies into jail. Including Huggybear. Our quote-unquote asset.

I knew he'd sing within about five minutes. So before the FSB can turn his apartment upside down, I have our people plant a few items. Notes, in a facsimile of Huggybear's own handwriting. Stuff about procedures in case we need to exfiltrate him in a hurry. Phone numbers. And a vague but revealing note about a US cyberpenetration of their electoral infrastructure.

Why would I do something like that? To make Putin go ballistic. So he'd think that Trump had double-crossed him. And wouldn't interfere again on Trump's behalf.

So there you have it, Herb—the alpha and omega of the deep state's dark op: to get Russia not to interfere in an American presidential election. Pretty nefarious, huh?

For a while I thought it had worked, she said. That I'd finally gotten it right. Putin canceled the visit, wouldn't take Trump's calls. He's pissed. Mission accomplished.

Then Oleg called you. And yes, Herb, I was listening in on your phone calls. Which was completely illegal. Enough to land me here in FCI Wingdale. You could teach me napkin folding.

By now I was past caring. But some small part of me that hadn't rotted away from cynicism warned me that the president might be in danger.

Now I learned that Oleg was done waiting for you and

gerbil-man to repeal the Glebnikov Act. And was going to release the "take care of" Katya tape on Facebook. On Halloween. Perfect.

You told me about it. The tap on your phone wasn't necessary.

The rest you know, she said. What I told you that day in the Sit Room, after we watched Putin take out Oleg. Crafty old Putin. He swallowed his anger and did the smart thing. Four more years.

She touched my arm.

And you, poor old Herb, what did you get? Nine years.

I told her about early release. She started to cry. She shook her head and muttered something unflattering about Mr. Trump. I gave her a napkin folded in the shape of a swan, to dry her tears.

She got up to leave.

I said, Miriam, if I put all this in a book, won't you get in trouble?

She smiled. Write it, she said. She gave me a hug and left. And died a month later. She obviously knew about the cancer when she visited me. Dear Miriam. She was past caring about legal repercussions.

Today is the second Saturday of the month. Hetta's coming. She's been terrific these years. Brings me nice things to eat. The food here is not what you'd call "fine dining." I can always tell if she's been stewing in one of her *you-shoulda-listened-to-me* moods because she brings borscht. I pretend to enjoy it, because she's been so great. I'll say this: it beats the shit out of kelp.

I'll end with the most recent letter I have from someone I've grown fond of over these past four years. He and I have to phrase things in a certain way, but we've both learned to read—and write—"between the lines," so to speak.

Friend Nutterman, greetings!

Thank you for your ultimate letter, which reached me here a mere two months after you wrote it. A new record! Imagine what voluminous correspondence we would accumulate had we access to emails. But there is something to be said for old-fashioned letters, don't you think? I do, though I wish they supplied us with better quality paper and implements of writing. As you see, they allow us only dull pencils. So we cannot assault the guards with sharpened pencils and escape!

I exult that you have decided to write your memoirs. I have been writing mine. The superintendent here, a fine fellow named Feliks Mussachevki, confiscated my first chapters. At first I was upset with him, but now I see that he was right— brevity is a virtue. We literary Russians—I refer of course to my fellow writers Tolstoy, Dostoyevsky, and Solzhenitsyn— are in truth not known for our brevity. But with Superin- tendent Mussachevki's guidance, I will continue cutting and editing until it is just right. Fortunately, there is no rush, as three years remain on my sentence. Meanwhile, what do you think of my title: *I Demand a Recount.*

How exciting, this news we hear that Trump Junior will take over the presidentura of the USA from his father. And without a normal election! Certainly he will keep America great. Just as our own dear Vladimir Vladimirovich continues to keep Russia great. I am in awe of his continuing energy. How fortunate are we to have such great leaders, eh?

Of course young Trump will have large shoes to fill. In his place I would tremble. Alas that he will not have you for his chief of cabinetry, to give wise counsel. But probably by now you have had your fill of public life. And you have your book to write. I look forward to reading it. Perhaps someday we will meet. I would like that.

I shall close there. I send you fraternal greetings, Herbert Abrahamovich. Write me again. The address remains the same!

Anatoli Ivanovich Zitkin
23-8949
Lefortovo Detention Facility No. 2
Ulitsa Lefortovskiy Val, 5
Moscow, Russia

Acknowledgments

Kind thanks—and then some—to Dr. Katherine Close and comrades John Tierney and Gregory Zorthian. Kind thanks, too, to Maria Mendez, Faren Bachelis, and Sherry Wasserman.

The Order of Lenin, first class, to Jonathan Karp and Amanda Urban. And to Natasha Simons for not smearing me with Oil of Oleg for that deplorable first draft.

About the Author

Christopher Buckley is the author of nineteen books. His first national bestseller was *The White House Mess*, published in 1986, a fictional memoir by a presidential chief of staff. Buckley renounced political satire some years ago on the grounds that American politics had "become self-satirizing." As they say in Washington, he wishes to revise his prior statement. Now, thirty-four years later, he returns to the scene of the crime (as it were) with *Make Russia Great Again*, another fictional memoir by a White House chief of staff. If enough people buy it, he promises to retire permanently from political satire.